where it began

where it began

ANN REDISCH STAMPLER

Simon Pulse

New York   London   Toronto   Sydney   New Delhi

SIMON PULSE
An imprint of Simon & Schuster Children's Publishing Division
1230 Avenue of the Americas, New York, NY 10020
First Simon Pulse hardcover edition March 2012
Copyright © 2012 by Ann Redisch Stampler
SIMON PULSE and colophon are registered trademarks of Simon & Schuster, Inc.
For information about special discounts for bulk purchases,
please contact Simon & Schuster Special Sales at 1-866-506-1949
or business@simonandschuster.com.
The Simon & Schuster Speakers Bureau can bring authors to your live event.
For more information or to book an event contact the
Simon & Schuster Speakers Bureau at 1-866-248-3049
or visit our website at www.simonspeakers.com.
Designed by Mike Rosamilia
The text of this book was set in Bembo.
Manufactured in the United States of America
2 4 6 8 10 9 7 5 3 1
Library of Congress Cataloging-in-Publication Data
Stampler, Ann Redisch.
Where it began / by Ann Redisch Stampler. — 1st Simon Pulse hardcover ed.
p. cm.
Summary: After she is in a horrific car crash when drunk, Los Angeles high school student Gabriella Gardiner assumes she stole her rich boyfriend's car and smashed it into a tree, but she cannot remember anything about the events of the evening.
ISBN 978-1-4424-2321-3 (hardcover)
[1. Traffic accidents—Fiction. 2. Alcoholism—Fiction. 3. Dating (Social customs)—Fiction.
4. Peer pressure—Fiction. 5. High schools—Fiction. 6. Schools—Fiction.
7. Los Angeles (Calif.)—Fiction.] I. Title.
PZ7.S78614Wh 2012
[Fic]—dc22
2011011726
ISBN 978-1-4424-2323-7 (eBook)

For Rick and Laura and Michael,
again, still, always

where it began

part one

I

THIS IS HOW IT STARTS: SOME HAPLESS GIRL IN A skanky little tank top lying on her back in the wet grass somewhere in Hidden Hills. She is gazing at the stars through the leaves of a eucalyptus tree. The trunk of the eucalyptus tree is wrapped in Billy Nash's blue BMW. Midnight-blue. The girl is trying to figure out what's going on, beyond the more obvious facts: a mouth lined with a sick combination of beer and stale vodka, a crunched-up car with black smoke pouring out of it, a night sky filled with glassy constellations and a big white moon.

There are certain unavoidable conclusions.

Even so, the girl is trying to remember the particulars. The keg, maybe. The crash. She is trying to remember who she is and what happened to whoever that person might be.

She is trying to remember she is *me*.

★ ★ ★

When I wake up, I am wired to machines. Everything looks somewhat gray. I check to see if my toes can wiggle and I start counting my fingers, which proves to be more challenging than you'd expect. I'm pretty sure they're all there, but I keep having to start over around finger number six.

Someone speaks, but it doesn't make sense, pieces of words and random syllables. It occurs to me that I might be on some fairly serious drugs. Then I go back to counting my six fingers.

Just after this, or maybe way later, it is hard to tell, someone else says, "Good morning, Sunshine."

I start to say, "Good morning," but I end up throwing up instead. Which is evidently a good thing. I am surrounded by happy, blurry, celebrating people in scrubs.

Someone grabs my hand and yells "Good morning!" again, enunciating all the consonants in case I'm deaf or speak Serbo-Croatian. My name remains a mystery of life, but I do remember this horrible story about a gray-haired old lady discovered locked up in a mental hospital in Chicago or someplace, where she'd been stuck since she was sixteen years old when a policeman found her wandering the streets speaking Serbo-Croatian. Only nobody knew it was Serbo-Croatian so they decided that she must be crazy and locked her up basically forever.

Whoever I am, I'm pretty sure that I'm not her.

Then it occurs to me that all these greenish-gray, blurry-looking figures I've been thinking of as people might actually be space aliens doing a bad job of pretending to be human. I try to go back to counting the fingers, but this is hard with the big happy alien clutching my hand as if she is afraid that I might make a break for it and cut out of the mother ship if she let go.

I try to get my hand back, which is cause for further celebration.

The hand-grabbing alien is wearing a V-neck scrub shirt with bunnies all over it. "Can you tell us your *naaaaame?*" she yells over and over.

I am still trying to reclaim the hand.

I hear myself saying, "Bunnies."

They all echo me and someone writes it down, or writes down something. I can hear the ballpoint scratch against the paper, harsh and loud.

"That's very *goooooood!*" someone else says. I have made the space clones ecstatic. "You've been in a *car accident*, Bunny," she shouts cheerfully.

The car. I sort of remember the car.

"You probably feel a little sick, but you're going to be *fine*. Dear? We need to know your last name too. What's your last name, Bunny?"

By now I am overwhelmed by the mystery of the situation. Although, I am in command of several key facts:

1. My name is not Bunny.

2. I have ten fingers, or at least I have six, and none of them actually seems to be missing.

3. I might or might not be in a hospital somewhere.

Ideas float through my head like big, goofy cartoons. Elephants and bunny shirts and bags.

"My ID," I say.

"Heidi!" they say. "That's great! Are you Heidi?"

"ID," I say. "Look in my bag. Give me my wallet."

All right, so I have no idea who I am, but at least I'm not stupid. This is something of a relief.

"I'm afraid the paramedics didn't find it, honey," Bunny Shirt says. "Let's see if you can tell me what day it is today."

This seems like an exceptionally stupid, random question under the circumstances.

"Calendar," I say.

They seem to be missing a lot of important items around here, such as calendars, and where is my bag? I remember my bag. It is the small, black fabric Prada bag, the kind with the leather strap and not the woven cloth one. The kind you can buy somewhat cheaply on the Internet and look somewhat richer than you really are. Unlike Louis Vuitton bags, which are always fake on the Internet and everyone can tell you bought some cheap, fake bag and you just look like a poseur.

There: car accident, toes and fingers, no name, no ID, and an encyclopedic knowledge of bags. I try to think about bags. What else do I know about them? I know I want mine back. Did they leave it in the car?

"Look in the car," I say.

The aliens chirp and huddle, letting go of the hand. I think about escaping, but I don't seem to be able to move. Also, there are tubes coming out of the back of my hand and the crook of my elbow. There are wires glued to my chest.

"Okay, Heidi," Bunny Shirt says, turning back with a great big toothy smile that makes her look like she might want to suck blood out of my neck. "The car you were driving is registered to Agnes and William B. Nash. Could you be *Agnes?*"

"Billy!" I say.

I remember Billy. Billy Nash. William B-for-Barnsdale Nash. I remember him in glorious and perfect detail, his hair and his shoulders and the salty smell of him.

"Is Billy all right?"

The nurse-like creature strokes my arm. "You were the only person by the car, dear," she says.

All right. So just after I was in some car crash that I don't remember, I was kidnapped by helpful aliens. The first part makes about as much sense as the second part. And oh, right, I did all this without my bag, which I ditched somewhere just before losing my mind.

"Can you tell me your whole name now?" the nurse asks, still stroking my arm. "Can you remember who you are?"

How could she know that the second I remembered Billy, I knew who I was too?

So I tell them my name and they all go scurrying off some-place to celebrate without me.

II

MOSTLY I SLEEP THROUGH ENDLESS DAY. THE ROOM is always light and everybody still looks slightly gray. Every time I open my eyes, I expect to see Billy—only he would be golden. He is, when my eyes are closed.

But it's just Vivian.

She is sitting in the corner on a green plastic chair, maybe too far away for me to see her clearly. Or maybe in her quest to look as if she's made of ten-years-younger, wrinkle-free plastic sheeting, my mother has found a way to get herself permanently, cosmetically airbrushed so *nobody* can see her all that clearly.

I think about her face melting into a fuzzy, greenish blur, and then I start thinking about the mass quantity of drugs that must be dripping into me through the IV and about how to speed it up.

This is when Vivian puts down her magazine and wafts across

the room to loom over my bed. I can see that she is wearing her tasteful mauve and plum makeup with the matte finish and matching mauve, no-sparkles nail polish she wears for funerals and teacher conferences, and it hits me that I might actually be in a real hospital on the verge of death.

I wonder what would happen if I just sort of reached up and squeezed the bag that's feeding the IV tube.

What I say is, "Where's Billy?"

Vivian gives me her strained imitation of a cheery smile.

"Hey, Gabby," she says, as if she were some happy, sappy character from *Mister Rogers' Neighborhood*, as if she were pretending to be somebody's mother. "Let's take this one step at a time, okay? Let's just get you okay and out of the hospital."

Brain-dead as I am, I know and she knows and everyone who ever laid eyes on me since September knows that I'm not going to be okay without Billy.

For a second I have this horrible thought that maybe the nurse is lying and something bad happened to him. Maybe Billy was run over and is crushed and dead and laid out behind a William Barnsdale Nash plaque in the Nash family crypt where we made out, Billy dressed up like a vampire and me a cross between a really slutty French maid and a zombie, on Halloween.

Otherwise, why wouldn't he come see me?

"Where's Billy?"

Vivian leans over the railing that's supposed to keep me in the bed. "Maybe you should have thought of that before you plowed his car into a tree," she says softly, as if this could pass for some form of a helpful suggestion.

I can tell that I am crying because a tear is blazing an acid trail down the side of my face.

"Don't touch!" Vivian lunges through the tangle of tubes and wires toward my seriously bandaged hands.

"What?" I say. "What happened to my face? Oh God, do my hands work? What did I do?"

The bed bobs and lurches like a space raft floating in the gray-green sky. I can tell that the nurse is injecting something soothing and potent into the tube that goes directly to my veins. I can tell that Vivian is saying something soothing and insincere. I open my eye and Vivian whirls into the distance in the plastic chair, her hair streaming behind her. The doctors multiply in kaleidoscope formation, at the center of which is the tiny white light that they shine into my eye.

Before sunrise, when the room is vibrating with pale fluorescent light, I can see the space debris that's been floating in the corner of my eye is a bouquet of ugly Mylar balloons. The watercolor clouds are flowers, mostly half-dead, showy ones, with cheesy stuffed animals stuck in the crooks of branches stiff with curled, dry leaves.

I have been here long enough for flowers to wilt.

I rattle the railing on the side of the bed, wondering what happens when my feet touch the floor. If I can walk away.

As it turns out, I can't.

Bunny Shirt and her minions tuck my legs under a warm blanket so tight I can't move. Then they crank up the railings.

"Gabby," Vivian whispers, "do you remember what you did? Even the tiniest, teensiest detail?"

Nope.

"Well, the doctor says that with this kind of head trauma and all those, um, substances, you might not remember . . . I guess you might not remember yet."

Then she tries playing games.

"Okay, Gabby, let's try this: When I say 'party,' what pops into your mind? Just go with it. Don't even try to think about it."

As if I could *think*.

"Okay, what if I say 'Songbird Lane?' Okay . . . *Songbird Lane* . . . Gabby, will you please just try this? The police want to talk to you, and I'm not sure how long I can hold them off."

Songbird Lane?

I would tell her if anything was in there.

Maybe I would.

Voices drift in through the doorway.

"Even if I let you talk with her, what would be the point?" somebody murmurs. "It's a closed head injury and she just rambles. Good luck making sense of it."

My injured head rolls toward the sound, and there is Bunny Shirt in silhouette. Bunny Shirt and someone with a gun.

"Look, I know you're just doing your job, but this won't take long," the lady with the gun says.

"You're not going in there."

"I just need to take her statement," Gun Lady says. "It'll take three minutes, tops. Can't she talk?"

"Sure, she can talk," says Bunny Shirt. "She thinks her name is Heidi and she lives in Mister Rogers' Neighborhood. Come on. You've got her blood alcohol level. They brought her in with car keys in her hand. What else do you need?"

You would think some part of this would have made a lasting impression.

You would think that after Billy didn't show up and my mother kept hissing about what I did and averting her gaze, it would occur to me that there might be some serious problem here.

You would think.

III

WHEN I COME TO, VIVIAN IS READING THE CARDS
that are stuck in the flower arrangements, writing down who sent
them in the tiny spiral notebook she carries around.

"Everybody sent you flowers," she says. You would think this
was a good thing, but you can tell it isn't. "Everybody knows."

"Did Billy send me something?"

"They sent you a lovely bouquet," Vivian says, not looking
up. "The Nashes did." She flicks away a helium-filled balloon dog
that is hovering over the foot of the bed and starts foraging for
the Nashes' lovely bouquet.

I start looking around for some sumptuous floral extravaganza, given that the Nashes could basically afford to send me
a whole tulip farm and a live-in Dutch florist if they felt like it.
But it turns out they'd come up with a particularly weird combination of green and red oversized lilies that look left over from

Christmas with a smiley face card that says, "Wishing you all the best for a speedy recovery!!!" signed, "The Nash Family."

Which is when it happens: when the story of my life starts to show up in mosaic splinter flashes in my head. Which is when Agnes Nash shows up in my head—with horns and a red pointy tail and little cloven hooves and an Armani suit. Which I take to be a drug-induced yet totally insightful vision of her.

You could see her making her assistant's assistant go order this bouquet and this particular card, the most impersonal, meanest thing she could think of that wouldn't make people jump to the conclusion that she was the Great Satan of the Three B's— Bel Air, Brentwood, and Beverly Hills—where, in my personal opinion, you have to try pretty hard to be the really Great Satan and not just some random devil due to all the competition.

Did I mention Billy's mother doesn't like me a whole lot?

Apparently, it takes more than a eucalyptus tree to bang this particular fact out of your head.

Agnes Nash's face the first time I saw her.

Agnes Nash's eyes the first time she saw me with Billy.

Billy, who walks three inches off the ground, is the mainstay of the Winston School water polo team, and gets anything he wants out of anyone he wants it from because he is just so charming and gorgeous and basically the first person you notice in a room full of people only you look away really fast because you don't want him to think that you're staring at him, which you are.

Every time Agnes sees me with him, she kind of looks me over and makes a little face like once again, she has considered my many fine attributes, and once again, she can't figure out what Billy is doing with me.

We have these generic little conversations in which she says, "So, Gabriella, are you thinking about college?" and I can tell I'm supposed to haul out some Ivy League fight song or start panting "Oh Stanford, oh Stanford, oh give it to me Stanford, oh *Stanford!*"

But instead, I just sort of stand there muttering something incoherent about art school. How there is a really good art school just down the road in Pasadena.

Big frown. Agnes is maybe as enthused about art school as my parents.

Well, Rhode Island School of Design is supposed to be good and it's right next door to (bow head and genuflect) Brown, right?

You can tell she has to exert a lot of effort just to keep her eyes from rolling. You can tell she'd be a whole lot happier with Billy hooking up with the kind of girl who is going to cheerlead her Advanced Placement butt into (angels playing harps) Yale. Not the kind of girl whose reach school is some art school next door to (bow your head) Brown but not actually (well, you know) Brown, and who probably is going to end up in some pokey college in South Dakota with a bad art department because, in the first place, my parents would never pay for me to go to art school, and in the second place, no doubt even art school can figure out who is sub-regular.

The kind of girl who isn't me.

Still, as long as I don't interfere with Agnes's plan for Billy's life—*Do Not get kicked out of Winston School; Do Not, no matter how plowed, do lines in front of Coach; Do Not get caught violating your probation; Get into* (drum roll) *Princeton*—she is happy enough to give Billy the keys to the beach house and look the other way when he takes me there.

Even trapped in this electric hospital bed, dizzy, smelling sour, and with Swiss cheese for brains, I can see where if she didn't like me all that much back when I was just some ordinary, stupid excuse for a girlfriend, she might be even less happy with me now that I'm Billy's drunken car-wrecker girlfriend.

Still, it seems north of cold that Billy is staying away from me now, which I suddenly decide—probably as a result of my bruised brain sloshing from one side of my head to the other and not as a result of actual thought—*has* to be because of Agnes.

Or, it occurs to me: Vivian.

What about that? Her Rule to Live By *is* that no one gets to see you when you Don't Look Good. As far as she's concerned, if you look fine and you send Everything-Is-Fine vibes out into the universe, then everything will magically *be* fine.

Right.

Only you're not supposed to think *Right* in a dubious frame of mind. You're supposed to go, *Everything is freaking swell.* Because: If you give the universe the slightest hint that things suck, such as by slouching around being realistic about the fact that your life actually *does* suck, then the planets will converge in celestial agreement and you'll be locked in astrologically inevitable suckdom forever.

"This isn't even from him," I say, eyeing the gross Nash flowers. "Where is he? Did *you* tell him he couldn't come?"

But Vivian is not the kind of mom who likes to sink into a club chair with a lovely cup of tea and gaze into your eyes and talk things over. She is the kind of mom who likes to pretend everything is fine until the badness of it hits her on the head. Then she turns into the kind of mom who runs around crazed, trying to fix things—which would actually *be* swell, except that her ability to size up any situation with me in it, let alone fix it, is severely limited.

Vivian glides to the railing of the magic bed and gives me this deeply deeply understanding caring sharing look. Farewell to *Mister Rogers' Neighborhood*. Now she is trying out for the even more dramatically satisfying role of Florence Nightingale, Angelic Nurse. In the climactic scene when Angelic Nurse Florence figures out how demented and completely brain-dead Mashed on Head Girl is.

How brain-dead would I have to be to think that Vivian would do anything but toss rose petals and gorgeously wrapped condoms on Billy Nash's path to my bed? Because: Being Billy's girlfriend is the only thing I've done since I turned twelve years old and got into Winston School that comes close to fulfilling her destiny as mother of a daughter she can stand.

IV

"HEY, SLEEPING BEAUTY," THE DOCTOR WITH THE ponytail says, completely on top of the Fantasyland aspect of the situation but apparently oblivious to the critical fact of the missing prince.

She is young and cheerful and inordinately pleased with herself.

Inordinately?

I am young and entirely cheerless, a bruised repository of random SAT words and fragmented memories that keep flashing behind my closed eyes like stray clips of some lame documentary: *Scenes from Teen Life in the Three B's.*

Such as the scent of incense and Anita Patel holding up a vocabulary flash card, feeding me slices of plums roasted in honey and spice in a vain effort to turn me into the pride of Winston School.

Such as lying on my back on the hood of the Beemer next to Billy in a field near the airport, holding hands and watching airplanes disappear into the darkening sky.

Such as Agnes Nash glaring at me.

The doctor flicks her ponytail over her shoulder and sits poised to see how much of her inane quiz I am going to fail this time. You can tell she was the pride of wherever *she* went to high school.

I keep meaning to cram for her questions with Vivian, to write the day of the week and the date and the numbers backward from one hundred by sevens on my palm, but I forget and fall asleep instead.

"So," she says, making penetrating eye contact and smiling encouragingly, all the while bracing herself for my daily failure. "How are you doing with your name today?"

"Sleeping Beauty?" I say.

She smiles again, this time anxiously, not sure if this is a cute joke or perhaps the total breakdown of my grasp on concrete reality.

"Gabby Gardiner," I say, going for extra credit. "Gabriella Bingham Gardiner. Gabster. Gardiner. Gabs."

The doctor is grateful, but not grateful enough to go away. "And the day of the week?" she says.

I'm thinking Tuesday. I'm thinking there's a one-in-seven chance that this will give me two for two. But it doesn't. As for the month, if it's still spring, maybe April?

I am vague on the name of the hospital, the president of the

United States, which you have to figure I'd know, and a reasonable version of how I ended up in an unnamed hospital, on an unidentified day of the week, unable to do simple math.

"It's not coming back," I say.

The doctor tells me not to worry and pats me on the leg. If my brain were vaguely capable of telling my legs what to do, I would kick her.

"Think of those rich images that keep popping up," she says brightly. "Think of all the important things you've remembered." It's true, the whole array of kindergarten facts, the parts of the body and the names of all the colors in the big, jumbo box of Crayolas, is still in there. That and the complete, unabridged guide to Billy Nash.

But I am thinking more of the important things I *don't* remember. Such as how this happened to me.

I say, "It's not ever coming back, is it?"

"What?"

You have to wonder if she's even paying attention.

"About the accident," I say. "About what happened that I don't remember."

The doctor shakes her head. I watch her ponytail whip back and forth. Scrunching up her face in what's supposed to pass as sympathy, she skewers the clasp of her clipboard with her pen. "Classic retrograde amnesia," she says. "But never say never."

But you can tell that is exactly what she's saying.

V

VIVIAN, MEANWHILE, IS IMPERVIOUS TO THE SLIGHTEST hint of any fact she doesn't like. This is just how she gets through the day. She is waiting for my missing night to reappear, whole and perfect, in what used to be my memory. She is waiting for me to tell her all about it. She keeps leaning over the railing of the bed so the end of her nose is six inches from the end of my nose.

"Don't give up! Try to remember!"

I try to remember, but the DVD that was my former life goes spinning along up to the big front door of the party house on Songbird Lane, splutters, and picks up, raggedy and dim, with me on my back in the wet grass three and a half hours later, a new movie with a whole new plot.

"Try to remember!" Vivian says, as if I'm holding out on her.

★ ★ ★

This is what I remember:

How everything leading up to the party is nothing special.

Me and Billy in the front seat of Billy's car with the Andies making out in the backseat because Andy tried to teach Andie how to drive his stick shift and she stripped the gears, and now Andy's car is at the Porsche mechanic's semi-indefinitely and Billy has to drive Andie and Andy everywhere.

Me wearing a black silk stretchy tank top and a bra with lime-green ribbons for straps. Which Billy keeps fiddling with and touching and getting all twisted up, his index finger tracing the green ribbon strap closest to him, as we drive out on the 101. That much I remember perfectly. That bra strap and my jeans. How I was wearing low, low tattered jeans that came washed thin and papery from ritzy Italian-designer washing machines, hand-shredded in designer shredders, tight as shrink-wrap.

Me pressing my hands up against the roof of the convertible that Billy puts up because it's drizzling when we drive out of Bel Air. Billy kissing the underside of my arm. Me wondering if the underside of my arm is too flabby, but too blissed out to care all that much for once. The sound of one of the Andies unzipping something in the backseat.

Billy pulling his car onto the front lawn of the house on Songbird Lane under a security light. Girls in jeans and camisoles and high heels loping past toward the big front door that opens and then shuts out three and a half hours of my life.

My life, which, by the time I wake up wasted, lying dead

drunk on the ground clutching the car keys with my head bashed in and heading for the hospital, is pretty much over.

Only I don't know that right away.

Billy is gone and no one will let me look in a mirror, but I still can't figure it out.

VI

WHAT IF?

This is quite the scary game under the circumstances.

Given that Billy is not exactly famous for being with girls who Don't Look Good: What if?

Vivian isn't saying anything, but it doesn't exactly strain the intellect to figure out what she's thinking. It's not as if she has that many Rules to Live By, and as far as I can tell, whenever I drift off, which is most of the time, she is out foraging for remedial beauty supplies that she stashes discreetly behind all the dying flowers in giant striped Sephora shopping bags.

I say to Ponytail Doc, "So, what's the deal with my face?"

You can tell that she is clenching her teeth so as not to say, *Oh shit.*

I say, "It's not like I'm going to get upset and yank out the IV and die. Let me see."

I watch her running back through the entire contents of Relating to Teenagers 101 in her mind, trying to come up with a really good way to say no.

I am clenching my teeth, but *oh shit* is the least of it.

She takes a breath. She taps her toe. She stares down at her pager as if she is trying to get it to beep through sheer force of will.

I say, "I want a mirror."

"I know this is hard for you," she says, "but you're in a state of flux. A mirror would capture *one* moment in time but your situation is . . . um . . . dy*n*amic."

Lovely.

Dy*n*amic.

The asshole orthopedist with the stuffed marsupials hanging off his stethoscope carries on at length about his reconstructive genius and how he'll have me throwing pots, playing some imaginary accordion, and keyboarding fast enough to be some other asshole's secretary any minute. But when I get to the part about my face, he clutches his koala bears, grimaces at Ponytail, and flees.

"You have to tell me what's going on," I say to Ponytail. "Am I coming out of this as Scarface or what? You *have* to tell me."

"Healing takes time," Ponytail says, infinitesimally edging back toward her usual state of bizarre cheerfulness while carefully sidestepping the question. Not that she isn't manaically thorough: Orbital fracture. Reconstruction. Hairline fracture, broken, chipped.

My face is like the table of contents in a how-to book for surgeons.

"Dr. Rollins already reset your nose; it's going to be almost perfect. Same tip." She smiles, but I do not smile back. "And that gash—almost entirely behind the hairline. So assuming you're not planning to shave your head . . ." She grins at me, but I am so so not amused. "Invisible."

Almost perfect.

"What do I look like?"

"You look like a pretty girl who ran into a tree at thirty miles an hour without a seat belt and got pummeled by air bags and the tree. So what you'd expect. Bruises. Lacerations. A lot of swelling and some discoloration."

"So basically I look grotesque. Is that what you're saying?"

The ponytail is whipping around in the coiffure version of an anxiety attack. "You look exactly like someone on the way to having the same pretty face she had before," she says. "Just not yet . . ."

I feel as if I've been transformed into a giant scary lizard or some frightening mythological creature that turns people to stone when they so much as glance at her because that's just how bad she looks. You can't help but notice that no one is saying when I'm going to attain *almost* perfection either. No one is saying when I'm getting out of here or how messed up I'm going to be.

Ponytail is so not good at this.

"You're going to look more like yourself in a few weeks, maybe a month. And in a couple of months, my goodness . . . ," she drones on. "As soon as you feel up to seeing your friends, you know they're going to come support you through it. Believe me. A lot of patients feel this way, but your friends are friends with *you*, not with your face. People won't care how you look."

People. Won't. Care. How. You. Look.

You could tell that she spent all of high school being home-schooled, studying honors bio on her kitchen table, not looking up long enough to notice the first thing about real life.

Meanwhile, *Gabriella Gardiner's (slightly mangled) Scenes from Teen Life in the Three B's* is just rolling along in my head, jumping back and forth in no particular order from one bit of my real life to another.

There it is, with a *Before* and *After* that make more sense than the actual present, which comes after the *After*, the *after-After*, shooting off in a whole other direction.

I close my eyes, and there it is.

Right there, the embarrassing *Before*, my own personal prequel.

Look:

There I am, getting into Winston School, ripping open the envelope and spilling the good news onto the kitchen counter. There is green and gold confetti in the envelope.

Twelve years old and I'm thinking, *Hey, Gabs, this is pretty damned great.*

But not so much as my dad.

Zoom in on my dad, out on the balcony that overhangs the canyon and runs the length of our house, which is shaped like a big cardboard carton built into the downslope of a steep, ritzy hill in Bel Air, from which we get to look down on L.A. He is shuffling up and down the balcony congratulating himself while Vivian chases him around squealing and providing him with an endless supply of Bloody Marys.

"I knew being a Gardiner had to mean something," he crows, tossing the celery from his Bloody Mary into the canyon so some poor coyote can get plowed too. "I'm so proud of you."

Proud of me has been a long time coming, given how when I didn't get into John Thomas Dye, kindergarten of the rich and famous, he went into deep mourning for the next seven years.

Proud my last name is Gardiner, a clan filled with rich and famous members, not including us despite my dad's efforts to play the Asian stock market at three a.m. Despite his efforts to sell zillion-dollar houses to foreign guys who don't know any better, taking out really expensive ads in the *Kuala Lumpur Daily Gazette* or wherever, and driving the big Mercedes we can't actually afford but looks good in carpool.

According to my mom when she's pissed off, if the *über*-Gardiners didn't throw my dad a bone once in a while and use him as their real estate agent when they bought ten-zillion-dollar buildings in Las Vegas resulting in the occasional monster commission checks that keep us afloat, we'd be the only family in Bel Air subsisting on cat food and mac 'n' cheese. We would have to move to the Valley where, according to her, we'd be like royalty in exile in a vast, smoggy wasteland. Unlike here, where it's hard to miss the part that we're the dregs of Upper Bel Air.

But now Winston has opened its gates and I'm *in*.

I can finally go to the right school, meet the right people, get into the right college, become incredibly successful, smart, popular, and rich, be star of the school play, captain of the soccer team, president of my class, homecoming queen, and valedictorian. I can be the cheerleading, honor roll, never-a-bad-hair-day girl whose papers get read aloud to classes years later as examples of super-galactic perfection.

As if he actually believes that if only I'd be that girl and if he drove that big car over to Winston School, we would all be magically transformed. As if parents who pay the humongous tuition out of leftover pocket change would leap out of their even bigger cars, bang on the Mercedes' slightly darkened side window, and beg him to sell them a strip mall in the Philippines.

Because a guy with such a perfect kid must be hot shit.

It is as if he's never actually met me, an ordinary student with the normal amount of friends, who doesn't like sports, and is somewhat good at art.

Art?

Did somebody say *art*?

Hell no.

After Winston, I would be attending the totally impossible

college of my parents' dreams. Biz school from the sound of it, between Bloody Marys. Because: Do you know what twenty-three-year-olds who graduate from Wharton make even in this economy? Six figures!

Gabby Gardiner, shake hands with your totally impossible, not-going-to-happen future.

VII

IN ACTUAL FACT, THE HIGH POINT OF THAT YEAR AT
Winston is when Miss Cornish, the art teacher who does the
crafty part of art—ceramics and pottery and sculpture—puts my
ceramic spoon holder on a pedestal outside the teachers' lounge
because it is an outstanding example of really good glaze.

At my old school, I had always been this sort of regular person.
At Winston, I figure out quickly that I am *sub*-regular. Basically,
everybody else is either gorgeous or super-smart or incredibly
good at something important, born with the popular gene or
richer than God. And I'm not. So, big surprise, I do not get a
whole crowd of popular friends and a round of applause when I
walk down the hall.

Look:

There I am, telling myself all these helpful affirmations such
as, *Oh Gabby, you really are smart. Oh Gabby, you're totally normal*

and everything is fine. Oh Gabby, aren't you just the most adorable thing that ever got out of bed in the morning?

Only if any of this were true, it is hard to explain why I'm standing around Winston School watching Billy Nash and the Slutmuffins lounging in the Class of 1920 Memorial Garden, owning benches and tables and patches of grass that are instantly cool just because they own them, watching the smart kids and the *über-*rich kids and the weird kids in the manga club all hanging out together in big happy clumps, while I am alone with my unimpressive grades and no one to talk to except for Lisa Armstrong and Anita Patel.

"Your little friends called again," Vivian says from what sounds like far away across the vibrating green room.

Friends?

You would think that after all these enlightening sessions with Ponytail Doc trying to get me to tell her all about myself, it would be easier to connect the dots.

I open my eyes, but everything stays in a lot better focus when they're closed. "Who?"

"That Lisa and Anita," Vivian says. "*Those* friends."

Making her little puke face as if having to be reminded that her daughter is once again reduced to counting these poor excuses for fashionable teens as her only friends makes her physically ill.

As if she can't stand to remember.

★　★　★

32

What I remember is the smell of burnt, melted bittersweet chocolate and charred marshmallows. The backs of their heads—Lisa's strawberry-blond fluff and Anita's black braid—blurring in the smoke that billows from the wall oven in Lisa's kitchen. Grabbing for the mitts and the fire extinguisher and waving magazines at the smoke detectors to try to get them to turn off.

How long ago was that?

There I am, thirteen years old and slouching around Winston School in the shortest blue uniform skirt in the history of man over tiny black bicycle shorts. The only cute thing about this skirt is the pocket on the butt. Anita is wearing a similarly truncated skirt over a pair of leggings, which is also, God help us, a Winston School style, except Anita is wearing them because her mother made her. Lisa is the one person still wearing the baggy khaki uniform pants that no other girl has ever worn to school after the first day of seventh grade. Lisa is also the one person at Winston School who admires me for something before I get Billy after four years of total obscurity.

It is October of seventh grade and I have just figured out that art is the *only* thing I don't suck at, but it turns out to be the only thing Lisa does suck at (apart from her apparent inability to shop for clothes that don't have some Disney character or strange-looking appliqués on them) and that she really really wants to be good at. This is because her parents are seriously religious cinematographers who value art just a notch below how much they value God Almighty.

It is November and Lisa has started following me to assembly and sitting next to me and Anita, who actually has the potential to be completely regular, except she has to take Hindi language class and Indian dance class and learn to play weird-looking musical instruments and entertain old ladies from her extended family who are visiting her from New Delhi for months at a time. She has to figure out how to modify her uniform in a way that keeps her mother happy but does not involve social suicide.

At least the stuff she has to do to keep her mom happy doesn't involve getting people to think she's hot.

There we are in December, about as hot as egg salad sandwiches or, in Anita's case, completely vegan soy wraps. There we are, sitting three in a row, invisible enough to slouch there in the back of the auditorium eating contraband snack food, while Mr. Piersol, our idiot headmaster, slogs from one alarming story to the next in his mind-numbing weekly ascent up Cliché Mountain. Not to mention, Mr. Piersol would appear to be scrounging all his information on teen life off a shady website for urban legends.

News flash: Boston high school girls caught in pregnancy pact!

Oh no, boys and girls: Children having children! Look before you leap!

"Children having icy pops. Look before you lick," Anita whispers, gazing up at Mr. Piersol, hunkering down in her auditorium seat to eat the lime icy pop that she smuggled in.

"Anita!" says Lisa. "That could have such double meaning."

News flash: Catty clique of mean cheerleaders in Texas cause sad, chunky cheerleader to leap from bridge!

Oh no, boys and girls: If you can't say something nice, don't say it!

"If you can't say something nice, welcome to Winston School," Anita says.

"That is *so* mean." Lisa says. And then she snickers. "Are you by any chance a member of a catty clique?"

"I want to be in the catty clique!" I say. I am not completely joking.

"Sorry," says Anita. "I think you might have to be pregnant first. And you have to look like a Slutmuffin."

We don't look as if we're members of the same species as the Slutmuffins, as if we are fit to inhabit the same planet, as if our skin is made of the same dewy membrane, or that our hairs were ever genetically programmed to spring out of our scalps and line up in perfect order like theirs.

Cut to a montage of sleepovers at Lisa's house with everybody sitting in their sleeping bags watching old Technicolor movies with Doris Day and Debbie Reynolds and making large sheets of semi-inedible marshmallow fudge, shooting at each other with Silly String.

I don't know. Maybe all over the country, this is what deliriously happy teenage girls are doing Friday nights, but it seems as if all of the people worth being at Winston are engaging in somewhat less boring activities involving sex and drugs and rock and roll.

What I want is to be one of those people.

But I am stuck in my *Before* and I have no idea, not a clue or an inkling, that I am even going to get an *After*.

VIII

I AM SO DEEP INTO *GABRIELLA GARDINER PRESENTS Scenes from Teen Life in the Three B's,* trawling through it looking for some faint clue as to how I ended up like this, that it is seriously annoying when people show up to take my pulse and check my blood and squirt mildly hallucinogenic drugs into my IV bag.

Ponytail Doc, possibly because she can't stand the pressure of trying to keep me from getting a look at myself in the crystal of her watch or the lenses of her big retro Italian glasses, has sent in reinforcements. An occupational therapist named Wendy shows up in my room pushing a green metal cabinet on wheels through the door, grinning as if she hasn't heard that (1) I am not in a good mood, and (2) I do not have an occupation.

"This is a mistake," I say. "I don't need an occupational therapist. I go to high school."

But Wendy, it turns out, is a pediatric occupational therapist whose goal in life is to help little damaged, hospitalized children play. This is so sad that I can hardly stand to think about it.

"I'm a playologist!" she says.

There is some possibility that I am the oldest person Wendy has ever dealt with. To prove it, she hauls out coloring books, glitter markers, peg boards, and stickers with Elmo in a wheelchair. She has faded clay that is squishier than Play-Doh. She is so chirpy and perky that you have to figure even someone a lot nicer than I am would want to poke a glitter marker in her eye.

Wendy tries to find some space to unload her stuff on the counter between the botanical splendor and the shopping bags of beauty supplies, but I end up with tacky kindergarten art supplies piled on my stomach.

"You've got Barbie and Midge paper dolls," I say.

Wendy is over the moon that I can name Barbie and Midge. When I ask her if she's got Ken and Skipper, she is one orgasmic playologist.

It is so weirdly easy to please these people.

She hands me a pair of blunt scissors and admires the way I cut things out. I cannot believe that I am lying here cutting out paper-doll clothes.

"Do you have any actual art supplies?" I say after what seems like hours of this, when it seems like my right hand at least is somewhat functional and I could actually draw something. "Like real paper and good pencils or charcoal or anything?"

Wendy admires how precisely I have cut out Barbie's tiny high-heeled shoes, which I am kind of seeing quadruple but are nevertheless perfect.

"I mean it," I say. "I'm an actual artist."

"Of course you are, dear," Wendy says.

"Seriously," I say. "I really am! Werner Rosen is my art teacher!"

Wendy looks deeply impressed, but when I think about it, I remember how deeply impressed she was about the Barbie shoes, and I can't even tell if she knows who Werner Rosen is. But she does go scuttling off to get more stuff.

So I can sit there by myself with my auto-closing eyes and miss the art rooms at school. I miss Miss Cornish's and Mr. Rosen's art rooms, all right?

Look:

Me and Lisa and Lisa's semi-boyfriend, Huey, hanging out in Miss Cornish's art studio at Winston. Back when I think Huey is the artist and not me. Because photography counts but I am mostly good at throwing pots and glazing ceramics, which I kind of think doesn't count much.

Close-up of Huey running around with a giant classic camera from the 1940s strapped around his neck over his father's ancient Grateful Dead T-shirt, which hangs on him like an old, raggedy dress.

If Huey had given off the slightest hint that he cared what other people thought, the jocks would have ripped him to pieces before he had a chance to finish middle school. But what Huey wants is to take spectacularly weird pictures that fill the spectacularly uncool Winston School Wildcat yearbook and that hang in the Winston School gallery (aka the hall outside of the gymnasium) and that win prizes.

We are all in the art room because Huey is briefly interested in making big papier-mâché animals out of computer-enhanced photographs. Lisa finally has a buddy who can't paint either to hang around the easels with. Then they both start standing around watching me paint and throw pots, which is somewhat creepy. I am perfectly fine with Lisa hanging on my every brushstroke. I understand the part about not wanting to disappoint your parents so much it makes perfect sense to watch somebody else drag their paintbrush up and down a canvas for hours at a time. But Huey is taking pictures.

"Jeremy Hewlett," I say. This is Huey's actual name. "This is creeping me out. You have to stop it."

"I'm recording the creative process," he says.

"Well, go record somebody else's creative process."

"Maybe you didn't notice," Huey says, "but this is Winston School. Nobody else has a creative process. Except Lolly Wu, and the shutter clicking messes with her concentration."

Lolly Wu plays the cello. Why she isn't going to school at Crossroads, where they have an entire orchestra of kids who know how to hold their instruments right side up, is just another mystery of life.

"Yeah, well, when I become an art goddess, you can compare me to Wu."

But I let him keep taking pictures. Leading Vivian to tell me that I can't be a complete social leper if I have so many pictures of myself in the yearbook.

"Right," Huey says. "I'll just sit here and finish up my swan until you change your mind."

This is the first time I see Mr. Rosen up close and personal, when he shows up in Miss Cornish's art room in search of turpentine and a rag at that exact moment. He is like a hundred years old and a real artist, paintings in museums, the whole famous artist thing, who lives down the street from Winston, and somehow they convinced him to show up three times a week to Mentor the Next Generation. It is hard to imagine how a famous guy who deserves all his glory like Mr. Rosen—who, the headmaster keeps telling us, is some kind of official German national treasure—could fall for that, but he did.

When Mr. Rosen spots Huey turning his hundreds of black-and-white photos of women into that papier-mâché swan, the camera swinging perilously close to the bowl of liquid paste, he marches up behind him and sucks in his breath.

Huey just sits there frozen, holding a paste-soaked photo, gazing over at Mr. Rosen, with his googly green eyes open wide, as if he is waiting for spiritual enlightenment to come his way in a German accent.

"Did you take these photos?" Mr. Rosen asks, thumbing through the stack.

Huey says, "Yessir."

"Well, they're very good." Mr. Rosen waves at Miss Cornish.

"Look, Elspeth, see what nice composition?" he says, blurring his *w* sounds toward *v*'s, pointing at the black-and-white grainy picture of a freakishly large woman getting on a bus.

"You should take more photos," he says to Huey. "Forget this duck."

"It's a *swan*," Lisa says.

"Werner," Miss Cornish says, visibly steamed, her skin getting whiter and her freckles standing out. "Jeremy has important things to express about beauty and metamorphosis in three dimensions."

"Huey," Huey says. "For Hewlett. Jeremy Hewlett the Third."

"Cheremy Hewlett!" Mr. Rosen says. "Your mother took the raccoons out from my attic."

Huey nods as if this were normal. He doesn't even seem to be embarrassed about his spectacularly embarrassing mother, Bel Air's bizarro answer to Saint Francis of Assisi, who is constantly coming to pick up Huey in the carpool line with an animal-rescue goat or a couple of ratty chickens and a three-legged pit bull in the backseat of the Bentley.

"You take maybe five hundred shots. Maybe six hundred. Then you bring me ten. Only the best." Then he marches out with his turpentine and Miss Cornish's blue rag.

Then he comes back.

I thought it was to give Miss Cornish back her rag, but it isn't. It's to look at my bowl that just came out of the kiln. "Beautiful glaze," he says.

Lame as it is, this is my best day of school ever until Billy.

IX

ANYWAY, ACCORDING TO VIVIAN, IT ISN'T JUST LISA and Anita who are bugging the hell out of her. Huey is phoning every day too, calling the nursing station and demanding to know how I am. He is leaving messages from Huey, Jeremy, and Mr. Hewlett on the off chance that he'll come up with a name so appealing that somebody will talk to him.

But Vivian is having none of it. She is spending her days hanging over the side of my bed trying to jog my unjoggable memory and then running off to go shopping to cheer herself up. She is buying me vats of goopy makeup that she waves in front of me, as if it's going to make me happy. (Except that when you open up the jars, they smell like toxic waste.) She is much too busy stirring the unappetizing mess into a lumpy paste to spend a whole lot of time chatting with Huey.

But Wendy takes time out from cajoling me to get up and

sit at a table and draw and not fall over to tell me about Huey's many calls. My head feels roughly like a bowling ball in a vise and sitting up just makes it worse; I do not want to discuss how upset and concerned Huey is.

Except that Wendy thinks he's my boyfriend.

"You're one lucky girl," she says, trying to get me to squeeze these stupid, squishy rubber balls as hard as I can with both hands, only I can't. "You have very persistent friends and they all seem to care about you a lot. Especially your nice young man. And your boyfriend's mother wants to know if she can bring a visiting therapy dog to see you!"

Huey's mother and the gimpy pit bull! Which, combined with the failure of my *ac*tual boyfriend to call, write, text, or show up, makes me cry for what feels like days on end, except with everything including time and the days of the week blurred together so much, it might have been more like forty-five minutes.

So where is he?

Where is Billy?

"That's it," Vivian says to the roomful of medical residents who want to hear me try to count backward from a hundred by sevens some more for a laugh, shooing them all away. "Look at her face! She's completely unhinged. How can it possibly be good for her to talk with the police looking like that?"

Even flat on my back, hooked up to a bottle of liquid narcotics, and amusing myself by making the electric bed go up and down, I can tell that talking with the police would not be good.

Until I forget all about it.

Although the way I look has not left my consciousness once in, basically, forever.

"You know what, Wendy?" I say. "I think I want to sculpt my head."

Wendy is such a paragon of guilelessness and I am such a shameless liar, I'm pretty sure that this is going to work. There is no way you could make an ashtray with sides that stand up out of this mushy clay, let alone sculpt a face. Not to mention, if you actually want to sculpt a face, it's helpful if your left hand doesn't have to lie useless in your lap because the steel pin in your ulna seems to send out shock waves when you so much as try to curve your fingers around a dinner roll you're trying to butter. But I'm pretty sure Wendy can't tell.

"That sounds wonderful!" she says.

I almost feel guilty.

Almost.

"Yeah," I say. "Only, I don't think I'm supposed to touch my face. I might have to look at it and extrapolate to 3-D. Do you think?"

"You're the artist!" she says, just beaming away. "If you think you can do it, then I'm sure you can."

"Only, I don't have a mirror . . . Do you have a mirror?"

She does.

This is how I look: like a scary thirty-second community service ad for seat belts that can only run on late-night between info-mercials and porn because it is unsuitable for children and adults with weak stomachs. Oh, and the color-blind. Because it's hard to justify exposing anyone to all that gore and medical handiwork—the stitches, staples, bandages, and butterfly Band-Aids arrayed across my face—without giving them the psychedelic thrill of the color palette. Purple and black and violet around the eyes, the left eye sinking into greens, banana-yellow down the cheekbone, interrupted by a splash of white bandage with a crusty brown trim of blood and unidentified gray ooze. Bluish eyelids rimmed with perfectly dyed eyelashes, my eyelashes, the only recognizable, remaining portion of what used to be my face.

And I think: *How is it that I'm going to go from this to normal?*

And I think: *How did you do this to yourself?*

And I think: *Even if Billy is sitting around watching porn after a quick run to the Westwood Cannabis Club on Le Conte with Ian Brodie's dog-eared med club card, even full of Master Kush-laced, semi-legal, double-chocolate pot muffins, it is not an entirely bad thing that he isn't here to see this.*

Which you would think would make me feel somewhat better about his being somewhere else, the silver lining of the disappearing boyfriend.

You would think.

My eyes close and I don't feel anything.

This is what happens when you are lying on your back in a hospital gown made of coarse retro-print cotton, when your current life ranges from swirling fog to basically unbearable: Your eyes close and you are still you, only somewhere else.

My eyes close and there's Billy, driving too fast around the curves on Mulholland with open bottles of old scotch on the front seat and a couple of girls from Holy Name riding in his open trunk. Then Agnes shows up, fuming, to drag him home from the police station. Not that there is the slightest possibility that anything bad will ever happen to him, or he'll get kicked out of Winston. It isn't as if he stuck actual Winston girls into his trunk.

But as it turns out, when Billy says, "Let's violate some probation," every time he lights up, he actually means it.

There we are sitting on Billy's bed, throwing darts at his conditions of probation. Billy keeps the thirty-two conditions of his probation—*Maintain a 3.0 average; Do not exit domicile between the hours of six p.m. and six a.m. without permission of parent or guardian; Do not consume controlled substances or alcoholic beverages of any kind; Do not cavort with known underage users of said substances*—on the bulletin board over his desk. We are sitting on the bed trying to hit his favorite ones.

We are sitting on the bed and he is nuzzling the back of my neck.

"Follow the light with your eyes," Ponytail Doctor says, glancing down at her clipboard, reviewing my daily mental state as ascertained by one of her eager little intern helpers, dropping Wendy's mirror into her giant pocket and leaning in toward me in the mistaken belief that we have anything, including human-looking heads, in common.

She tilts her head to consider my face.

"The swelling will come down," she says, staring down at the bandages some white-coated flunky plucked off, depositing them, soaked in bodily fluids and livid orange antiseptic, on a stainless steel tray so I could admire them.

"I *saw* it," I say. "You know I'm screwed."

"This is why I didn't want you to see it when it's still like this," she says. "This is only temporary. Look—"

"I *did*."

Wendy is bringing up the rear and I'm pretty damn sure she won't be getting her mirror back any time soon. "You're going to be just as smart and beautiful as before!" she says with a cheerleading fervor that leaves Ponytail's usual baseless enthusiasm in the dust.

Ponytail looks as if she wants to stuff the entire playology supply of mushy modeling clay down Wendy's throat.

"It's hard to see yourself like this," she says. "Of course it is. But it's going to be all right. It might not seem that way right now but—"

But *what*? You have to wonder what Ponytail could even come up with that would make this even vaguely all right, now or ever.

But she doesn't have to.

"You go to Winston School!" Wendy says. "You're on Student Council! The world is your oyster." She avoids Ponytail's eyes. "Remember that."

Winston School is hard to forget, and even if you could forget it, no one else will let you. But the Student Council part is a memory I was just as happy living without. And oysters, which I have only ever eaten with Billy at restaurants he finds and drives me to and orders for me and I slurp down with a smile on my face, are pure slime.

I close my eyes and wait until their voices recede into the whirring and annoying background.

I close my eyes and keep them shut until they go away.

And then, even before I look up, even with the hospital banging and the disembodied voices in the corridor, the humming and clicking of the equipment I'm tethered to, I can hear John breathing. He is standing there staring at me, braced against the green wall, with tears running down his face and disappearing into the tiny dark houndstooth of his shirt.

Vivian hisses, "John-o, get a grip. Shhhhhh! You're scaring her."

But he is completely silent, stoned and still, and you can tell that Vivian is who he's scaring the shit out of. Because a catatonic drunk staring straight up from a reclining leather chair is a lot easier to deal with than a sloppy, barely standing one with watering cans for eyes.

Not to mention, a mother who is pissed off that you did what you did but is determined to remain unnaturally normal is a lot easier to deal with than a father who acts like your screwed-up life is his own personal Greek tragedy.

I close my eyes and I go back to watching *Gabriella Gardiner Presents Scenes from Teen Life in the Three B's*. Back to watching the scene with Billy and me throwing darts from his bed to the wall. Feeling his phantom fingers touch my cheek back when it didn't hurt to touch my face, back when my face didn't have scabs and ridges where the stitches used to be.

But not for long.

X

BECAUSE: THE MINUTE THE BUTTERFLY BANDAGES are off and my face is semi-unveiled, Vivian is even more obsessed with making me look semi-normal.

She pulls out the bags of camouflage supplies and we gaze at all that product.

"My poor little prizefighter," she says, sitting on the side of my bed with a crate of tiny little sea sponges, a species I am probably personally responsible for pushing over the brink of extinction by my inordinate use of its posthumous services. She pulls out a jar of sewer-scented Brazilian cover-up with the consistency of mud. Not the makeup version of pouffy masque-mud either—actual mud.

"Look at this," she says, swirling a sponge in the monochromatic glop. "This is such a nice color."

"For that semi-alive look," I say.

Vivian frowns with the lower half of her face, careful not to crease the skin around the eyes. Apparently I was unconscious long enough for her to develop a meaningful relationship with the makeup genius at the Lancôme counter at Neiman Marcus. His idea of how to reduce the appearance of swelling involves brushing three shades of blush onto my cheeks, and then, given the inevitable failure of this clever technique to turn a battered pumpkin into Heidi Klum, distracting people with more eye makeup than they've ever seen on one person.

Vivian tries to get me to let her apply eye liner, but it feels as if she is slicing off my eyelid with a meat cleaver.

"It kills me to see you like this," she says, mostly to herself. "It kills me to be doing this. You were so beautiful. You were. But you have to stay positive. I'm really making inroads here."

"Can Lisa and Anita maybe come over?" I say. "Now that this is getting covered up?" In a burst of baseless positivity, I am vaguely optimistic about how I'm going to look smeared with beige mud and all that multicolored blush.

But Vivian is so busy trying to figure out the finer points of making purple, green, and yellow skin look normal that she's not exactly taking in what I'm saying.

"Don't worry," she says, surveying the wreckage with a sour look. "They can try all they want, but they have to get past me. You don't have to see anyone looking like this."

Which, of course, is the story of my life: Vivian making decisions about how to organize my life based on how I look.

Setting in motion my *After*.

* * *

This is how my *After* starts: It is June. It is the summer before junior year. It is last summer, not even one whole year ago, which in the warp of hospital time seems like it happened in some other century, and Vivian decides it would be a good idea if I could look like someone else.

This is not as far into the realm of the truly bizarre as it sounds, given that my actual appearance, not to mention my actual life, is so not in Vivian and John's satisfactory column. And she can pretty much tell that no matter how much she tells me to stand up straight, brush my hair, and slather on zit cream, it's not going to make a dent in my sub-regularity.

"A makeover?" Lisa says. "Like, you get a new hairdo and a personal shopper? How can you spend a whole summer doing that?"

"You should at least do something you can put down on a college application. You can't have a blank space the summer before junior year," Anita says, not because she's a complete pain, but because if she doesn't get into someplace a lot better than UCLA, her parents are going to make her go to UCLA and live at home and let them check her outfits every morning.

"It's not like you have to cure cancer or anything," Lisa says. "Not that you couldn't."

Anita is more realistic. "How many mani-pedis can you get in one summer before you want to jump off a bridge?" she says. And then she says, "Oh no! You're not getting implants, are you? Do you want me to find you some articles about how unhealthy that is at our age? You can't even tell how big your boobs are going to get for years."

"Not that there's anything wrong with them now," Lisa says.

"Of course not," Anita says. "That's not the point. The point is that having plastic surgery before junior year is insane."

"Not that you're insane," Lisa says.

"At least give yourself two years to think about it," Anita says. "At least if you do it between high school and college, everyone won't *know*."

Vivian probably *would* have had me redone surgically if she hadn't blown all those bucks on my vast collection of bazillion dollar T-shirts I didn't exactly fill out. Seriously. For a couple of months, I was the only kid in the Three B's who wasn't anorexic whose mother wanted her to pack on the carbs on the off chance that all those extra calories would somehow migrate to my chest—until it became obvious it wasn't going to work and she wanted me to go back to subsisting on carrot sticks and cartons of Trader Joe's soy milk.

Look:

Wave while other people fly off to camp or their family's cute little cottage or castle or villa or whatever on Majorca for summer vacation.

Watch while I go off to Yuko System of Beverly Hills and get seven hundred dollars' worth of chemically straightened hair. With extensions. And shimmering blond highlights with color-coordinated low lights. It takes all day.

Then someone named Rolf, who is nevertheless Japanese and

wearing extremely tight leather pants, teaches me how girls who have forty-five minutes to blow-dry their bangs, blow-dry their bangs.

And while we're at it, why not drag me someplace to get my eyelashes dyed in a process that creates so much by way of stinging fumes that I am seriously worried I'm going to be a gorgeous blind girl?

Soon a color consultant with an actual office and a receptionist and everything, as if picking out colors were an actual profession, gets all excited about the perfect color of my now slightly fried eyelashes.

My entire wardrobe, on the other hand, has to go. All this time, I have been recklessly dressing without regard to my season. All those spring T-shirts and summer sweats when I was really an autumn. No wonder I looked like crap. Only now I have to wear a bunch of new stuff that is slightly orange.

"Copper!" the color consultant says.

Oh.

And I can't get just any old new slightly orange stuff that I happen to like. No, I have to get a personal style. And I have to get one quick before they do my makeup so my face won't get done in some clashing style that is stylistically hostile to the personally stylish, autumnal skirts I am about to buy to show off my improved stylish legs.

The style consultant, after foisting off a style on me that she keeps describing to Vivian as "kicky," is all agog over the mother-daughter aspect of turning me into a person my mom can stand to look at. This gives her the overwhelming urge to find Vivian her own kicky yet sophisticated style so we can match. But Vivian is not about to chuck all of *her* clothes, even if it would enhance my personal stylishness to have a matching mother.

"No," Vivian says in this pseudo-motherly, pseudo-wisewoman, totally fake voice. "I've had my turn and now it's Gabby's turn."

"Your *maman* is *magnifique!*" the color lady says in an accent I imagine her practicing for hours on end while standing in front of the mirror in her color-coordinated high-rise condo on Wilshire Boulevard. "What a *rite de passage* for you, little one."

By which I figure she has to mean something other than dyeing almost every hair on my body and becoming kicky, since it is hard to extract some big spiritual thing from hair dye. Vivian meanwhile is patting me on the hand and getting off on whose turn it is.

My turn for what?

To turn out like her, mother of a kid who needs an army of exterior decorators?

To live in Bel Air in a shabby house on stilts that is probably going to slide all the way down to Sunset Boulevard the next time the earth quakes or we get a really big rain?

To hang with some guy like my dad who can't even make it from the bedroom to the den if there isn't a pitcher of margaritas waiting for him on his desk by way of motivation, and who doesn't even seem to like her all that much?

Oh yeah, sign me up for *that*.

The thing is, as totally fake as I know it all is, and as much as I don't want to turn into some pseudo-pretty grown-up stuck in

Three B Hell, I look really good. My eyes look huge and sleepy and my mouth is big in a good way, even if it is slightly orange. My eyelashes look like the lush tips of mink paintbrushes.

And the hair: It doesn't even feel like hair. It feels like a silky rabbit. Somehow the hair-dye guru has managed to make it look as if light is radiating from my head, like a saint in a medieval painting.

And even if none of the carbs I am now supposed to forget even exist actually regroup at their intended location, a couple of hours at Victoria's Secret and everything I have that can possibly be pushed up is pushed up and defying the minimal gravitational force that affects such small mass.

The only downside beyond feeling totally fake is that I am embarrassed that everyone will think that I'm trying too hard and I'm a deeply superficial person who only cares about the way she looks. I am embarrassed to walk around outside in case anybody sees me. Not that it isn't embarrassing enough inside my own house. How totally crazed Vivian is to get me back to Winston so people can see her handiwork and how she keeps carrying on about the New You.

Meaning the New *Me*.

XI

THEN, AT THE END OF AUGUST, LISA AND ANITA GET home from their uplifting summers of fun that will look great on a college application, and Lisa starts phoning me.

I kind of avoid her phone calls until I can figure out how I feel about looking like someone else, but eventually I answer my cell phone when she calls from a blocked number, and I am trapped into girlie coffee in Westwood.

And here's the thing: When I walk into Starbucks, Lisa and Anita look up—and then they look down again.

I'm not completely sure if my friends not recognizing me is a good thing or a bad thing, but I am sort of fixated on the bad thing aspect of it, thinking about turning around and leaving fast if I can just come up with a not too obvious way to do it, when Lisa yells.

Everybody looks up from their laptops and their lattes and

the people they're flirting with to stare at me. People no doubt come out of the bathroom to stare at me.

"Gabby, you look so different!" Lisa hurls her arms around me in some kind of a frenzy. All I want to do is to sit down and be inconspicuous.

"You look really, really good," Anita says.

"You do," says Lisa. "Not that you didn't look good before."

"You know what I mean," says Anita. "How did you get your hair to even do that?"

They both sit there googly-eyed, staring at the New Me and I basically want to go into the bathroom and rip my face off, or more accurately, peel it off.

But I change the subject instead. "How was camp?"

Lisa had been on a religious Outward Bound where she learned how to survive if she ever gets stranded in Wisconsin with only dehydrated stew, a toothbrush, and a pocket Bible. She met a lot of boys with great tans and six-packs but, given that she was somewhat streaked with dirt and smelled sort of funky the whole time, she was not exactly ripe for romance.

"And then there's Huey, of course," she says, looking down.

All right. She has been hanging out with Huey, making the discreet, religious version of goo-goo eyes and getting her picture taken maybe two dozen times a day ever since seventh grade, the pictures lined up chronologically and perfectly cropped in little plastic albums that Huey, besotted and creepily well organized, buys by the truckload at Rite Aid and hauls to school to show her every time he fills a new one. But given that she would appear to be completely and unnaturally fine with the fact that she isn't allowed to wear clothes that show any cleavage or go on car dates or think thoughts with body parts in them, and given that she is not exactly open about how she feels or what they've been doing together for the past four years, it's hard to tell what, if *anything*, is going on.

Anita had volunteered to help out orphan children in New Delhi all summer where she lived with her grandma and learned once again that (1) she is Indian, and (2) things are a lot better back in L.A.

"But," she says, sipping her mocha Frappuccino, "I met someone."

Tragically, he is an extremely cute French guy from Marseilles who was in India emulating Mother Theresa because he is thinking about becoming a priest, which makes the chance of his taking up with an underaged Hindu girl somewhat remote. Which is especially annoying since the chance Anita's parents will let her go out with some cute older guy they didn't more or less pick out back home in Beverly Hills is even more remote.

"They wouldn't even let me go to a kickback at Derek Dash Sharma's house at four o'clock in the afternoon yesterday. Because his mother wasn't home, if you please. But look at you," Anita says. "You look like a completely different person! Also more confident. With very good hair."

Lisa and Anita have both had these supposedly transformative summers doing all this deeply meaningful stuff that is going to change their lives and get them into college, but we can all tell that after three months of beauty salons, color consultation, and Pilates, I am the one who is transformed.

"I'll bet your mom is happy," Lisa says.

"Orgasmic. I look just like a Slutmuffin."

Lisa and Anita shake their heads and deny what we all know is true. The whole Winston School Slutmuffin crew would have nodded to me in the street if they didn't figure out who I was first. That is how hot and totally debauched I look.

Still, it's hard to miss the part where Lisa, who has signed on for a life as Untouched Godly Girl, has Huey following her around, and Anita has to be forced to turn down invitations to cavort with cute Indian boys, while I, having spent the whole summer being doused with Elixir of Sex Appeal, only ever have physical contact with males who are working on my hair, and my hunky yet gay personal trainer.

"You know," Anita says. "At the beginning of the year, so many people are at loose ends. You should run with this. Before things get organized."

I just keep hoping I won't screw this up before somebody figures out that I'm the same sub-regular girl with nothing going for her as before I showed up looking hot.

XII

AND THEN SCHOOL STARTS.

It's that perfect SoCal scene with the matching Jaguars lined up in the carpool line, inching through the stone gates with their ivy and red bougainvillea and pink geraniums, sunlight glinting through the palm fronds and the flat blue sky that makes people from Back East want to throw up or move here.

The ironic thing is that we start off the year reading Thoreau in non-AP, non-honors, sub-regular English Lit. The part where he says you should beware of any enterprise you have to get new clothes for? Clearly, this does not apply to Winston School. I have two inches of cleavage, thanks to my slightly orange Wonderbra, and by lunchtime Billy Nash is looking down it.

"So, how do you like it so far?" Freaking Billy Nash is making eye contact with my chest. It's a freaking miracle.

"Excuse me?"

Billy sticks out his hand like a politician who is pretty damned sure he is going to get my vote. Then he flashes me The Grin. The smoldering, adorable grin. Like he knows that I'm going to race from precinct to precinct and vote for him over and over all day long.

"Billy Nash," he says.

"Uh, Gabby Gardiner," I say. Why not?

"Whoa," Billy says, with the faintest look of recognition. "You're not new. I know you, don't I?"

"Not really," I say. This is basically the weirdest conversation I have ever had, although it does prove for all eternity that I really was invisible as plastic wrap with nothing in it until I streaked my hair and got professional eyelash consultation. Which I already know but do not exactly *want* to know.

"Weren't you in my Spanish class?"

"Eighth grade," I say, feeling the way you feel when you've just jumped onto a ski lift and it's pulling you up quickly over the crowns of pine trees and the air is thin and cold and you're afraid you might fall off and die but it's just so amazing you really don't care. "Who remembers?"

"Who wants to?" Billy says. Billy Nash, who has been bathed in golden light, as far as anybody knows, since birth. "Did you get a nose job or something?"

"No, I did not get a nose job or something."

And I realize we are walking together, actually walking down the hall toward the cafeteria together, we are actually walking through the door and people keep saying hello to him and nodding to me, and I am actually walking around with Billy freaking Nash.

As it turns out, Billy has just broken up with Aliza Benitez, the queen of the Slutmuffins, and is trawling for firm young flesh. Or so he says. It is one of those jokes that isn't really a joke.

"Aliza's great," he says. "But let's face it, she's very high maintenance. And, let's face it, life with Aliza isn't exactly a day with the Andies."

I nod and try not to look as if I am memorizing it all.

Slutmuffin: good.

High maintenance: bad.

Day with the Andies: good.

Day with Aliza Benitez: not exactly good.

Benitez *gone*: The firm young flesh sitting right next to Billy Nash in the Class of 1920 Memorial Garden is *Me*.

My flesh: *good*.

I keep wishing that lunch would extend for the rest of the day, or possibly the rest of my life.

By the time I get to the art room for back-to-back ceramics and painting, I am in an altered state of consciousness.

Miss Cornish, although she doesn't come right out and say it, seems slightly taken aback by the New Me. When Lisa comes in late and sits next to me in the chair I was saving for her, Miss Cornish beams and looks relieved that I'm not trailing Slutmuffins in my wake. Then she tells me that I should probably wear a smock, which somewhat defeats the purpose of free dress day, and I'm not sure if it's the newly unveiled cleavage or the fact that the mega-expensiveness of the new blouse is obvious even to her, a woman who comes to school in large plaid shirts thrown over Lakers T-shirts.

Mr. Rosen, of course, doesn't notice a thing. If I'd shown up naked, he probably would have figured that Winston had a radical new figure-drawing policy and made everybody sketch my naked body really really fast before some angry parent made sure the policy switched back and we only got to draw heavily draped figure models, who might just as well not have had any nipples for all we got to see of them.

He comes up to me and he says, "So! Gabriella, you're working on portfolio, yes?"

Well, no.

Even though Winston School goes basically apeshit whenever anyone wins pretty much anything and our portfolios are constantly being pillaged by the prize-whore faculty and submitted to every contest in the galaxy, I am so so done with that.

I am done winning diddly art ribbons, the same tacky red ribbon as one hundred and fourteen other pathetic losers in L.A. County who can also draw a pastel bowl of fruit, while the bouncy, organizing-10K-walks-to-cure-obscure-diseases girls are getting commendations from the mayor, the governor, the Secretary General of the U.N., and the Queen of England, and everybody else is too busy to attend the commendation ceremony because they are all tied up becoming National Merit Finalists, AP Scholars, Presidential Scholars, and Masters of the Universe. And Lolly Wu keeps showing up at assembly to play the sonata that took the audience by storm and won her a gold medallion in Romania.

So unless someone is planning to crown me Worldwide Queen of Glaze: no.

Just no.

But I don't tell *him* that, and he spends the period sticking stuff in front of me and making me draw it for five minutes, and moving it slightly and making me draw it again, and putting it in a glass bowl and making me draw it again. It is very hard to concentrate, given that all I can think about is Billy Nash.

"Oooooh! I'd love to draw the feather and those eggs," Sasha Aronson says, staring at the ratty old objects on my still-life table as if they were pirates' booty.

Mr. Rosen tells her to keep drawing her hand, which you have to figure is going to get old pretty fast.

"You have slides of all those pots you make for Elspeth, yes?" he says to me.

Well, no.

"Tell Camera Boy, very fine resolution and well lit to show the luster."

To which Huey, the aforementioned camera boy, is not going to object because he is slavishly devoted to Mr. Rosen and because he gets to look all cool and technologically proficient in front of Lisa while she sits there trying to throw bowl after sorry bowl on her potter's wheel.

Not that I'm not slavishly devoted to Mr. Rosen too, sort of, but it is as if my slavish devotion compass has suddenly been thrown off course by an irresistible magnetic force and all I can think about is whether I'm going to run into Force Field Boy again when class lets out.

Which I do. He is waiting for me after class.

He says, "Hey."

I say, "Hey." Thinking: *Do not screw this up, Gabriella. Do. Not. Screw. This. Up.*

He says, "So, are you coming to Kap's?"

I say, "I don't know, Nash. Why would I go to Kap's?"

Billy puts his hand into the back pocket of my tiny denim skirt. "Because his father scored a copy of *Gorgon III.*" (Which isn't out yet. Which is supposed to have the world's most gruesome special effects. Which up until that point I had no plan to ever see because I don't care all that much about gruesome special effects.) "And maybe other reasons . . ."

I am leaning in toward him. I know and he knows and anyone in their right mind knows what other reasons.

I say, "What other reasons, Nash? Could you perhaps elaborate on that?"

The elaboration is the pressure of his fingers on my ass.

And even though I am the same person, living in the same place, going to the same school, and driving the same ratty Toyota, I am magically someone else.

XIII

"LOOK AT YOU," PONYTAIL DOC SAYS, GRINNING AT me like a drunken baby. "Wendy tells me you're reflecting on your life, and your brain is going a mile a minute."

Meaning: Not only did I remember to ask Vivian the day of the week when she came with some kind of remedial lip liner in a giant tube with a rubber grip this morning before Ponytail showed up, but I told Wendy to go away because I was thinking due to the fact that I was glued to *Gabriella Gardiner Presents* and I didn't want to be interrupted. Then, when given no choice but to open my eyes, I told Ponytail it was Friday—when, ta-da, it *was* Friday—and she wrote it down.

I am just racking up the bonus points.

Except that all I want to do is keep my eyes closed and lounge in what appears to be my actual past with Billy Nash in it looking a lot like my actual boyfriend, as opposed to sitting here in this strange, hospital present where Billy Nash is nowhere to be found.

But Ponytail's unbridled enthusiasm for my progress as an ever-so-slightly sentient vegetable is unquenchable. "I saw your sketches," she says. "And your mood chart is stellar."

This is the chart on which I circle a number for my mood, from suicidal number 1 to buzzed-on-IV-morphine number 10. When you circle a number between semi-jolly 7 and drugged-out, ecstatic 10, people in white jackets stop coming by your room to cheer you up. But circle a 4 and there they are, trying to force you to ex*plore* your lack of cheer and making you take happy pills.

It's not that I'm opposed to happy pills in principle, it's just that they make it hard to work your way from one end of a thought to the other. Which makes you feel so sadly brainless, it pretty much defeats the purpose of the pill. You would think. Part of which I evidently say out loud.

But Ponytail, having lost Miss Congeniality to Wendy, is going out for Miss Empathy. "It can be hard to feel smart after an insult to your brain," she says. "It's common even for very smart people—"

I feel a precipitous dip below semi-jolly 7 coming on, but I am too completely whacked to keep my mouth shut. "How do you even know I'm smart?" I say.

Ponytail Doc looks stumped.

"Gabby," Vivian asks in her Florence Nightingale, long-suffering nurse voice. "Do you know any little kids who might be calling you? Do you tutor a small child for community service or something?"

I don't remember anything vaguely like that, but who knows? Maybe I used to be a paragon of tutoring homeless kids with sad, incurable diseases. Maybe I'm the poster girl for Why Bad Things Happen to Good Teenagers. Maybe I just haven't gotten that far in *Gabriella Gardiner Presents*.

Still, it seems pretty unlikely.

"Well, do you?" Vivian wants to know. "Because some little girl named Andrea keeps calling you."

"Andie Bennett is calling me?"

"Is that *Heather* Bennett's girl? The pretty one with the shoes?" Vivian is impressed. "Maybe you should call her back."

Because if you're pretty enough and you have enough different-colored pairs of quilted Chanel ballet flats, you are right up there on Vivian's automatic speed dial.

"Did she say what she wanted?"

Vivian looks perplexed. "She sounds a lot younger," she says. "And it was hard to understand her."

My eyes close themselves and I am right back in my *After*—*after* I get made over into an adorable, hot girl; *after* I get Billy; *after* I become designated decorating slave on the Student Council decorating committee; *after* I start spending my leisure time in Kap's pool house (which is more of a pool villa) with the future Ivy League water polo and lacrosse gang and trying to figure out what the hell Andie Bennett is even talking about.

The *After* that comes before the hospitalized *Present*.

The *After* I'm not even sure I'm still in.

I am right back to watching the Andies float across my brain in Technicolor splendor, lit up the same way they used to be when I stared at them at Winston from afar for all the years when I didn't actually know them, back in my *Before*.

But the problem with the Andie and Andy reel of *Gabriella Gardiner's Smashed Brain Presents Scenes from Teen Life in the Three B's* is that it's hard to tell if it's going to be some weird parody of Teen Luv or a creepy Lifetime drama about sick sick codependency or what.

Look:

There they are floating down the hall, their hands all over each other, so into each other that the only reason they don't bump into people is that people get out of their way.

There they are in a tight little threesome with Billy, walking around with their arms draped over each other's shoulders, and whatever Muffin Billy is with right then is running along slightly behind them to keep up, no room on the walkway to be four abreast.

Back then, you had to wonder if the rumors were true.

Turns out, they were. Andy and Andie have been into each other since Sunny Hills Preschool where they spent their leisure time slipping snacks to Billy in time-out.

Turns out, Andie doesn't actually have to dial or do *any*thing else by herself because Andy does it for her.

Turns out, Andy is very smart and gets Andie through all of her not-what-you'd-call-difficult classes (not even sub-regular normal American Lit, but super-unbelievably easy Topics in Literature, in which Mr. Mallory stands on a chair and applauds if anyone finishes a book. Any book, including graphic novels and Classic Comics) by teaching her everything in really simple sentences and making color-coded index cards.

Andie is very well dressed, mostly in pink, and it has nothing to do with whether pink is the new black. Also, she likes getting little pink presents. This works because Andy likes giving her presents. A lot. What they don't like is drama.

"Allergic to drama!" they say.

It's like they're the only good marriage any of us has ever seen. Even though all four of their parents have been married about nineteen times each, including once in the fifth grade when Andie and Andy narrowly escaped a future fraught with incest because Andie's mom was married to Andy's dad for about twenty minutes. This was not even long enough for Andie to pack up her little pink bedroom and move into the new joint house that never happened.

There she is, opening a set of Hello Kitty pencils in their own matching pink pencil case, only you can't tell if this is a campy little joke or what she wants for real.

"They're so nice! Thank you, Kaps!"

Then she looks over at Billy who is sitting with his legs draped across my lap on the low wall behind the Class of 1920 Garden loading up on Cabernet before AP Spanish Language.

"You should get Gabs a present," she says. "How come I get all this stuff and she doesn't?" She puts her hands on her hips and makes a monkey face at him and the possibility that I am going to come out of this looking like present-free Pathetic Girl seems to be rising off the checkered blanket like the bouquet from the wine in the thermos and the Dixie cups.

"I don't know, Bens," Billy says. "We could get you pink shoelaces and you'd be happy, but she's a hard one to figure."

Andie rolls her eyes. "Well, you could always ask her what she wants, you know." She looks over at me, dying on the blanket, pouring Dixie cups of Cabernet down my throat. "Well, he could, couldn't he?"

And I say, "I don't know, Nash. Could you?"

The thing is, by Christmas, he can ask, and by Valentine's Day, he knows without asking, and when Andie gets another in a series of velvet, heart-shaped, lace-trimmed cushions that you figure her bed must be buried underneath by now, I get my little silver heart-shaped box with my initials on the lid and one slightly melted candy kiss inside.

Propped up on pillows in the small green room, I want to close my eyes to avoid the close-up of how pathetically choked up I was, fondling that candy kiss, but they are already closed.

Not to mention my current state of choked-uppedness because nothing makes sense: that Andie Bennett has figured out how to phone me in the hospital from Cute World while Candy Kiss Boy might just as well have been sucked into a black hole with no cell phone reception.

Explain *that*.

"You should call back this little girl when you feel up to it," Vivian says. "Because she sounds like she's going to cry if you don't."

Everyone in the whole world that I don't want to talk to is just calling calling calling. And then there's Billy, who isn't. Who is, for all I know, out there sitting around with Andy and Andie and some shiny, new piece of firm young flesh that Andy and Andie have nothing to say about because they're so into each other that they don't even notice that she isn't me.

I slip from Paranoid Fantasyland into Homemovieland without even a glitch in the continuity.

See:

It's the first time I actually *meet* Andie and Andy *after* four years of being in school with them and just standing around watching them, that first lunch with Billy that first day of junior year on the lawn in the Class of 1920 Garden, and they don't actually look up.

Not that I care.

I just keep smiling.

You have to figure that if I could smile through entire weekends of *Singin' in the Rain* and a cavalcade of Disney classics with marshmallow-speckled fudge because that is what my actual friends like to do in their free time, there is no reason I can't deal with *this*. Even though I know I don't remotely belong on the perfect checkered blanket and even if I did, I could never be as perfect a girlfriend as Andie because I will never be as cute or as nice or as rich or a congenital idiot.

You go, Gabs, I tell myself in buzzed affirmation. *You're just the second-cutest thing ever and you fit right in. Just let out your inner babe and no one will notice you're just a sub-regular girl with good hair.*

Right.

So then I go, *You go, Gabs. Billy Nash has his hand on your thigh, and that's all anybody will notice.*

Which turns out to be more or less true.

Not to mention, if Billy is the Andies' oldest friend, then he has to be somewhat nice, right? He does start saying hello to my friends purely in honor of me by the end of the first week of eleventh grade, which is not what you'd call a challenge, given that there aren't all that many of them. But still. He says, "Hey, Anita," "How's it going, Lisa?" all the time, not even looking over to see if the Slutmuffins are curling their lips. And he is already nodding his head whenever Huey bounces by, more, it seems, out of friendliness to my semi-buddy than out of recognition that Huey is another mega-rich boy from the same zip code.

All right, he is definitely somewhat nice.

XIV

MEANWHILE, MY PARENTS ARE SPONSORING A Gardiners-Have-Made-It Fest complete with a great many banana daiquiris and pretty much everything except Mexican sparklers.

Watch:

The first night Billy pulls up to my house in the midnight-blue Beemer and Vivian spots him getting out of the car and slinging his little black daypack over his shoulder and flexing his back, she is pretty much ready to fall to her knees and yell "Hallelujah!"

She doesn't even try to hide how excited she is. For years I'd been this disappointing nonentity, a sorry clothes rack for expensive little wrong-season outfits from Sunset Plaza, but now I have a pretty damned cool approximation of a boyfriend.

Hallelujah, all right.

My dad, who pretty much hasn't said squat to me on a regular basis since father-daughter Indian Princess at the YMCA broke up in second grade and we retired our stupid leather Indian Princess medallions, says "Nice ride." While making eye contact.

It's unnerving.

Somewhere out there, somewhere in the Midwest maybe, with cornfields and silos and sheep, there are parents who are all concerned about the age when their children should go on a date, all worried about whether they'll kiss with tongue before marriage. These are no doubt the same people who think that having a cute lime-green bra strap sticking out of your tank top puts you one step away from working in a brothel in Hong Kong.

Or maybe these parents are in Hong Kong and in their minds the brothel is here in L.A.

Or maybe these parents are from Utah and their imaginary brothels are littered all over the other forty-nine states.

Wherever they are, they don't have kids at Winston School.

Unless they're from some exotic land filled with ethnic diversity, but clueless about pimping your kid for popularity. But still, you can tell that even Anita's mom is eyeing that cute Derek Dash Sharma when he rolls through the Winston gates in his nice little red tricked-out Audi TT, so who knows? Although you can't help but notice that Anita's mom is afraid Derek will ravish Anita at four in the afternoon if his mother isn't home to stop them, whereas Vivian would drop everything to drive me straight over there if Derek Dash Sharma—whose family is in the richer-than-God category that she and John are so fond of—so much as cocked his head in my direction.

There stand my parents, grinning like grateful idiots when Billy comes through the front door of Casa Gardiner. He is golden, with that pale blond hair reflecting light. He says, "Hey, Vivian. How's it going, John?" And it is as if they are turned on.

But not as turned on as me, the original grateful grinning idiot.

He is so absolutely, undeniably perfect. I go: *Why me? Why me? Why me?* about six hundred times in the five seconds it takes me to walk across the living room to the front door. And then, by the time we are out the door, by the time his arm is draped around *my* shoulder, I don't even care why or how or anything. And the only thing in my mind, arranging myself in the passenger seat of the midnight-blue Beemer, tying my hair back so the wind won't blow it into the shape of a tumbleweed, is my increasingly insistent mantra, the one about how I'd better not screw this up.

Lisa and Anita are completely nonplussed. Even though I am pretty sure that everyone else kind of wants to have what I suddenly have—cute skintight clothes and a spot in the Class of 1920 Garden drinking wine out of paper cups at lunch with Billy Nash—I have somehow managed to cozy up to the only two friends who are a special case. They seem more amazed than covetous, like they want anthropological field reports of the inner workings of hot, elite circles that they themselves don't actually want any personal part of.

Sitting in a group study room trying to teach me SAT II math facts, Anita says, "It's just that I see you with someone more, I don't know, more arty."

Before now, the idea that she saw me with anyone at all would have been highly flattering and also highly unrealistic.

I say, "Huey is arty."

"Someone *normal* and arty. Someone, I don't know, more intense."

"Billy is intense."

"Not that kind of intense. Not jock intense."

I've barely known him for a month, but I am pretty sure that he's the perfect intensity. I am pretty sure that even if this is like Zeus coming down from Mount Olympus to frolic with some clueless shepherd maid, I don't want to wreck the frolic with major analysis or—yay Vivian and the power of positive thinking—think one single negative thought to mess it up.

"It's not like he's a *dumb* jock," I say. "He is going to *Prince*ton."

Anita slams her ten-pound AP Bio book down on the table. "Don't be naive," she says, as if anyone could stay naive for five minutes at Winston. "It's not like people who know they're going to Princeton fall of junior year are getting in because they're Albert Einstein."

"Anita!"

"Some people actually have to study and get a four-three GPA and build a nuclear reactor in their basement to get into an Ivy. And some people don't."

Which is obviously true. Which is why Peyton Epps, famous for being mean and stupid but whose whole Epps dynasty has large buildings named after them at every high school, college, and hospital in Southern California, is going to Brown instead of Cal State Bakersfield.

"At least Cal doesn't have a quota on Asians," Anita says.

Which is why Lewis Wing, who actually got a prize for taking and acing more APs than anybody else in the history of Winston School, is going to Cal instead of Brown.

"Okay," I say. "I get it. Life is unfair and also sucks. But my life, for once, doesn't suck and it's not as if the ticket to Princeton is his fault."

"I'm just saying," Anita says. "Don't go confusing him with Wallace Schaeffer."

Wallace Schaeffer has been taking engineering courses at UCLA since he was fourteen. There are completely credible rumors that Wallace Schaeffer got a likely letter from MIT when he was still a sophomore. The only reason Wallace Schaeffer is even at Winston and not hanging around with all the other certified geniuses at Harvard-Westlake—which Winston tries to pretend is our crosstown rival, ignoring the tiny facts that (1) it is not across town, and (2) it is better than us in basically everything except equestrian team and cheerleading—is that the Harvard-Westlake middle school carpool line is routed past his house and his mom's hobby is waging war to make them stop blocking her vast, circular driveway.

But Wallace Schaeffer is not the one driving me around in his midnight-blue convertible:

That would be Billy Nash.

Lisa and Anita try to be nice to him. When we drive past them in the parking lot, they wave while looking at their feet.

Not that there's any way that I can tell them what I'm doing with him up in his bedroom, when he knocks the homework off the bed with his bare feet and strokes my hair, and my forehead, and my eyebrows, and my eyelids. When he runs his fingers down the back of my neck and down my spine under my blouse and I want more and he wants more and I just want to give him more. Because: Even though getting him off like that might not technically be sex, they would still be completely grossed out.

But there we are, by the side of the bed, his fingers on my shoulders, me unzipping him, me with my clothes still on because every time I think about taking them off, all I can think of is Billy looking down at my naked self going, *Jesus, what was I thinking?* And the whole time, I'm going, *Whoa, Gabriella, this is actually more than somewhat fun. Whoa. This is freaking amazing.*

And trying not to look so into it that he'll think I'm a skank.

Only you have to admit, Billy is Gorgeous Boy from Planet Irresistible.

Eating frozen yogurt together after sculpture, Lisa says, "I wouldn't mind sculpting that." That being Billy from behind. Also, not being totally unobservant, she says, "Watch your back, okay? Not that you have to."

She is thumbing through a college catalog from Davidson that she got from the college counselor—the one who I never go to visit and am pretty much planning never to go visit. The one whose official job is to make pronouncements about how your sub-regularity severely limits your future options, college choices, happiness, success, viability as a resident of the Three B's, and potential for shopping at stores other than Ross Dress for Less once your parents stop supporting you.

"What's Davidson?" Anita asks.

"It's a really good college that I'm not going to attend," Lisa says.

"How is anyone supposed to make decisions from a catalog anyway?" Anita says.

"Great catalog," Lisa says. "I just have other plans."

"My plans don't extend beyond this weekend," I say.

Lisa sighs. "You're an artist, so you're in a completely different category than the rest of us. Your portfolio is going to be amazing." Lisa thinks that any doodle you aren't outright embarrassed to sign is amazing, which makes her very supportive but not entirely realistic about my stature as an art goddess. "Do you know where you're going to send it?"

Well, no.

Whatever brains I once had have been sucked out through

my new and time-intensive good hair, my energy devoted to precision blow-drying and Billy. But even if I'd still been skulking around Winston with sub-regular hair and no boyfriend, it is not as if I would have been out there whoring it up with extra-sexy extracurriculars to fill out great-looking lists for the (close eyes and wince) sub-regular, second-tier colleges that would even consider a person like me.

The portfolio seems like a bizarre little sideshow to keep my mind occupied so I won't have to contemplate how fast I'm going to plummet in a highly entertaining yet predictable nose-dive from the high board into a very small bucket during the main event. How I am going to spend the spring of senior year congratulating everybody else for getting into (loud applause from God Himself) Harvard while I pretend I want a gap year.

Anita says, "It's junior year. Shoot me if this sounds too mom-ish, but don't you need to start making a plan?"

Well, no.

How much strategic planning does it take to get rejected from Penn, laughed out of the Wharton School of Business applicant pool, and left rotting and Ivy-free up on Via Estrada with only your totally shattered dad who has run so amok with his stupid, unrealistic plans for your future that even a pitcher of iced margaritas is not going to take the edge off?

My only plan is to climb onto Planet Billy and only occasionally glance back down at the debris of my soon to be previously sub-regular life. Because even though I can tell that high school is only temporary, I just don't care.

Anita says, "You know, Gabby, you should run with this. You should go out for student government right now."

Which is not as bizarre as it might sound. Because: Student Council is always getting both halves of cute couples elected to it. And because Winston has its Student Council elections at the start of the school year instead of in the spring, presumably so that if someone gets fat or their social status suddenly tanks during the summer, the cool kids on Council won't be stuck in a room with them all year.

And right then, two weeks into being with Billy, a meteoric rise to super-regular Student Council Girl Appendage to the Gorgeous Hot Boy seems as unremarkable as crossing the street.

"Right now," Lisa agrees. "Not that you have to."

Right now, before you screw it up with Billy Nash, is what I hear. Which is *so* not happening. Because pretty much my whole way of life involves thinking about how much I adore Billy Nash, and adoring him, and doing all this cute domestic stuff to keep him happy and not screwing it up.

XV

I AM MAYBE THE WORLD'S BEST ASPIRING GIRLFRIEND.

Billy likes blue Pilot pens; I always have one handy. Billy wants to cut out of school and get coffee at Starbucks or some boysenberry/wheatgrass thing at Jamba Juice; I am out of there in a flash. Billy likes fat oatmeal cookies with currants and not raisins; I am a fat-oatmeal-cookie-with-currants-and-no-raisins baking machine.

Vivian even helps me. We have mother-daughter pimp-your-kid bonding over cookie sheets and baking powder.

"Don't think you don't deserve this," she says, spraying sticky nonstick grease onto the cookie sheets.

I say, "Huh?"

"You look darling," she says. "And you're a very sweet girl. People like that."

And for like thirty seconds, kneading the dough for sugar

balls, standing next to Vivian in a cloud of powdered sugar, I am in a state reserved for actual darling-looking, sweet girls whose mothers really like them. I am beaming and inhaling sugar and Vivian is sort of looking at me strangely.

And then I go, *Shit, Gabriella. Really? Are you freaking delusional?*

Because: It is more than slightly difficult to forget the part where I was the slightly less darling-looking, sweet girl she didn't like all that much before she got me slightly reupholstered and I got such a hot boyfriend.

"People like what?" I say.

"Oh crap, Gabby," she says. "Don't do this. Let me support you, all right? I just don't want you to squander your opportunities."

"What opportunities?"

Like we both don't know what my one and only opportunity is, and what kind of car he drives. I just want to make her say it out loud.

"What opportunities?" I whine.

"Just to be with people who might be more, uh, fun for you," she says, not looking up, lying as fast as she can while measuring the flour. "Just to have the chance to be a little more, uh, out there. You know, The New You. So more people can get to know how wonderful you are."

I don't think she even said anything like that to me when I was a tiny kid at the young age when everybody really *is* wonderful. Or maybe I'm just not wonderful enough, or my head is too bashed in, to remember. Maybe I would remember better now if I hadn't smashed my head against a tree, greatly reducing my wonderfulness as well as my crowd of fun people.

Not that I exactly make a bunch of fun new girlfriends once being with Billy turns me into who I was before I ran his car into a tree.

The obvious people to be my new girlfriends are Aliza Benitez and Charlotte Ward and their little pack of Slutmuffin hos and maybe the whole taste-impaired Student Council decorating committee once it turns out that Anita is right, and I get elected even though the only thing anybody knows about me is that Billy has his hand down my back pocket.

But Billy had dumped Aliza Benitez, popular ho royalty, just before he hooked up with me. So: The princess posse is even less likely to throw a Welcome to Our World party for some outside, unpopular, clueless girl they've never heard of, no matter how good I look and how good I am at slinging crepe paper after they relegate me to the status of newbie slave on the Council decorating committee.

Actually, one of the good things about moving into Billy Nash World from total obscurity is that I don't have to worry about getting tight with a whole lot of new friends I could screw it up with.

The Andies are so busy with every detail of each other that they just sort of accept I'm there and go back to gazing into one another's eyes. And the Slutmuffins aren't exactly begging me to make time for little shopping trips down Montana Avenue with them.

I actually think that the fact I'm not brown-nosing around makes me somewhat less abhorrent to them than if I'd been a more obvious wannabe, panting around their thin, tan ankles, all eager and wagging my tail. Not to mention I am completely terrified that if they do get to know me, they'll figure out how sub-regular I am and tell Billy.

They sit right in front of me, three of them sprawled on the corner of the Andies' checkered blanket in the Class of 1920 Garden and have what passes as a conversation while looking straight at me but acting as if I'm not there. Not so much an invisible person like before, but more like the Serbo-Croatian-speaking crazy lady who can't be expected to follow even the simple English dialogue of brain-dead hos.

I could just reach out and knock them over, but I don't.

"Are you coming to shop at Ron Herman or not?"

"Not. I have my French tutor."

"So blow him off."

"What does Ron Herman have anyway? Those dresses are heinous."

"Crimes against humanity."

"I thought you were coming."

"I'll wait for you at CPK. I'm too gross to try on right now anyway."

"So you're going to binge on CPK barbeque chicken pizza, skank? Come try on."

"No, they don't even like me in there. That big redheaded salesgirl—"

"The one with the split ends?"

"She just keeps following me around like I shoplifted a T-shirt or something."

"No way! Why?"

"Because she shoplifted a T-shirt or something."

"I spend so much money in there, they ought to be *giving* me T-shirts."

This is not as hard to take as you would think, given all the Chardonnay I consume with my egg salad sandwich. Still, you would think that after breaking up with Billy, Aliza would maybe want a little more distance, or at least, if she is going to jiggle her T and A in his face on the same blanket, you'd think she would want to come across as halfway appealing and marginally gracious. But apparently she is just so secure in her God-given place as Slutmuffin bitch queen that she doesn't even care.

When I actually have to show up and try to get the decorating committee not to make things look any uglier than they have to given the large quantity of gaudy balloons and tinsel they have stockpiled, when all they will say to me is basically, "Please pass the glue gun," I just go, *Gabriella, you do not have to hang with these bitches, you have actual friends. You have Billy and they don't. Everything is Perfect. Back away from the glue gun and go make a crepe paper flower and shut up.*

They go back into their little huddle, as if they think they're magically inaudible. Or maybe they just don't care.

"Kaps says Nash wants us to let her do the posters."

"But we're already tracing the Elvis poster."

"Just because he's hooking up with her, she doesn't get to take over."

"It's just a poster, Char. And she's got plenty of time for it. It's not like she's in AP Physics."

"Yeah, and do *you* want to tell Nash no? Because I don't."

I just keep telling myself that as long as I keep Billy happy, I can ignore them back. I can just wander around glowing faintly with light from his star.

Which makes me more noticeable.

All of a sudden, I am cuter *and* smarter. Dr. Berg says that I'm "building up steam" in non-AP, non-honors, sub-regular track chemistry (although I have to say not as sub-regular as Andie, who is taking Topics in the Environment for which she gets extra credit for figuring out how to send away for a poster of a humpback whale from Greenpeace) when I am doing exactly the same as always.

Sure I'm building up steam; I am smoking from hotness by association. *Sure* I have a whole lot more going for me, the entire whole lot consisting of Billy and my new wardrobe. If Billy likes me, suddenly everybody but a few stray Muffins like me. Not that they actually *like* me like me, they just act like they like me. And it isn't as if I mind all that much.

Mind—*please*. I want more all the time. When Billy walks by in the library when I'm sitting there with Anita trying to figure out the workings of the periodic table and he bends down and blows just faintly on the top of my head and ruffles my bangs with the tips of his fingers, I have to bite my lower lip just so I won't shiver with joy in too obvious a way.

XVI

IF I HADN'T BEEN SO CRAZED ABOUT MAKING SURE that Billy would keep liking me around the clock, it could have been completely fun.

It definitely eliminates any shred of boredom or dead time in my life because the thing about being with Billy is that you have to be made up and ready to roll 24/7. He likes to drive and he likes company.

"How is it you've lived in L.A. all your life and you've never been anywhere?" he says.

And he doesn't mean chic places on Sunset with bouncers, where I also haven't been. He means the best Pho 999 for Vietnamese noodles so far out on Sepulveda, it is almost at the far end of the Valley; he means hickory burgers on the red faux-leather stools at the counter at the Apple Pan on Pico; ribs with bikers who seem to have dropped in from a 1950s time warp at Dr. Hogly Wogly's;

Versailles for Cuban plantains and black beans in Culver City; and tacos at La Canasta, which is somewhere so far south and east of downtown that it looks like some whole other country. He means that field in Westchester where you can lie on the hood of the Beemer and watch the planes taking off from LAX at night and the Cajun place at the Fairfax Farmers' Market that has homemade yam potato chips fried up and ready to eat by ten a.m.

I remember that perfectly: the taste of the yam chips and their crunchiness and the grease on my fingers, how you couldn't get enough, and at the end, you dig the last little shards out of the corners of the little paper box they come in.

"How do you know all these places?" I say. "Do you just cut school and drive around Monterey Park looking for pork bao?"

"I get bored easily," Billy says. "You want to roll?"

He likes to tell Agnes that Andy is helping him study for precalc. And then driving up to Santa Barbara for hotdogs and sauerkraut at the only dive on State Street open after midnight, then turning around and driving back. He likes telling Agnes that he is doing community service (Condition of Probation #17) at a fictional downtown homeless mission and then driving to San Juan Capistrano to listen to ska at a bar—only, he has to bribe the ticket guy because even though Billy has the excellent ID of an actual twenty-two-year-old guy named Lars from St. Cloud, Minnesota, I don't.

He could have told Agnes he was going on an overnight NASA expedition to Mars and she would have bought it.

I, on the other hand, don't have to make up anything. I just say, "Going with Billy. See ya." Vivian couldn't have cared less if I had my head in his lap all the way to San Diego on a school night, which I didn't, just so long as the stick shift wouldn't mess up my makeup and reveal the un-cute Old Me lurking underneath, thereby jeopardizing my girlfriendhood and metamorphosis into a kid she actually might want.

"How is it that you've never had a corn dog in Eagle Rock?" he'd say.

And I would say, "Beats me."

And he would take down the rag roof of the Beemer and that would be our destination.

The other thing is sports. Endless sports. Obviously, I have to attend water polo matches near and far, which turns out to be a not un-fun game to watch, with a whole lot of splashing and yelling, and muscular boys in Speedos. It soon becomes apparent that Billy's one area of school spirit involves sitting around at all Winston varsity events and patting his friends on the butt. Who knew that all varsity jock boys have a fixation that makes them watch all other varsity jock boys play all other sports except golf? This includes fencing, where they all pump fists for the other team's guy by mistake half the time because they can't figure out who made the touch.

"How is it that you go to Winston and you've never been to a home game?"

"I'm not that into sports, Nash. I mean, I like them now. I like watching you rule the pool and all. I just wasn't that into it before you enlightened me."

"Well, what are you into, Gardiner, other than eating international junk food and decorating things?"

"*I'm* into international junk food? Have you ever noticed who's leading these fun expeditions to Rooster Shack to eat fries with the Crips?"

"That would be Americana," he says. "Have I taught you nothing?"

"I'm into art," I say. It kind of comes out of nowhere, but once it's out, it's out. Okay, I am into art.

And it seems like he can handle it because he says, "Well, I hope you're very good at art, because you are currently hanging with the undisputed king of water polo."

Apparently, this is not one of Billy's more egregious exaggerations. On our late-night jaunts, sometimes we end up at Sam Deveraux's fraternity house at USC, which seems to have a permanent, twenty-four-hour party going on, and where we are always welcome because Sam was the water polo equivalent of a linebacker back when he was a senior and Billy was a varsity starter in tenth grade.

"Yo, you gotta come *here*," Sam Deveraux says, more than slightly drunk but dead serious. "Fight on! We're number one!" His also more-than-slightly-drunk college water polo buddies stick up their index fingers in agreement. "We need you, man. Don't you want to be number one?"

"Dude. Nothing would make me happier than staying in town," Billy says. "But, man, I've gotta go to . . ." (drumroll drowning out even the permanent, twenty-four-hour party music) "Princeton. You know how it is."

"*Damn* Agnes." Sam drapes his arm around Billy as if Billy could somehow steady him, which, I can tell you from my vast experience with my dad lurching through the house beyond help, is by that point in the evening totally useless. Then he turns to me, which is slightly frightening since he is extremely large and I figure he could crush me if he fell on me, which seems like a strong possibility.

"Whadda bout you?" Sam says. "Don't you wanna come here and be a Theta and Billy can be king?"

And you know, even though the thought of spending four years at Crazed School Spirit U and being a Theta (if I could have gotten in, which I couldn't) kind of makes me want to go throw myself into a ditch, if Billy was going to be king of college at SC instead of Princeton, all hunkered down and happy in his dad's old eating club, I totally would have signed right up.

Billy sticks his shoulder between me and Sam, which could have saved my life if so much as a slight breeze had hit Sam from behind, causing him to pitch forward. "She doesn't do sorority chick crap," Billy says. "She does *art*."

Sam runs his hand up the wall as if he is looking for a handle. "Theta could do art," he says. "She *could*. 'Member Becca French? Theta does product *de*sign. Tolja."

"She doesn't do that kind of art," Billy says. "She does real art."

Okay, so you would have to conclude that he does know something about me, right? And even though I am pretty sure it's all about the incredibly expensive hair extensions and the perfect makeup and the gravity defying Wonderbra, something like this would give a reasonable person cause to think he actually did kind of like something about me that my mother didn't spend the summer buying for me. Right?

Which is what makes it so hard to tell if the eucalyptus tree on Songbird Lane has done some actual damage to my chest, or if I am just some metaphorically heartsick, delusional bimbo in a hospital gown with no sense and, coincidentally, no boyfriend.

Explain that.

He has completely vanished. I am lying in a mechanical bed with the sides up while he is no doubt out at Johnny Rockets eating a medium-rare burger with curly fries with his water polo boys and girl school prostitots from Holy Name.

Only, it is hard to reconcile any of this with what I actually do remember, which I am pretty sure is true.

XVII

THIS IS HOW A PERSON FALLS IN LOVE WITH BILLY NASH.

The part of the *Gabriella Gardiner Presents Scenes from Teen Life in the Three B's* where a person wants to slow it down to keep it from lurching precipitously toward the mysterious and annoying Now, to hold it on pause and watch it slowly, frame by frame, in an imaginary present in which we, Billy and I, are both in the same room.

Unlike the *actual* present, in which we aren't.

By October of junior year, I know that it is right in front of me. He holds my hand by the lockers more often than he doesn't. He plays with my hair on the Andies' blanket every day at lunch time, casually, as if it were a natural and easy thing to do, and I just have to keep breathing, or at least not stop breathing so much that anyone would notice.

I tell him, "Stop it," but I don't really mean it and he looks at me and I smile at him and he knows I don't mean it and he says "Really?" and I say "Not really," and he doesn't stop playing with my hair and behind my ears and the back of my neck out in the open where anyone can see that he is claiming me.

After school, up in his room, we lie there on the floor doing homework, and on the bed, not doing homework, throwing darts at his conditions of probation, just rolling around and kissing and kissing and kissing. Sometimes he takes off his shirt, and he is muscular and pale and perfect, with a smooth swimmer's torso and muscles that ripple when he raises his arms as if he were cutting through the water. And when I press my head against his chest, when he cradles my head there, his skin tastes like salt.

The issue of *my* shirt is more complicated. He likes to slide his hands underneath it, his fingertips feeling their way along the edge of my bra, and then over the edge, and then under it. I imagine us there, perfect and naked on his bed all the time, except that, of course, I'm not Perfect. I *really* am Not Perfect, and I don't want him to see that I'm Not and go find someone else who Is. The thing is, as long as he can actually touch underneath anything he wants to move aside, he is happy. I wear extremely stretchy underwear on purpose. I am happy as hell.

And he says, "Hey, you want to go to the beach?"

I say, "Like the *beach* beach? Like now? You want to surf?"

"Like the beach house," Billy says. "You want to go right now?"

And I say, "Yeah, Nash. I do." And I do. I do. I so so do.

Billy drives us to the end of Sunset, speeding around the curves, and onto the Pacific Coast Highway. It is sunset and the sky is pink and orange, orange flames reflected in the water just off the edge of the highway. The beach is just a little strip of sand with the tide pounding over the traffic noise, pounding in my ears.

And it feels as if after waiting forever, waiting my whole life sort of bored and ready for something else, I am finally getting my something. It is as if it is Billy's sunset and he is feeding it to me with a big spoon. The ocean, too, all blue and roiling: mine. My day, my spoonful of sunset, my boyfriend, finally my boyfriend, and my decision.

Why not?

Billy and the Beemer and the ride up the coast. His parents' beach house by the water near Point Dume with the glass doors open to the dark Pacific and the first stars and the big, white rising moon.

Mine.

We pull into the garage, and Billy turns off the car and gets out and opens my door. He kisses my neck.

"Oh yeah," I say. "You're very good at that, Nash."

"You sure?" he says, pulling away. "Are you sure?"

"Pretty damn sure," I say, and he does it some more, leaning over the car, leaning into the front seat.

It is getting dark. I am almost sure I could do it in the dark.

"We should celebrate," Billy says, unlocking the door and taking me into the house with still enough light to see the ocean and the foam where the waves hit the beach. "Would the lady care for champagne?"

Champagne. All right, it's a total cliché, but I completely don't care. He looks so good and he tastes so salty. He gets two champagne flutes and he carries them upside down between his fingers and the champagne bottle in the other hand, up to the bedroom with its white bed and its pale-green comforter, silky and sweet-smelling.

There is the bite of the champagne, all those little bubbles, all that sweet liquid, and my camisole over my head. Billy's body, which is pretty much perfect, and me. Billy is looking down at me, the lamplight shining off his pale, blond hair, his arms reaching for me, his fingers tracing my eyebrows and the edges of my face down the sides of my neck and across my collarbone.

And I reach over toward the lamp, to turn it off, so the bed will be a soft, dark nest for us, but he holds my wrist.

And he says, "Gabby, you're so beautiful." He is looking right at me in the yellow lamplight, he is seeing me in the yellow light, he is sliding my jeans down over my hips and I am arching my back and this time, I don't distract him with some fun alternative. This time, it is both of us, together. This time, I don't say stop it.

There it is, and I like it. He says yes and I say yes and he says yes and I say yes, and I just go with him, like he is taking care of me. The condom, obviously. I giggle at it and he looks at me and I shut up and go with it some more. And I say, "You are really good at this."

And he says, "Beautiful. You're beautiful."

And that is all it takes.

I had never been beautiful before this moment, but now I am. I am beautiful because Billy says I am beautiful. I am beautiful because Billy gave me that, and I am still beautiful from that, even now, underneath all this makeup, after everything, sort of.

I am beautiful, I am happy. Basically, disgustingly icky as they are, if we could have turned into Andie and Andy right then, I would have signed up for it. Right then, before I get my camisole back on even, before I comb my hair in Billy's parents' bathroom.

I feel like a love-crazed puppy, all wagging its tail and its tongue hanging out of its mouth, all love me love me love me. I want to lie around on the green comforter, just kissing him and looking at him and holding his face for days, not going to school, not going home, nothing. To hell with everything but him, just to be with him, on the bed in the beach house. Just clinging to Billy Nash, inventor of my beautiful.

But he doesn't say, "I love you."

And in the throes of my decision, when I am drunk and a virgin, I don't care.

And then, when I am beautiful and drunk and completely in love with Billy Nash, I do.

Maybe I should have said it. Maybe I should have grabbed him and told him: *I love you forever. I'll do anything for you. I swear to God, nothing else matters.* Maybe everything else would have turned out differently if I'd just told him and asked him and he'd told me one way or the other.

The thing is, I am not a complete moron. I know what every other halfway normal girl in the U.S.A. who ever watches TV or reads *Seventeen* knows: Cling to Gorgeous Hot Boy and you're dead in the water.

Even if you Do It, afterward, if you act like you want him too much or you need him just a little or you think he's perfect, unless you're Andie from Cute World with a free pass from God to worship Andy Kaplan right out in the open and Kaps still worships you back and gives you Hello Kitty earrings, the guy will run out the door and he'll never even look back. Even if you're beautiful. Even if you love him.

Especially if you love him.

And I say to myself in half-crazed affirmation, *Gabby, you are just so secure and mature and wonderful. You don't need him to tell you what you already* (kind of) *know. You are just the most secure and mature and wonderful girl since Coke in a glass bottle, so if you want to keep this going, you'd better just back the hell off.*

Because: Everybody knows that no matter how much you need to talk to Gorgeous Hot Boy, if you phone him fourteen times between ten and ten thirty p.m., by the time he gets to the third message, he'll hate you, and by message number fourteen, his mother will have a restraining order taken out against you and you'll be in court-ordered Stalker Recovery Twelve Step before you even have time to make call number fifteen.

So I don't call him. I don't even try to cuddle. Not even.

So I don't presume to follow Billy around or hang out next to him on Monday at school, curved into his side, hooking my fingers through his empty belt loops. Not me. I stumble around watching for him, longing for him. All I can think about is how his body feels, smooth and naked and a little bit damp, pressed up against me. And when he passes me, when I am close to him, the faintly salty smell of him fills me up.

"Hey, Gabs," he says in the cafeteria the Tuesday after that Sunday in the beach house. "Don't you like me anymore?"

I am shaking. I am afraid I'm going to drop my tray.

"What do you think, Nash?" I say as casually as possible under the circumstances. "You think you own me now or something?" Thinking: *Own me own me own me.*

Billy reaches over and he put his fingers through the hair behind my ear. "Yeah," he says into my ear. "Oh yeah, I own you now."

XVIII

THE DIFFERENCE BETWEEN SECRETLY, CONSTANTLY wanting Billy to own me and Billy taking actual possession is that now he just assumes I'll be there, like his wallet and the keys in his front pocket.

It feels safe in there, like I am some indispensable but ordinary thing he can't do without, because who doesn't need pocket change and their school library Xerox card and gum? Who doesn't miss that ordinary, indispensable stuff if they can't find it? He would look up and there I would be, the everyday, always-there girlfriend.

I am Billy Nash's girlfriend and even when he doesn't have his hands on me, I am still her.

It's perfect.

In my psychology elective, which is a lot less interesting than you'd expect, we are studying the minds of babies, how when you put their toy behind a barrier so they can't see it, they supposedly forget all about it and don't even know it exists anymore. By Thanksgiving, though, I am pretty sure that even when Billy is at the Four Seasons in Maui and I am sitting at my Aunt Adrienne's country club in La Jolla eating dried-out, room-temperature turkey because being associated with my mother's side of the family is the kiss of death for edible food, listening to my father and my uncle complain about the weakness of the watered-down mixed drinks, even separated by three thousand miles of blue sky, I am still Billy's girlfriend.

I have my cell phone in my lap under the table and he texts me and says so.

> Billy: If I can't get out of this room and onto a surfboard soon I'm going to throw a coconut

> Gabs: Isn't it like 7 a.m. there? Y r u up?

> Billy: Forced family bonding. Caitlyn wants to teach for America. Grandfather thinks she's a commie whore

> Gabs: Isn't Agnes a big democrat?

> Billy: Don't tell grandfather that. Ok Caitlyn's about to throw tropical fruit

Gabs: Does throwing things run in ur family?

Billy: Yeah well I'm the one with the arm

Gabs: Ur Thanksgiving sounds a lot more entertaining than mine

Billy: This isn't Thanksgiving. This is breakfast. Gotta get out of here before they move on to me

Gabs: ?

Billy: Commie whore's not on probation. I am. Jesus here it comes

Gabs: Duck

Billy: Ag says teach for America looks good for law school. This should b good for 10 more minutes

Gabs: Can't u stretch out T for A until they finish eating and bounce?

Billy: Can't open mouth except to eat. Instructions from on high. Have to shut up and eat until Monday

Gabs: Yowza.

Billy: That's my line G. Wish u and me were on the beach. Need gf fix.

Gabs: Me too.

Billy: What r u wearing?

Gabs: Jesus nash it's family Thanksgiving. I'm wearing a silk dress and pearls.

Billy: A boy can always hope

Gabs: xx

Billy: U know it

By the middle of December, I know which Christmas parties we are going to, and where we are going to be on New Year's Eve. (At Andy Kaplan's father's party with Hell's Gate providing the music and Andy's latest stepmother wearing a dress held on by denture cream.)

There we are, on the terrace by Andy's pool, dancing to Hell's Gate and wondering how much punishment the denture cream can take.

"Andy, that is so not nice to say!" Andie says. "That dress is by Helen Chang. It's pretty, don't you think?"

"Too bad part of it went missing," Andy says. "Maybe Helen freaking Chang gave her a discount on a partial dress."

"Come on, Kaps," Billy says. "The woman will be gone by summer. I give her six months on the outside. They'll be in court by Labor Day."

"Well, at least she won't have much to pack," I say.

Andy is laughing so hard he snorts vodka out his nostrils and puts his arm around me.

"I praise the day Benitez jerked off Hank Peterson," he says.

"What?"

Billy says, "Shut up, Andy." But Andy is too drunk to shut up.

"When Benitez got friendly with Hank Peterson at Hibbert's party and Billy broke up with the bitch and we got you."

Billy says, "Will you shut up?"

Andie, seeing the possibility of impending drama, says, "All he's saying is that Gabby's really nice. That's all. Gabs is a really nice girlfriend."

Billy shakes his head and takes Andy's arm off my shoulder which results in Andy, who is not only too drunk to shut up but apparently also too drunk to stand up without assistance, being held up by Andie and a Doric column that is just poking up out of the pool deck looking decorative, and takes me into the pool house. Billy looks righteously pissed off.

"I am a really nice girlfriend," I say, leaning my face into his tight, pissed-off neck.

"I know, Baby," he says. "You don't need to listen to that shit."

I don't know what to say, but fortunately, it isn't necessary to say much, and even though I had been really looking forward to kissing him exactly at midnight, I don't even notice when midnight comes.

So here I lie, in the land of infinite gray space, hooked up to tubes of liquid and whirring machinery in a hospital gown, and *who owns me now?*

part two

Part Two

XIX

AN ORDINARY MIDNIGHT IN THE HOSPITAL IS LESS festive and a lot less eventful. The fluorescent light is still on when the hands on the green, glowing clock over the door click together for a moment until, quivering, the second hand sweeps by.

Vivian has left the room and gone home on the thankless quest for beauty sleep. I have progressed to the point that I can reach over and pick up the phone without throwing up or falling off the electric bed, big whoop, but the sides are locked in their full upright position 100% of the time. If I want to get out of that bed, I have to buzz the nurse.

I am so bored, I am thinking about pressing the buzzer. I am thinking about reaching over and phoning some random person, some late-night wrong number, just to hear a voice.

When Billy calls.

It is such a shock, it is so hard to breathe, that it hits me that in the back of my so-called mind, I really was hanging onto the idea that he was actually dead, that I actually killed him, the eucalyptus tree crushed him, only everyone is keeping it from me, like mirrors and friends.

"Babe," he says. "Are you alone?"

"Yes." Tears start pouring down my cheeks and rolling into my ears and soaking the pillow behind my head. "God, Billy, where are you?"

Billy says, "Shhhhhh, Gabs, don't say my name."

"Why not?"

"I'm not supposed to talk to you right now."

I have this sudden reprise of the Agnes Nash vision, the one with the horns and the pitchfork and the little cloven hooves.

"Jesus, Billy," I say. "I know Agnes hates me, but I'm in the *hos*pital. My *head* got smashed. Aren't you even allowed to show up and go 'hey, get well soon' and be somewhat po*lite*?" I am, I admit, somewhat shouting by then, unhinged, I guess, by the mashed head and the weird drugs in the drip bags and my general state of brainlessness.

"Shhhh, poor baby girl, poor Gabs," Billy whispers in his beautiful, gravelly voice. "Are you all right?"

"No. I'm not all right. I look like an ad for fastening your seat belt and I can't even believe this! You aren't supposed to talk to me! Your mom—"

You could hear Billy's jaw snapping shut, like it does when he is trying to gain control over things so dire that a person just can't get through them with his mouth hanging open.

"It's not my mom," he says. And in the three-second pause I think: *Oh my God, if it's not Agnes, it's HIM. He's calling to break up with me. Probably he isn't here because he already broke up with me and I'm such an idiot I didn't notice. My life is officially over.*

"It's my probation," he says. "You know how I'm not supposed to drink or be around drinking or go to parties with drinking, right? This is major. Major like I could go to jail. I have to lie low until we see how this shakes out."

No doubt my mouth would have snapped shut too had any part of my body been capable of fast action, if there was one single part of me that didn't go mushy and stupid as soon as I heard Billy Nash breathe.

"What are you talking about?" I say.

"I could end up in really deep shit here, Gabs. I have to be careful."

"I don't understand. Why can't you talk to me?"

"Gabby, you're the one they caught. With the car."

"So?"

"Babe. I am on serious probation and my PO could yank it. Remember? I can't go near drinking. Just thinking about you violates half my conditions of probation."

"Billy—"

"Come on. The underage person I was consuming alcohol with way after six p.m. outside my domicile when I was supposed to be serving bedtime snacks to the homeless downtown and then driving straight home. I'm dead. And what happened to the Beemer was not in compliance with the California motor vehicle code either."

"You think?" And I know which condition of probation it is, too, it's Condition #6, the one about associating with minors who use alcohol and a vast array of legal and illegal and semi-legal drugs. The one we joked about because it leaves out crack whores, street corner pushers, and the entire Cali drug cartel as long as the whores, pushers, and international drug lords are over twenty-one.

Which I, on the other hand, am not.

And I think, *Why me? Why me? Why me?*

And then I think, *I'm really screwed.*

I say, "What are we going to do? I mean, this is actually kind of insane if you think about it."

You can hear Billy breathing into the receiver, that's how quiet it is.

"Gabs, did you talk to your lawyer yet?"

"What are you talking about?"

"Jesus, Gabs, didn't your mom get you a lawyer yet?"

"Please. Vivian is sitting around reading *Vogue* and complaining about the bad coffee and how jaundiced she looks in the fluorescent light."

"You have to tell her that before you talk to the police or anyone, you need a lawyer. Do you . . . do you even know what you're going to say?"

This is the exact moment in the conversation when it occurs

to me that as much trouble as Billy says he might be in, I am the one who got drunk and crashed the car and I am no doubt going to have to do something about this unfortunate turn of events or God knows what is going to happen to me.

But I am too happy to care.

All I really care about is how to get Billy to forgive me and how to get things back to how they were.

You can call me a bad girlfriend all you want. You can call me a blue-ribbon, certified bad person. But I am actually glad about Billy's probation. I am over-the-moon about Billy's probation. Because: Godawful as it is, it means there is an explanation for him not hovering at my bedside wiping the sweat off my brow. Other than the explanation that he doesn't like me anymore.

I am actually somewhat happy.

"I'm sorry about your car," I say, bracing myself for him to get mad.

"Just a car. No worries."

"You are *so* nice, Billy."

"Don't cry, Gabs. Shhhh. Shhhh. Don't. I'm sorry about everything."

I say, "It's not like it's *your* fault. How are we going to be together if you can't even talk to me?"

"I'll think of something. Gabs, I will. How soon do you go home?"

"I don't know. How can I even see you?"

"Babygirl, we have to keep this private. It's not just Princeton.

I could end up locked in California Youth Authority somewhere. Somewhere bad, Gabs. Jesus, I do not want to be rehabilitated again."

"I am so sorry."

"So what did you say?"

"What do you mean? What did I say to who?"

"To the police, to everybody," Billy says. "It's not like any of this is your fault."

"I don't remember anything."

Billy says, "Come again?"

Why is it that nobody gets this? It's not that complicated.

"So far, all I've said is I don't remember anything."

"Really," Billy says.

"Yeah. What else am I gonna say?"

"Really," Billy says.

"Yeah. So?"

Sound of Billy breathing in a huge breath. Sound of Billy sighing. Sound of Billy going *mmmmmmm.* "Oh, Baby! You are *amazing.* That is so totally helpful."

As if I would tell some random law enforcement drone that Billy got drunk even if I did remember.

As if I couldn't figure out that getting Billy Nash locked up with the Mexican Mafia is not a stellar plan.

His whole tone of voice changes, as if things were sort of normal again, kind of, and he says, "Hey, Gabs, are you wearing one of those little hospital gowns?"

I say, "Yeah . . . so?"

"The kind that's all kind of open in back and it ties with flimsy little bows?"

I say, "What do you think, Nash?"

And it is almost as if, sour and dizzy as I am, I am back to being myself. All right, so it's a barely recognizable self. Sinking up to my held-together-by-stitches chin in unfathomably deep shit myself. Myself who has to get out of trouble and get Billy back.

XX

"VIVIAN," I SAY WHEN SHE COMES WANDERING BACK in, dressed in her dowager-queen-in-mourning mauve outfit again and offering up *People*, *Us*, *Cosmo*, *Glamour*, and a paperback novel in which some teen bimbo overcomes her drinking problem. "What do you know about me having to talk to the police? And do I have a lawyer?"

As it turns out, Vivian, who spent her life pathetically devoted to making it on TV until she hooked up with my dad, after which she devoted herself to pretending to be rich and making really good mixed drinks instead, who wasn't even all that convincing in dog food commercials, is a better actress than anybody gives her credit for. Because apparently she is pretty well versed in the specifics of what deep and serious trouble I am in but she decided it would be a bad idea to share this scary information with me beyond endless bleak hints just in case I would freak out and braid the thread from my stitches into an itty-bitty noose and hang myself.

In fact, armed men with badges have been beating down the door, and she isn't letting them anywhere near me, with the complicity of the helpful, alien nurses who have adapted to life on Earth well enough to appreciate gifts of really nice perfume from Saks. The conversation I overheard between Bunny Shirt and Gun Lady was evidently one of many.

Many many.

Thanks to Vivian, as far as the outside world is concerned, I have been barely conscious all this time, and when I do emerge from my foggy state, I can barely hum "Old MacDonald Had a Farm" or chew Jell-O jewels without drooling.

The thing is, as much as I don't want to have a meaningful dialogue with an armed person with handcuffs, I *have* to go home if I want any slight chance of ever seeing Billy. Billy even thinks that phoning me at the hospital is too risky for him, which, all right, being somewhat familiar with total paranoia, I can kind of see.

But my room at home is an electronic wonderland, and even in my altered state, I am prepared to text and message and learn to wipe my hard drive clean endlessly if that's what I have to do to talk to him. My dad is pretty much comatose half the time, my mother is out shopping, and Juanita is only there two days a week. I am prepared to hang over the edge of the balcony above the canyon and send him sappy yet un-clingy smoke signals if that's what it takes.

But going home, it turns out, is going to be a bigger production than just pulling out the tubes and wheeling me through the front entrance. Because of the teenage felon aspect of the situation, Vivian is pretty sure that I'm going to be charged with some kind of major crime as soon as I'm unplugged and we no longer have the nice ladies in the bunny-printed nurses' uniforms repeating "closed head injury" over and over and running interference whenever law enforcement types show up.

"How is a child whose head got smashed against a tree supposed to deal with the police?" Vivian says to anyone who will listen, just in case they don't have a handle on her version of the situation.

And then she says, "Look at you! How are you supposed to talk to them and not incriminate yourself in something *really serious*? He never said that you could drive that sports car of his, did he?"

And I go, *Shit, Gabriella. You stole the car. You're toast.*

Because: Billy would never let me drive that car. Billy wouldn't even let Kaps drive that car around the Winston School parking lot. And it is hard to see how I am going to avoid incriminating myself about taking the car since it seems somewhat obvious that this is how I ended up in the hospital surrounded by funeral-ready floral offerings and cheesy, ozone-wrecking Mylar balloons.

To accomplish at least the temporary postponement of consequences that are too scary to contemplate without feeling sicker than I already feel, my job is to pretend I am too out of it to think a straight thought.

Vivian, meanwhile, remains obsessively devoted to getting me to look semi-normal. Which, given my new goal of getting home and somehow getting Billy to want to see me, is not what you could call a bad thing. I really wish she would spend her time getting me a lawyer in between buying all the industrial-strength makeup, but I don't get too far with this completely reasonable suggestion.

I keep trying to explain to her that even if she gets me to remember what I did and look like Miss Teen America, it's not going to make it so I didn't somehow total Billy's car with like a 98% blood alcohol level.

But she's not listening.

"Daddy is working on it," she says. Which makes you wonder if she could even pick Daddy out of a lineup, because he would be the one standing there sipping the dry martini and not the one doing the meticulous research on the top ten criminal attorneys of the Los Angeles basin.

"Billy says I have to get a lawyer before I talk to the police."

"You talked to *Billy Nash?*"

I let her marinate in this for a few seconds. Then I say, "Yeah, but you can't tell anybody. He's not supposed to talk to me."

"Now there's a surprise," she says.

She is not even smiling.

You would *think* she would be happy about the (slight) return of Billy. But she is too busy protecting me from anyone who might think she has a funny-looking kid. Sitting there answering the phone and explaining to anybody who wants to see me that

I am too debilitated and emotionally overwrought to see them. Telling Lisa and Anita and Huey and the kids who just want to see a train wreck when they get the chance, "Not yet, dear."

As if I were anything other than numb and confused and waiting for Billy to figure out a way to call me again.

I can visualize the concerned faces on the other end of the line, Lisa and Anita and Huey and Huey's mother with her herd of visiting therapy dogs all pulling on their leashes and, weirdly, Andie Bennett, who you figure would be functioning on the level of those dumb Piaget babies from psychology, forgetting I even exist the second I get stuck in a mechanical bed somewhere beyond her field of vision, all kind of frowning sympathetically and gently touching their end-call buttons.

It doesn't matter.

It's not as if they're Billy.

XXI

WENDY SAYS, "THAT LOOKS LIKE PRINCE CHARMING."
She is so enthralled with the artistic possibilities of occupational therapy with a patient over four years old that she has taken to making daily deliveries of actual, good art supplies. Then she makes me squeeze a squishy ball a couple of times and writes a chart note. And never is heard a discouraging word because I really want all that nice paper.

I say, "That's my boyfriend." Although, I admit, I have made him kind of glowing and unusually golden for a human. And then there's the issue of the slightly green horse.

Wendy says, "Well, he sounds nice too."

And I think: *You can totally do this, Gabriella. Tell her. Just because he hasn't been calling you every five minutes and he isn't lurking by your bedside, doesn't mean he's not your boyfriend. Tell her.*

I say, "That's not my boyfriend on the phone."

Wendy starts lining up the pencils on the tray table.

I say, "I don't want him to see me when I look like this." Which you have to give me points for, which is semi-true. "I want to look vaguely like myself and I want to be thinking straight before I even talk to him."

Wendy says, "Oh," like she almost believes it.

I almost believe it, too.

Eventually, though, even the perfume-smitten nurses can tell that no amount of communing with Ponytail Doc, who keeps showing up in my room trying to get me to tell her all the four-legged animals I can think of in thirty seconds, is going to get me to remember diddly about what happened; when I have exhausted the limits of playology and Wendy has taped my portraits of every medical resident, intern, janitor, and candy striper at Valley Mercy onto the walls of the staff lounge; when no one can figure out what possible reason there is for me to be sticking around, going up and down in the cool electric bed, having makeup sponged onto my face without being able to remember one single clue regarding how my face got that way, I get snuck out the side door of the hospital by the freight elevator, as if a bunch of paparazzi and the whole LAPD were just hanging around in the hospital lobby on the edge of their seats waiting for me to make an appearance.

I am completely petrified, huddled in the wheelchair, not even wearing my own clothes because Vivian thinks I look more pathetic in a hospital gown and she is going for the all-season pathetic look just in case. I am waiting for someone to arrest me and throw me in a tiny cell with one sixty-watt lightbulb and a window in the door to slide in Spam sandwiches with wedges of sad iceberg lettuce. I am waiting for someone in a uniform to grab the handles of the wheelchair out of Bunny Shirt's hands and wheel me away.

But it doesn't happen.

Bunny Shirt helps me into the backseat of the Mercedes when Vivian pulls it up to the valet service curb. Then Vivian guns the motor, and we're out of there.

And when I finally get home, which is exactly the same as before, when I finally get into my exactly-the-same room, the only drama left is the drama of me lying in my exactly-the-same bed with my same laptop on my stomach, staring at my same dog-on-surfboard screensaver and waiting for Billy to show up online. Staring at the new cell phone and waiting for Billy to text. Staring at the landline and waiting for Billy to call. Waiting for the miraculous evaporation of Billy's Have-a-Drunken-Girlfriend-Go-to-Jail Condition of Probation so he can come through my door and into my bedroom and hold my hand and stroke my hair and make things stay the same.

I want to be back in my *After* and not in some weird *after-After* Purgatory, waiting to find out if I am Saved or Damned.

Staring at the row of odd little presents that Andie Bennett has been sending and Vivian has lined up on my dresser, including a pink blown glass horse, a Peppermint Patty PEZ dispenser, and a mauve Kate Spade pencil case. And you really have to wonder if the Department of Probation would actually drag Billy off in leg irons if he sent me a freaking mauve pencil.

I close my eyes, but it doesn't work.

I can't even get my private home movies to work. I am not sure if this is because I no longer have the interesting drugs dripping into my veins or because now that I'm home and right here, right now, in real time, this *is* my life. This is *Gabriella Gardiner's ACTUAL Teen Life in the Three B's* uncut, happening to me minute by minute, without chemical enhancement. I can't close my eyes and watch it because I'm stuck in it.

Except that Gabriella's actual teen life consists of lying in my room waiting for Billy to show up, which might not even count as a life, if you think about it.

To make things even more bizarre while I'm lying here, completely terrified about what's going to happen with me and Billy, not to mention me and the LAPD, it is as if after all those years of flying too low to be a blip on his radar, I've come up with something my dad can relate to: a problem with mixed drinks in it.

I am used to being in the house with my dad and feeling comfortably alone, not having any idea what he's actually doing closed up in the den *other* than drinking. But all of a sudden, I'm his New Best Friend. All of a sudden, he starts coming downstairs and eating breakfast with me in my room, not saying much except for jolly, totally off-the-wall things about how much he likes pink grapefruit.

After the third day of this, he gets up from my desk chair and walks over to the side of the bed just as I'm sliding my tray off my lap. He puts his arm around my shoulder and he squinches up his eyes and it hits me that he is silently crying without the sobbing again. And even though all along, since it began, since Songbird Lane, since everything, I had pretty much thought it was the end of the world, I was wrong: The actual end of the world is *this*.

His arm is just resting there, not moving, like a dead eel. I just want him to say whatever it is he's planning to say, assuming he's planning to say something, so this whole freakish father-daughter episode will be over and he'll reclaim the eel. But no, now there is some weird shaking thing going on too. I can't tell if this is John's rendition of Deep Emotion or if he is trying to pat me on the back but he can't quite bring himself to do it.

And I go, *Shit, Gabriella, this is your dad having a nervous break-down. You're supposed to feel something and do something and help him or something.*

But I don't. Short of wanting him to magically turn into someone who vaguely resembles an actual parent, all I want is for him to retract the eel and go away.

"Oh, Gabsy," he says, like the guy hasn't even noticed what people call me for the past seventeen years. "I can't help but think that if only I'd wrestled with my own demons sooner, you wouldn't be going through this."

Right.

Unless, of course, he's talking about the demon that makes him a sub-regular, totally incompetent businessman, which, if he could have managed to wrestle it into the corner and slide past its defeated husk and into the *richer* than richer-than-God category, I could have been popular even if geeky.

"It's not like it's genetic, Dad," I say, just wanting him to take the eel and go back into the den, only the fish-head hand has grabbed onto my arm, hard.

"You are so wise for such a young person," he says. Then he sighs with what sounds a lot like relief and he slinks away. Marking the end of our father-daughter breakfasts.

For a couple of days, I am so freaked out by the possibility I'll run into him somewhere other than dinner where Vivian provides the complete antidote to any kind of emotional gushing, I only come out of my room to eat French toast in the kitchen really early with Juanita, like I always did before. Watching the *telenovelas* that got me my one and only flat-out A—other than the A's in art that don't even get calculated into your academic GPA—in Honors Spanish.

Juanita, who my mother has hired full time for the week supposedly to help with me but really so Vivian can go shopping without feeling too guilty, doesn't go in for all this pointless affirmation: I don't even think *you go, girl* translates as a Salvadorian expression. What she does is make me a lot of hot chocolate with high-cal whole milk she carries up the hill to our house in a little paper bag with contraband canned whipped cream and tiny marshmallows. Which is the highlight of my day.

This is so not turning into the best extended spring vacation ever.

XXII

THE ONLY PERSON WHO MANAGES TO GET THROUGH
to me, despite Vivian's best efforts to keep everyone away until my
skin goes back to being unbruised and lifelike all on its own, is Lisa.

"The hospital said you weren't there anymore. Thank God!
You're out of your coma. You remember me, right?" She sounds
exactly the same.

"Duh. Who said I was in a coma?"

"Your mom. Kind of. And Gabby, people gossip. Everybody
knows. Are you all right?"

It is hard to know which aspect of not all right to start with.
"My face looks like it belongs in a body bag, but yeah. And no
coma. I just don't remember the crash."

"Well, people can probably fill you in."

"Yeah, people in police uniforms. I crashed Billy's car, so
apparently they're interested."

"What are you talking about?" Lisa says, clueless as ever. "I'm coming over there, okay?"

"Are you sure your mom will drive you over now that I'm Evil Delinquent Girl?"

"Gabby! You are not an evil, delinquent girl," Lisa says, delusional but perpetually supportive.

But even if she refuses to believe I am a wayward, felonious teen, evidently I still qualify as a charity project, because her parents are letting her jump into the Saab every day to come see me, which is a little unnerving because they only ever let her drive it to community service and youth group at her church. Not only that, she is bringing Anita, who is generally only allowed to sit in cars driven by moms and people over the age of twenty-five who are related to her and have Volvos with front, back, side, rear, floor, and roof air bags.

Lisa seems to find this all extremely amusing. She says she hopes I'm ready for a whole lot of salvation because unless she brings me some on a regular basis, she is probably never going to get to drive a car somewhere other than church again until she graduates from college, gets a job, and buys herself one, a fact that she seems weirdly fine with. Then she starts beating herself up about how she's a twit to talk about herself when I'm bedridden and mangled, and at the point when I am pretty sure she's on the verge of hauling out our Lord and Savior, I tell her it's okay but I'm too tired to talk.

Meanwhile, Anita keeps sending me text messages about how worried about me she is and am I having cognitive problems and do I want her to show me how to meditate or go back over the SAT flash cards we've already done. She doesn't sound amused at all.

I'm not all that amused either. In fact, Anita's text messages are making me crazy, not because there is anything inherently annoying about them, but because every time my phone makes its little got-a-text bleep noise, I think it might be Billy but it isn't.

Meanwhile, Lisa and Anita show up at the front door with one of those Save the Children blankies they make for godless, impoverished children with no electricity or blankies, with my name embroidered on the yellow silk border.

"You don't have to let them see you," Vivian whispers, sticking her head into my room when they are pounding on the front door. "It's not too late. Nobody has to see you like this. Do you want to put on more concealer?"

She is in the Vivian version of maternal frenzy, seriously concerned that my so-called friends will ditch me if they notice I'm not pageant-ready, trying to save me from this sorry fate—completely ignoring the actual looming disaster in which somebody shows up and arrests me for DUI and grand theft auto.

But I am only thinking *Billy Billy Billy Billy Billy*, so much so that all other thoughts, scary thoughts, no-lawyer-and-the-LAPD-is-on-its-way-with-sirens-blaring-and-handcuffs-at-the-ready thoughts, oh-no-I-look-like-crap-and-my-friends-won't-like-me-anymore-and-I'll-be-a-Bashed-in-Face-Pariah thoughts—except, whoops, that last one is *Vivian's* thought, not my thought—have no space to hang out.

Vivian is prepared to barricade the door on my behalf, but eventually, still unconvinced, she gives way for the gift-wrapped goodies, the fuzzy knitted scarf, handmade dangle earrings, and a bunch of pastel aromatherapy candles with names like "Sea of Tranquility" and "Mellow Morning." And all right, as miserable a cynical bitch as I feel like, boyfriend-less and very likely re-invisible, it still feels kind of good to be with people who actually don't care how I look or what I did and still like me. Even if Vivian thinks they're a couple of losers, not unlike the reappearing Old Me with the purple and green bruises that clash with the currently non-existent New Me's autumn season earth tones.

And did I mention board games?

"When I'm sick, I love to play board games," Lisa says. "And you're really good at board games."

"I'm not sick."

"Grumpy, aren't we?" says Anita, making a face that is supposed to cheer me up and cajole me out of grumpiness but doesn't. "Sanjiv says closed head injuries can affect your mood."

"You talked to your *brother* about me?"

Anita shrugs and looks somewhat sheepish.

"Come on, Gabby," Lisa says. "You got hit on the head. This is your excuse to kick back and be a kid again! Don't you want to play Boggle?" Well, no. Battleship? No. Connect Four? Parcheesi? Candyland? Chutes and Ladders? Hungry Hungry Hippos? Checkers? Chinese Checkers? Mah-jongg? Chess?

"We should play Hūsker Dū?" Anita says. "After a closed head injury, we should work on your memory."

And it's no better when Huey tags along, either.

Because Huey, as it turns out, is such a wreck in the presence of a banged up, debilitated person such as me, he can barely hold it together for long enough to figure out who done it in a game of Clue. Or maybe it's just the shock of being in a girl's bedroom.

"I'd leave him out," Lisa says, "but he really wants to see you. And I might not get to be semi-alone with a boy in a car again for years."

"You do know that your mother is insane, right?" I say. "No offense."

Lisa sighs but doesn't seem all that worked up about it.

"You call that insane," Anita says. "Hello. Have you met *my* mother? She's trying to establish a perfect simulation of small-town life in Punjab circa 1958. Only in Beverly Hills. And we all know how sane *that* it."

We have all been so severely indoctrinated to respect insane cultural differences that Lisa and I don't know what to say.

"Well, at least you don't have to cover all your hair like Asha," Lisa says weakly.

"Admit it's insane," Anita says.

We do.

Ironically, Asha, albeit covered head to toe, gets to jump into Huey's car every time they have to go do yearbook business because Huey drove down to Culver City and had a meaningful dialogue with her dad.

Whereas the mere sight of me has reduced Huey to cringing in my desk chair, barely able to push Colonel Mustard around the board.

"Boys are such babies," Lisa says.

"You look like you're in so much pain," Huey says, as if this or some variant of this is the only conversation starter he can think of. "How do you feel about . . ."—he scrapes Colonel Mustard into the library where he's been before and doesn't need to go again—". . . everything?"

How do you feel about everything? You have to figure that if Huey had been born into my family, Vivian would have drowned him back when he was still a pup.

"And what's up with your left arm?" he says.

"Huey!" Lisa says. "She's going to make a full recovery. She's lucky it's not worse."

"Lucky!" Huey basically howls. "Sorry, Lisa. I admire your outlook. No—I'd say I *love* your outlook. But lucky is not on the list of words that describe what happened to her."

"Hello, I'm right here. Hello. Bed to Huey . . ."

"She's a *potter* and look at her left arm!" he bellows.

Just to show him that there's nothing to discuss, I do the wrecked person's version of slithering out of bed. All right, so I have to will myself to smile when my feet graze the floor. All right, so I am somewhat limping. But if I suck it up and make myself put weight on my left foot, my walk isn't noticeably all that weird. And it isn't as if this is keeping me out of jazz dance ensemble. To keep being who I am, I just need both my hands to work.

I try to button up my robe, but this does not turn out as well as you would hope.

And I go, *Gabriella, you don't need to run around buttoning things up to show off. You can always tie the brace on your left wrist. Just not in front of anyone.*

Huey, who is watching me make my way across my bedroom to the bathroom, for once puts down the camera.

He says, "How could you let this happen to you?"

I say, "I don't know."

Also, "Shut up."

There are days of Clue and Monopoly marathons that I am pretty sure Lisa and Anita are conspiring to let me win. Days that last so long my mother makes Juanita stay late and cook us actual dinner instead of getting the bad Chinese takeout Vivian slaps on the table night after night. Days when I figure that I might actually die if Billy doesn't call me.

Not to mention, Lisa and Anita want to talk about *every-thing* too.

"About *what you told Lisa,*" Anita says. "We should talk about it."

"About you *crashing Billy's car* . . . ," Lisa says.

"Could we please, pretty please, pretty pretty please not talk about it?" I say. The thought of Anita trying to devise a scientifi-cally perfect way to kick my brain into gear while Lisa prays for me is more than I can take.

"Not that we want to be pushy or intrude on your privacy," Anita says. As if it didn't take until tenth grade for her to blurt out that if her mother made her spend another Christmas vaca-tion at a theme park, national park, or slogging through the Getty Museum showing off her Hindi language skills to an entourage from New Delhi one more time, she was going to run away by Greyhound bus and hide out in her brother Sanjiv's co-op at UC Berkeley.

"We know that you're a private person," Lisa says, even though she, herself, has never uttered one single word about what she and Huey have been up to since seventh grade. Despite the fact that Anita and I are more than slightly curious.

"We want to support you," Anita says. "But some things don't make sense—"

"Can't you just accept that I don't remember anything and I'm not planning to remember anything any time soon and just leave it there?" It is the embarrassing and horrifying truth.

Lisa and Anita exchange looks and gape at me.

"Gabby, please just think about it—"

"We want to help, but—"

"I mean it," I say. "So there's nothing to talk about. And there isn't going to *be* anything to talk about either."

So Lisa and Anita just keep letting me be the tiny Monopoly top hat, and we just keep playing.

XXIII

AND THEN, JUST AFTER MIDNIGHT, A FEW MINUTES
after Anita gets into Lisa's mother's Saab and they tool back up
Estrada with their board games rattling around on the backseat,
Billy's screen name shows up on my laptop.

I am drunk on the possibility of bliss.

pologuy: hey baby. how r u?

And I go, *Stay cool stay cool stay cool. Just try to be somewhat amusing.*

gabs123: life sucks. lying around getting turned into a
geisha with a makeup mask.
pologuy: geisha? verrrrrrry interesting. what r u wearing
geisha?

And I go, *Stop whining. Stop it. Do you want him back or not?*

gabs123: makeup. lots of makeup. don't even have to
get out of bed for it. vivian delivers.

pologuy: wish i could c

gabs123: so come see.

Why not? I know he won't.

And then I think, *OMG what are you doing, Gabriella? Do. Not.
Cling. Do not ask him where he's been or what he's been doing or why
he didn't call sooner.*

I am just so far back there in that awful place of not quite
knowing, it's as if I just met him. It is as if I am back where I don't
even know him again.

pologuy: did u have ur fun talk with the cops yet?

gabs123: FUN?!?!?!?!?!?!

pologuy: i've had several fun talks. i have my own
personal policeman

gabs123: what did u say to ur probation guy? r u ok?

pologuy: u first

gabs123: what can i say to them anyway? i don't
remember.

pologuy: r u serious? r u still gonna say u don't
remember?

gabs123: seems like a plan.

pologuy: yowza! they're gonna go apeshit

gabs123: y?

pologuy: r u kidding me?

gabs123: what am i supposed to do about it? all i can do is say sorry 500 times and cry. what can they even do about it? if someone could make me remember, they already would have.

pologuy: hold up. u actually said u don't remember to the cops? they really hate that. does ur lawyer know about this?

gabs123: i don't have a lawyer remember?

pologuy: and they bought it?

gabs123: nash, i don't even remember when i told them that i don't remember. but that's what i'm going to say. y wouldn't they buy it?

pologuy: u r freaking amazing

gabs123: duh

pologuy: and this is the plan?

gabs123: it's my plan and i'm sticking to it. do u have some alternate plan?

pologuy: i need to c u

Yes yes yes yes yes! I have become a makeup-application fiend waiting exactly for this. I am the reigning queen of camouflage. *Yes!*

gabs123: me too.

pologuy: i'd climb through ur window if ur house wasn't on freaking stilts

gabs123: big letterman. u could scale a stilt. romeo would have scaled stilt.

pologuy: romeo ended up dead in crypt, whereas i'm going to play polo at princeton. broken neck scaling gf's stilt is not in my plan

GF!!!!!!!!!!!!!!!

gabs123: ok, do u have a non-fatal plan?

pologuy: behind the castle? can u get there?

Like there was any place or time or way I wouldn't go see Billy.

Like this wasn't the first time I'd felt like a halfway real person with a halfway real life since my actual life went up in smoke with Billy's Beemer.

Like maybe if I could just avoid looking desperate and drooling all over him, I could get my life back.

XXIV

IN THE MORNING, IT IS TORTURE WAITING FOR VIVIAN
to get ready to roll down the hill to get her hair styled so I can
spackle on my makeup and get out of there. The only real question in my mind is if I should go with all the concealer so I'll
look halfway cute or if I should let some of the bruises show
through so I'll look battered yet brave.

I go with the concealer.

And as soon as Vivian pokes her head in to say she is going,
looking slightly guilty but pretty much as eager to get out of there
as I am, I lower myself gently into the tightest possible sweats and
head out through the back of the house, through the laundry
room, and down into the canyon toward the castle, trying to walk
like a human being.

The castle is what we call this enormous old Spanish house
at the end of a cul-de-sac off Via Hermosita. It has been under

reconstruction but mostly abandoned, half-finished, for my whole life. The place is gated tight from the street, but if you climb down the bank from the house next door, you can slip through the gate by the pool house. The pool is empty and there's graffiti in it, but behind the pool, the yard is terraced and wooded, so even if somebody did show up to work on the main house, they wouldn't see you down there unless they came looking.

I wait on a stone bench out of the sun, not for the coolness of the shade, but because I am afraid my face will look as if it's covered with putty in full sunlight, and I watch for Billy.

And it really does feel as if I were abducted by aliens, sucked into a time warp, and returned to planet Earth a long time later, looking (almost) the same, but entirely different. Like I can't quite remember how to breathe, and my heart isn't sure how to beat in the right rhythm, and I don't know how to focus my eyes so I can take it all in, and I can't tell how to feel beyond the rush of seeing him coming toward me finally.

It's been twenty-one days since I've seen him, and climbing down the neighbor's embankment, he looks as if having his car wrecked made him get even more gorgeous. He is wearing a dark, dark green T-shirt and these perfect jeans and ratty old black Converse without socks. I swear, his footsteps have to scorch the path.

"Oh, Babe," he says before he hugs me, looking at me through those blue eyes, through those dark lashes, the sun in that pale hair. "You look like you've been through it."

So much for the makeup. Carefully holding my head a little

bit away from his cheek so he won't get plastered with a big, greasy splotch of opaque beige glop, the rest of me feels so good, so at home, pressed up against him.

And I think: *Don't cling don't cling don't cling.*

I say, "Ya think?"

"Are you all right, G? You look so *thin.*"

Like this is a bad thing. "I just want this all to be over. . . ."

"I know you do," he whispers in my ear, so close I can feel his breath, feel it blowing my hair over my ear. "But it's going to be fine. It's all going to be over and in the past."

"Billy, it's not in the past yet! What happens if I tell the police I don't remember and they don't believe me? What if they want to put me in prison for stealing your car?"

"You didn't steal my car," Billy says. Snorts, actually, as if the idea that I did what I did is so ridiculous, it's snort-provoking. "No one in his right mind would believe you stole my car. Come on."

Except that I *did.*

"Your mother hates me," I say.

"Not that much," Billy says. "Not enough to tell the police you stole my car."

Billy starts to rub my shoulders, which kind of hurts, but I let him do it anyway. I want it to feel good. I want to believe that Agnes will go along with him and I won't be up for the part of hot-girl icon in Grand Theft Auto any time soon, but if he has so much power over her, then why are we hiding out behind the castle?

"What if they want to know the story of my life?" Meaning my life since the first day of junior year, given that before then I didn't have anything that you could call a life. "I can't just say I don't remember anything ever."

Billy keeps rubbing, only faster, so it feels as if the skin is going to peel off my shoulder blades leaving just bones and nerve endings. "Maybe you could," he says. "You got pretty smashed. Maybe you could just pummel the bitches with your drinking problem."

"What drinking problem?" This is so not what I need to hear from him. "You want me to say I have a drinking problem and I'm like permanently blacked out?"

"Whoa," he says. "Don't get defensive. You were pretty smashed is all I meant."

"Jesus freaking Christ, Billy!" I can tell that yelling is not a good thing, but I can't exactly help myself. "*Everyone* gets pretty smashed! It was a party. Everyone gets smashed at parties. The stoners blaze and we get smashed."

"You were kind of unusually smashed," he says. "You could hardly walk."

"Well, obviously I could walk well enough to get into your car and drive it into a tree," I say. Billy just looks at me. It is impossible to tell what he is thinking. "It would help if I could remember anything."

"Whoa," Billy says, eyeing me as if he were one of the detectives Vivian won't let me talk to. "You *really* don't remember anything? Not *anything*."

"Duh."

He stands there staring at me. "But it'll come back to you sometime, right?"

"Gone forever," I say. "That's what my dimwit doctor said. Some combination of my so-called binge drinking and the head injury."

Billy says, "*Whoa.* So you'll never remember what happened? It's gone forever? They can't even hypnotize you?"

"Gone forever," I say.

Billy just stands there looking kind of dazed but like he finally gets it.

All I know is that if I don't do something right away, if I don't make him want me right away, it is pretty much over. I know it before he even starts to elaborate on how being with me is a probation violation, which I already know and so do not want to hear about. How he's beyond grateful that I didn't finger him for being at the party, but unless his PO is a bigger moron than he thinks, he has to keep the guy from figuring it out and nailing him, and he can't have a girlfriend with a drinking problem who parties blah-blah because he's on probation for *his* so-called drinking problem and his many DUI's that his mom got him out of, and it's different for me because this was my first offense blabitty-blah but if he screws up again, he's screwed and he can kiss (drum roll) Princeton good-bye because he's going to be incarcerated somewhere with bars and Eight-Trey Gangster Crips.

"I don't have a choice," he says. "It has to at least look like I've cleaned up, or I have to kiss everything good-bye."

It is so obvious that he'd rather kiss *me* good-bye.

It is so so obvious that I have to find a way to keep that from happening.

I keep trying to tell myself what a wonderful person I am and how any reasonable boyfriend would just have to see that and just want me, want me, want me, but this is such a complete crock that it only makes me cry more.

"Don't, Gardiner," Billy said. "Shhhh. It'll be all right. Like I said, we just have to act like we're over until things settle down."

I don't even know what that means. Am I supposed to be hanging around Winston School pretending it's over when it really isn't over? If Billy can't see me or talk to me or be with me, how is it *not* over?

Billy takes my hand and gazes at me as if he is actually sad. "Look," he says. "Are you sure you even want to come back?"

"What?"

"You look so fragile and everything. And with me not being able to take care of you in public and everybody at Winston looking at you and trying to talk to you about it and everything . . . Would you be better off at Holy Name?"

My face is suddenly hot and I feel like I am going to pass out, and not in some adorable southern belle, gee-golly, Rhett-Butler-run-and-fetch-me-a-mint-julep-straight-up kind of way either.

"You don't want me to go to Winston?"

"Christ, Gabs, it's not about what *I* want," he says. "I'm thinking about what's best for *you* with everybody talking about it and bothering you and me not being able to help you. This is not going to be easy to pull off."

Like the nuns at Holy Name are going to fall all over themselves taking in a teenage felon after Easter of junior year. Like they aren't already busy enough explaining to their little coke whores how they shouldn't drive around the curves on Mulholland in the open trunk of Billy's car. A problem, come to think of it, that I have solved for them being as how now Billy doesn't *have* a car.

Like I am going to leave Winston and, from the sound of it, never see Billy again, but hey, it'll be good for his probation.

Like I am going to hang around in a Holy Name plaid pleated jumper for a year and a half and never see him at all, not even have the slightest chance of running into him, of catching a glimpse of him turning the corner in the hall.

Like I am ever going to let that happen.

"I can deal," I say. "I'll just say I don't want to talk about it. Because actually, I don't."

And I say to myself, *Gabby, what a rare genius you are, you are already saying you don't want to talk about it before anyone else thought of it. You can so totally do this.*

"I'll just be very Greta Garbo: *I vant to be alone, dahlink,*" I say to him. "You *so* don't have to take care of me."

Billy reaches over and puts his arm around me tight. It hurts like a bitch. He looks really concerned.

"Just think about it," he says "I don't want anything bad to happen to you."

"What could be worse than what's already happened?"

Billy runs his fingertips up and down between my shoulder blades. "Listen, would you break something if we, you know—?"

And I think, *Whoa!* and I don't even care what breaks.

XXV

BILLY DRIVES ME HOME IN ONE OF HIS DAD'S OLD classic Ferraris which you would think would undermine a person's ability to sneak around effectively, only around here it doesn't. He drops me off a few houses up the street, glancing over his shoulder to make sure no one but a couple of gardeners out blowing leaves down the hill with their illegal leaf-blowers spots him, and he kisses me again before I stumble back home.

It's the middle of the day but I am too tired to even undress. I fall asleep weirdly happy, and when I wake up, it's completely dark and my mother is trying to haul me into the living room as if I have to hurry or I'll miss the Second Coming of Christ.

"Vivian, I want to sleep. Just let me sleep, okay?"

She is spluttering and hissing, but I am too tired and too buried under plaster of paris makeup and too weirded out to get that Agnes Nash has turned up without warning and is standing on the front porch staring right into our house.

My parents are embarrassingly awkward—like they can't figure out that they're supposed to invite her in. It's unnerving.

Actually, Agnes seems inexplicably smiley given that I just burned up, what, $75,000 of Nash family sports car and got her baby boy into deep shit with his probation officer.

My dad takes her coat and then sort of forgets about it and drops it behind the ratty chaise. My mother can't even look her in the face.

"Can I get you something?" Vivian asks, leading Agnes nervously across the living room, scooping up stray pieces of clothes and sections of old newspapers that are strewn all over the place because Juanita is back to coming two days a week, and the other five days, stuff just piles up.

"Nice view," Mrs. Nash says, looking outside since it's pretty clear that her looking around at the inside of the house makes my mother cringe with shame over the state of our dilapidated box on stilts.

My mother pours gin and tonic into a purple tumbler and shoves it into her hand. Agnes Nash looks down at it as if it might be contaminated. Then her whole body gives a little shake, as if she has to pull herself together, and she looks up with an even more beatific smile.

"You know," she says, "Vivian, John, you have to believe that I know how godawful this is. Because, believe me, we've been there." She takes a slug of the contaminated drink, still holding it away from her body, and makes a little face.

My mother snatches the glass. "Can I get you a refill, Agnes?"

Mrs. Nash shakes her head no, but my mother refills the glass anyway, stirring frenetically with a purple glass straw. Agnes is mesmerized.

I am thinking, *Where did we get all this ugly stuff?* and wondering why I never noticed how tacky it is before.

Mrs. Nash takes the drink in its nasty purple tumbler and makes a face at it, so just in case it didn't know how nasty it was before, it knows now.

"I can't even count how many times we've been there." She looks at me, slouched in my extremely tight sweat suit that probably still has Billy's fingerprints in the nap of the velour, folding myself into the smallest possible size on the ottoman, trying to pretend I am somewhere else. "Gabby probably knows. Gabby, how many times would you say we've been there? How many, exactly?"

I have no idea, not the faintest hint, of what I am supposed to say to her or why she is here. I have no idea how many times Billy screwed up.

"Um, I guess we're all in this together," is what I finally say when it's clear that no one is going to stop looking at me until I say *some*thing. It is one of Mr. Piersol's favorite all-purpose clichés. Who says I'm not taking advantage of all the life-changing educational opportunities at Winston School?

"So," Agnes says, downing drink number two, "you're telling the police you don't remember?"

The idea that Billy is actually having conversations with his

mother in which he talks about me and tells her how I'm somewhat saving his ass by not telling the cops he attended what must
have been quite the fun party is not totally unpleasant. I kind of
wonder what else he's told her about me. I wonder what other
meaningless clichés I can come up with so she'll stop looking at
me like that.

A stitch in time saves nine?

United we stand, divided we fall?

The early bird gets whatever?

What I say is, "I haven't talked to them since before I remembered what my name was. But what else am I going to say?"

Agnes squints and peers at me, thrusting her empty purple
glass in the direction of Vivian. Then she looks over drink number three and beams at me. All right, it is definitely a more-than-
slightly-strained beam, but it is an undeniable beam. Given that
Agnes has never even so much as slightly smiled at me before, I
am completely discombobulated.

Unless there is some diabolical plot afoot and she is secretly
here to take me down and I'm just too wrecked to figure it out,
this has to be a good thing.

"All right, then," she says. "Let's roll up our sleeves and make
this whole thing go away. I'm going to say the same thing to you
I said to Billy when he started down this trail. You have a problem:
Deal with it." She starts ticking things off on her fingers until it
becomes clear that if she makes any more points, she'll use up so
many of those fingers she'll have to put down drink number three.

"There is a tried and true way to make this go away," she says, staring at me. "You have to take this seriously or it could seriously derail . . . well . . . what*ever* path it is you're on. You need a lawyer who knows what he's doing. Oh, and you'd better find her some really good psych treatment pronto or she could end up in a group home in South Central. Or out of state, God forbid."

It's surreal.

"I'm not saying that's what's going to happen to you," Agnes says, noticing that I am about to die. "Thank God we were able to keep Billy out of rehab and get him some nice psychotherapy with Dan Jackman out in Malibu this time."

My parents are just standing there nodding their heads like bobble-headed dashboard dolls.

"We're so sorry about the car," my mother says, cringing some more.

"The car is the least of our problems," Mrs. Nash says. "That's what insurance is for, that damned blue car. Had to be midnight-blue. We're certainly not going to make a fuss about it. You just keep doing what you're doing and as far as I'm concerned, he gave her the keys and that's that."

That's that? That's *that!* You have to give the boy credit. He is a parental manipulation god. And I am semi-officially the not-a-car-thief drunken girlfriend.

Sort of.

More squinting and peering from Agnes. "All right? Are we on the same page?"

But college, my mother moans. College college college. How will Little Thug Girl *ever* get into college?

Mrs. Nash sighs some more. "Oh puh-lease," she says. "Let me help you with this one. College loves a good sob story. Just make sure her grades improve a little afterward and then make sure she counsels others. Not now. Not yet. As soon as she deals with it, though, pronto. With her Problem, I mean."

"Are you sure, Agnes?" I swear, anyone with nice accessories offers Vivian a crumb of hope and she's all over them, kissing the hem of their garment and sniffing around for more crumbs.

"I paid through the nose to be sure," Agnes says. "We hired a consultant. Damage control for college. Mid-five figures. No reason for you to reinvent the wheel here. I'll get you his info; just run the essay past him."

"But Billy doesn't have to counsel others," I say. It just slips out of my dry, sleepy mouth.

Mrs. Nash gives me the same look she gave the nasty gin and tonic. "Hel-*lo*. At the Youth League shelter. He most certainly does."

Well, not exactly.

Student Council decorates the Santa Monica Youth League shelter for holiday parties. Billy, who is not exactly into crepe paper and plastic turkeys, doesn't even show up.

You can picture him standing around on the boardwalk under the pier in Santa Monica getting high while me and the rest of the Student Council are laying on the masking tape and festive poster-board snowflakes. I mean, the only helpful counseling he could possibly be doing would have to be arriving by astral projection via the psychic cat that's always out there on the

Third Street Promenade in a wizard hat making money for his half-zonked owner.

Still, it is always reassuring to be reminded that you aren't the only person in the Three B's whose parents aren't exactly familiar with you or what you do in your spare time.

Agnes whips out her BlackBerry and a little pad of paper and starts writing in a terrifying frenzy. Lawyers, doctors, people for the lawyers and doctors to contact at the LAPD and the DA's office, the college consultant, an army of people who are going to help me, by which she means people who can be pushed around to cooperate in the secret plan to get me out of the consequences for everything I can't remember.

And I keep thinking, she *can't* actually hate me that much if she's doing all this stuff for me, or why would she be doing it, right?

But then I see her looking up from the BlackBerry and glancing over at me and I see the expression on her face and I think, *Yeah, well, she actually can.*

Agnes leaves and my parents have another drink and sit there, hunkered down in the living room, staring out at the view, faint lights and the night-black ocean, streetlights and stars, completely awestruck and wiped out with drunken relief.

I sit there stirring cranberry juice and just the smallest drop of vodka with a suddenly tacky purple glass straw in a suddenly tacky purple glass tumbler, and Vivian says, "Gabby, don't clink," so she and John can take in what just happened in stewed silence.

"Are you going to get me a lawyer like she said?" I ask.

"You are going to do exactly what she said," Vivian says, as if this is what she's wanted all along and I've been holding out on her for no apparent reason.

I don't say anything.

What do I care if she's drunk and delusional, as long as she's going along with the Agnes Nash plan to save my ass?

It is as if every small suspicion I've ever had that the mega-rich of the Three B's know the Secrets of the Universe and can therefore get anything they want is confirmed, now that Agnes has swept down from the gated manse on Mulholland trailing the very secrets I need to get out of this situation, get back to Winston School, and (sorry, Agnes) get back with Billy Nash.

And you have to figure, Billy must have more than a little something to do with this given that even though Agnes is saving my life, you can tell she hates my guts, my parents, my house, and all our purple highball glasses, matching straws, and ugly furniture.

You have to figure that Billy has somehow charmed her into the car and down the hill with my address and instructions to save me.

And you have to figure that even if I have to stay away from him until he charms the hell out of his probation officer or what-ever it takes to get me out of the Probation Violation category and back into the Girlfriend category, he must still kind of want me.

My plan is to plow my way through the fastest rehabilitation in the history of mankind so I can give Billy Nash what you have to figure he still kind of wants.

XXVI

BILLY NASH.

I am in a haze of total adoration.

More than usual, to the extent it is possible for my mind to be any more hazed over than it already is. And then, in one of those perfect moments of perfectly fulfilled wishes, when I am staring at the screen of my computer and playing auto-solitaire trying to calm down and wishing he was there, there he is.

pologuy: r u feeling better now G?
gabs123: ur a god and your mother is, damn, i
don't even know what she is. seriously. i don't even
believe this.
pologuy: believe it. how do u think a dangerous guy
like me is still walking around?
gabs123: well thanks for sending her my way.

pologuy: my pleasure

gabs123: exactly nash. i'd like to thank u in person. In the interest of ur pleasure. i was thinking the door by my laundry room might have some potential.

pologuy: sorry juliet. might not get out of this house until the princeton letter is bronzed. fml. she went berserk when i was at the castle. she bribed the guy at the guard gate and kap's housekeeper to rat me out if i show up there after 6 p.m.

gabs123: too bad the KGB went out of business. she could run it.

pologuy: thx for the fun fact. will it b on AP euro?

gabs123: u know what i mean.

pologuy: i know. it's child abuse. i'm in rooster shack withdrawal. among other things

gabs123: what things would that b, nash?

pologuy: u know what things

I do know what things.

And I know where I have to be to have the slightest chance of getting a crack at those particular things.

Unfortunately, the prospects for my glorious return to Winston School, where I could actually be somewhat near Billy without sneaking through someone's abandoned shrubbery on Via Hermosita, close enough so he could actually figure out what things he still kind of wants *in person*, are looking kind of grim.

Unfortunately, the Agnes Nash plan for avoiding all consequences of bad behavior entails meetings with a cast of thousands of helpful professionals who have to sign off on my every move, and going back to school is apparently on the bottom of the juvenile delinquent to-do list.

Something it is difficult to explain to Anita and Lisa.

"Okay," Anita says, sitting on my bed eating the carrot cake Lisa made. "I know you don't want to talk about it, but do you know when you're coming back? I mean, you've already missed two weeks of school, not even counting break. Everybody wants to know how you are."

Lisa has actually collected my books from my locker, a get-well card organized by Sasha Aronson and signed by everyone in permission-only advanced painting, and horrifyingly detailed assignment sheets from all my teachers. My math teacher, Miss Lewin, had written, "No pressure. Just do what you can and we'll deal with makeup work as soon as you get back," as if the concept of no pressure makes any kind of sense in connection with trig.

"I have to see a bunch of people first."

"Neurologists?" Anita asks.

It is all just so embarrassing.

"Do you have a good lawyer?" Anita asks.

"I haven't seen him yet."

Lisa and Anita exchange looks. "I'm sure your parents are totally on top of this and it's all going to work out," Lisa says. "But do you want me to ask my uncle? He's a lawyer in San Francisco."

"My mom knows some law professors," Anita says. Her mom is an ethnomusicology professor at UCLA and an expert on South Asian percussion, so unless there are some law professors drumming up a storm and banging gourds together down in Westwood, this doesn't sound like much of a plan.

"Thanks for the thought, but I'm pretty sure my guy is decent. Billy's mother found him."

Lisa and Anita exchange more looks, as if the first annual Nonverbal Communication Fest of Casa Gardiner is in session but I'm not invited.

Anita clears her throat. "Are you sure this is smart?"

"Of course it's smart!" I say. "Why wouldn't it be smart? Billy has a lot of experience getting out of this kind of stuff."

"Yeah, but don't you want to get a lawyer just for yourself?" Lisa asks.

No.

What I really want is for this whole thing to go away and never have happened and for Lisa and Anita, who have never so much as shoplifted a peanut butter cup and whose entire knowledge of the criminal justice system comes from watching *Law & Order* reruns, to stop giving me legal advice.

XXVII

I HAVE MY HANDS FULL WITH LEGAL ASSISTANCE
from Vivian, which turns out to be one of those hideous life les-
sons in the Be Careful What You Wish For category.

Vivian is so enthusiastically down with Agnes's directives, you
would think she was gearing up for a shopping trip to the fash-
ion capitals of Europe. Apart from the fact that she keeps coming
back from Barneys with the world's ugliest clothes and forcing
me to put them on, such as a bottom-of-the-unwashed-bowl-of-
oatmeal-colored cashmere sweater Amish women would wear if
they happened to shop Wilshire Boulevard.

"There," she says, picking at some oatmeal-colored fuzz balls
because God knows how long this puppy has been languishing
on a remote shelf. "Demure." She looks me up and down. "Agnes
says you can't miss with demure."

The Barneys trip, it turns out, is just *part* of her agenda. She has a calendar; she has a list; she has a telephone voice so obsequious and kiss-ass that you'd think she was trying to get me off death row. My life is now dominated by the Agnes Nash Get Out of Jail Free flowchart that Vivian has fastened to the refrigerator door with retro magnetic pineapples.

And first on the agenda for the upscale delinquent youth of today is a visit with the lawyer. All I can think is: *Okay, Gabriella, you can stop being freaked out now.*

But it doesn't work.

The faint but persistent hope that now the whole thing can maybe start to be over is completely overwhelmed by the less-than-faint fear that getting too optimistic might not be such a great idea. So I get dressed for the occasion, trying not to flip out, getting dizzy when I look down to pull on my sandals.

Unfortunately, Vivian's idea of looking demure for this lawyer is not exactly what you'd think Agnes Nash had in mind. She comes back from Sunset Plaza holding out a little burnt-orange suit with the kind of boring jacket I'm not planning to wear until I turn forty and a six-inch-long pleated skirt. But before I have a chance to point out that I can't wear it or anything like it, I am wearing it and in the car on the way to Century City to see the lawyer Agnes picked out for me.

His office is in one of the towers with the thirty-eight-dollar valet parking, and Vivian doesn't even try to get around this by parking for cheap under the shopping center next door and walking over.

His suite is so big that the elevator opens into his reception area, acres of massive Persian rugs and soft lighting, and two receptionists who either have to be earning mega-bucks for answering the phone or some lawyer's hot mistress based on the size of the giant diamond studs in their earlobes.

It's hard to believe that springing teenage thugs could be such a ritzy profession, but according to Billy, all the best law firms keep someone on hand who can spring their top clients' little thug kids and someone else who can hide their money and scare the shit out of their old wives when they want to get new wives.

Vivian heads to the shiny mahogany counter and says, "We're here for Ted Healy. Agnes Nash sent us."

This perks the receptionist right up. She comes out from behind the counter, possibly just so we can see that she's wearing Manolos and we aren't, walks us over to leather chairs big enough to swallow and digest us in a single gulp, and sends the assistant receptionist to get us cappuccinos.

To add to the surreal experience, when Mr. Healy finally ushers us into his gymnasium-sized office, he looks like an extremely well-dressed, ginormous teddy bear. This is probably why he got stuck doing juvie, where it doesn't matter if your flaky little clients sit there marveling that you can even find pants that big and wondering just how much you have to eat to fill out those large pants. Probably the DA takes his plea bargains because he's afraid that Mr. Healy will sit on him and squash him like a Swedish pancake. Although, thanks to Agnes, we are probably going to get our own personal, cooperative DA.

"Well," Vivian says, leaning into the giant, shiny lawyer desk, fluttering her eyelashes as if being really, really charming will help make my little legal *problema* go away, "Now what, Mr. Healy?"

"Well, Vivian," he says, disgustingly charming right back at ya, tilting his head to one side and pursing his lips. "That depends on Gabriella here."

"Gabby," I say, in what comes out in too much of a sullen teen voice under the circumstances. Pissed off as I am to be walking around in tiny little mincing steps for fear the tiny little pleated skirt will fan out and show off my panties, I am not so brainless as to miss the part where this guy has to more than like me.

Why else would Vivian have stuck me in the six-inch pleated skirt in the first place?

But Mr. Healy, presumably familiar with the sullen disposition of teen thugs in strange outfits, doesn't seem to mind. "Gabby it is," he says. He is quite enthusiastic about this, actually, as if having a nickname is an asset for the youthful offender.

Then he gives us this big, dopey spiel about how he's my lawyer blabitty-blah until Vivian figures out he is tossing her out of the room and she wriggles out the double mahogany doors as if her dress itched. It is extremely embarrassing, but Mr. Healy seems to be enjoying it.

So then he can give me his even bigger dopey spiel about how for him to be able to work with me effectively, I have to level with him when he asks me a question.

"But I don't remember anything."

He looks mystified.

"Gabby," he says carefully. "I'm not sure I'm clear on what you're trying to tell me here."

"It probably doesn't matter anyway," I say. "It's just that I don't remember anything to level with you about."

"Really?" he says. Only it's more like *REALLLLLLY!?!?!?!?!?!?*

"Yeah, like if I said I remembered what I did, I'd be making it up."

"Oh, I *see*." Mr. Healy leans back in his big leather chair, which creaks pathetically, as if it were hoping that someone would put it out of its misery. "Then you really will be comfortable telling the police and probation that you don't, in fact, remember?"

Like I'm going to be comfortable telling anyone anything.

"I guess," I say. "I mean, I'm definitely not going to be comfortable having a big courtroom scene where I have to take an oath and have to . . . you know . . ."

By now, the guy is grinning from huge ear to huge ear. "I don't think we have to worry about what would happen if you were testifying in the kind of trial you see on TV," he says. "I think we can work this out without that. As for what happened on, er, Songbird Lane, your mom was kind enough to fill me in, and, unfortunately, the facts do seem to speak for themselves."

Drunk blabitty-blah car wrapped around a tree blah-blah car keys in my hand blah-blah-blah.

This is the part where Mr. Healy tips all the way back in his immense leather chair and explains in detail how if not for the vehicular pyrotechnics, maybe I could get away with being a penitent-yet-dopey teen led astray by peer pressure and a low, low tolerance for canned, chilled daiquiris. But now, in the eyes of the State of California, if I don't deal with the Problem that led to all these hijinks fast, next thing you know, I'll be off on a drunken vehicular rampage. If someone doesn't rehabilitate me immediately, a life of crime, mixed drinks, battered sports cars, and carnage spreads before me where some mediocre college and a sub-regular career used to be.

As a result of the State of California's unfortunate opinion of me, the helpful helping professionals Agnes Nash has picked out for me have to love and adore my perfect self. Because: If I'm not really really convincing, I'll be singing my sad, alcoholic ballad of teenage depravity in a locked juvenile rehab jail in Arizona.

He has the brochure.

I'll be taking wilderness walks in a one-hundred-and-ten-degree desert wonderland. And I'll be doing it sober. Which would pretty much work for me since I only drink at parties north of Sunset and gated ones in the Valley on streets like Songbird Lane, and all right, also at picnic lunches in the Class of 1920 Garden, which involves white wine in tiny Dixie cups and shouldn't even count, or just something relaxing with Billy and company after school, which seems a lot more like a bonding activity the Brady Bunch would go for after turning off the cameras than a hard-core criminal activity. But even so, I sort of doubt they have anything like that in locked rehab facilities no matter how many zillions of dollars your parents have to pay to get you in there and, more importantly, to keep you out of California Youth Authority where they have actual gang members and where Mr. Healy seems pretty convinced that someone like me could actually get killed.

XXVIII

"SO," MR. HEALY SAYS, "ARE WE ON THE SAME PAGE?"

Given that the only other page involves me going to juvie jail and being a car-thief drunk-driver with a criminal record for about ten minutes until a gang girl stabs me to death with a stiletto-sharp, rat-tailed comb, you bet we're on the same page.

But now that I can barely breathe because it feels as if my throat is closing up, there's The Bright Side. It's my first offense; nobody got all that hurt; and probation is a real good option.

This is so so not totally reassuring.

"So," he says, making a brave but unsuccessful attempt to push his sleeves half an inch up his arms. "When you were arrested, do you recall what you said to the police?"

"I was *arrested*?"

"You don't recall being arrested?" Mr. Healy starts thumbing through the files with increased interest.

"Uh-uh."

"This is interesting," he says, plucking papers from the file. "Let's see what we have here. . . . Wait a minute, is this the LAPD or the sheriff or what?"

I am trying to look as calm as possible while waiting for this to make sense.

Mr. Healy looks perturbed. "I don't see an unbooked DUI, I don't see a citation. . . . Wait . . . okay, this paperwork is not in your name."

"What isn't?"

Mr. Healy heaves a giant sigh. "Tell me you didn't give them a false name. Heidi?"

"No way! It must have been the nurse or someone, seriously. I was delirious. I was in some kind of coma." It is hard to tell if he believes me.

"We're going to have to fix this," he says, frowning at my file. "I'm going to have to take you in there."

I'm too scared to ask what the *this* we have to fix is, and where we have to go to do the fixing.

"And you weren't handcuffed to the hospital bed?"

"*What? No!*"

Mr. Healy shakes his head. He looks somewhat disgusted with the wrong-name paperwork, or me, or both. "Okay, do you remember talking to a sheriff at the hospital?"

What I remember is the gun lady and the vigilant nurse. I remember telling people who, when you think about it, had no reason to be there if they weren't police, things like "I don't know" and "I don't remember" and "I *really* don't remember" and shutting my eyes and pretending they weren't there and falling asleep. I remember drip bags full of clear liquids that greatly enhanced the possibility of falling fast asleep in the middle of a sentence.

"Well, I know they wanted to talk to me. But the nurses kept telling them I was comatose and they couldn't come in. And that they had my blood alcohol level so what else did they need."

"I see," Mr. Healy says, apparently pleased with this turn of events. "Blood draw. Blood draw? I see the blood draw. What I don't see is a warrant. And I don't see a consent form. And I don't see that a certified nurse or a phlebotomist did the draw either. You don't recall signing a consent form, do you?"

"Uh-uh."

"Well, well," Mr. Healy says. "This might give us something to work with. No bottles in the car or at the scene. And maybe no usable blood work. Just maybe they're going to have to break more of a sweat than they like breaking to find someone who saw you putting it away."

"Good luck with that one," I say. "No one will say they saw me. Are you kidding me?"

"Pardon?"

"No one will *ever* say anything like that."

Mr. Healy looks up from the file. "How can you know that?"

How could he not know that? That no one would ever tell. That Winston and every place else like it is a sacrosanct no-snitch zone, the Citadels of Silence of the Western World. Even in seventh grade, when Buddy Geiss and his eighth-grade a-hole pals were sticking little kids' heads in the toilet and flushing for no apparent reason and everybody hated his guts and was afraid they'd be the next upside down, little seventh-grade kid with pee in their hair, nobody said a single word.

And because I'm Billy Nash's girlfriend, sort of, if anyone does say a single word, they'll come out of this looking worse than me, which is, all things considered, someplace pretty damn far south of happy.

Not to mention, it seems somewhat beside the point given what you would think any reasonable lawyer would have to see as the main event of the Gabby Gardiner Crime Spree and Amnesia Fest: the car.

"What about the car?" I say.

"Well, insurance should take care of that," Mr. Healy says, not even looking up. "And you won't be driving for a while, of course."

Excuse me?

"Because I took the car?"

"Because you drove it drunk into a tree," he sighs. "Okay, let me explain this to you again."

"Wait! My boyfriend . . . my former boyfriend is like Mr. DUI and he's still driving," I say. The thought of being stranded in that house on Estrada with Vivian and John and no possible means of escape is somewhat horrifying. "When can I drive?"

Mr. Healy hems and haws and makes a lawyer joke about how my former boyfriend's lawyer must have something on the DA hardy har har. "And even if the blood alcohol is out as evidence," he says, "then we've still got some pretty reckless driving on our hands."

He seems determined to completely avoid the thing with me stealing the car, which seems like it *could* be a serious crime.

"The car?" I say again.

He just sits there in the squeaky chair looking concerned but clueless.

"Uh . . . stealing the car . . ."

"You stole a car!" Mr. Healy says, trying to sound calm as his chair squeaks back to its full upright position.

"There's no way Billy would have given me the keys to that car. That car is his baby. I mean, it *was* his baby. Before I wrecked it. So it seems like I must have just, I don't know, sort of *taken* it. Won't the police figure that out?"

Mr. Healy is suddenly taking a lot of notes. "And, uh, what does Billy say?"

"Pretty much nothing. He pretty much says not to worry about it, and his mom pretty much says the same thing."

"This would be *Agnes Nash* who says not to worry about it?"

"Uh-huh."

At which point, Mr. Healy puts down his yellow legal pad and smiles at me.

"Okay, then," he says, settling back down into the chair which squeaks an even more hideous protest. "You just might not have anything to worry about on that aspect of it. The police and the prosecutor haven't brought it up, and I don't think we'll be bringing it up either, eh?" Hardy har har.

So if nobody says anything about the car, we can all join hands and have group amnesia together?

Like if no one says it happened, then it didn't happen?

As if Billy had said: *Here, drunken girl, take my stunning and incredibly expensive car and wrap it around a tree.* Or maybe he was so drunk he just tossed me the keys, but who is going to go there? I'd still be the drunk girl who drove into the tree, and he'd be in a worse ring of Probation hell.

"Right," says Mr. Healy. "I think our focus here needs to be helping you get past the Drinking Problem so everyone can see that you Take Responsibility and it isn't going to happen again. I need you to be a model girl. I need you doing everything you're supposed to do, everything all the mental health and rehab people you're about to meet tell you to do, on time, and with a smile on your face. Can you do that?"

"Yeah, I can do anything."

"Anything *le*gal," he says. "Anything legal, moral, and looks good in a probation report. What about school? Do you have a disciplinary record at school I need to know about?"

"No, nothing," I say, trying to figure out quickly how to let him know what a paragon of perfection I could look like on paper if desperate enough. "I'm on Student Council!" I blurt.

Mr. Healy does not look all that impressed. "They never caught you so much as smoking a cigarette behind the gym?" he says. "You're not one of the usual suspects, notorious bad girl, sketchy friends, the works?"

"No!"

"Because if we need to send you to another school, I've got one up my sleeve, and we can slip you right in. Fresh start and all that."

"I don't want a fresh start!" I say. "The only thing I could be notorious for is this, and it's not something I do a lot of."

"No drunk and disorderlies are going to pop up in Orange County with some Jane Doe-linsky ID? And by the way, if you have a Jane Doe-linsky ID, I need you to melt it down. Today."

"I don't. But if I did, I would. I get it. I can be completely perfect for as long as you want, but I really have to go back to Winston."

Mr. Healy looks suspicious. You could tell that he'd heard protestations of teenage perfection before.

"All righty," he says, sounding completely unconvinced. "Best-case scenario, you'll get some favorable probation recommendations, the DA buys it, you'll live at home, you'll get some treatment, you will not so much as sit behind the wheel of a car until your license is restored, you'll act like your conditions of probation are the Ten Commandments, and twelve, eighteen months from today, you won't have a record."

"No record?"

I feel as if I've stumbled into the Magic Kingdom of making things go away. I want to kiss Billy Nash. I mean, I always want to kiss Billy Nash, but now I *really* want to kiss Billy Nash just after ripping off this awful suit. Except that how I can get myself physically close enough to Billy Nash to plant my kiss is a Mystery of Life because even in the Disneyland of best-case scenarios, I still can't *drive*.

Mr. Healy looks very pleased with himself. "Expunged," he says. "You'll need to follow the rules of probation punctiliously. Because worst-case scenario, you're spending some time in that residential facility."

Okay, out of the Magic Kingdom and into a black-and-white girls' prison movie with catfights and sadistic butch matrons with cattle prods.

"Well, young lady, this is what's going to happen," he says in a jovial tone that seems spectacularly inappropriate under the circumstances but I really don't want to piss off the guy standing between me and total doom by pointing this out. "We're going to get you arraigned. You won't have to say anything except to verify your name and address. And we're going to make sure this citation isn't screwed up in a way that could bite you. And from what you're telling me, you can honestly say you don't remember a thing no matter what they ask, so no sweat there. By the time they get around to finishing up your probation report, we'll have you squared away."

I don't even want to know what it means to be squared away in Mr. Healy's world. All it brings to mind is a perfectly square cell or maybe a cube-shaped cage with bars all the way around.

"All righty, then," he says. "Let's get your mother back in here. Let's get you into Twelve Step and coordinate the psycho-babble. Let's talk to the police. Let's get the show on the road."

XXIX

YOU WOULD THINK THAT AFTER WEEKS OF LYING
around petrified and chanting *I want a lawyer* over and over, I would
have been a happy little camper now that my show *was* on the road.

You would think that now that I didn't have to man up to
put weight on both feet without flinching, and my left hand—
although it would have been pretty much a straight-up catastrophe
if it had been my right hand, but it wasn't—was semi-functional
and filled with prickly sensations that were actually quite the
relief compared to feeling pain or nothing, I would have been
striding toward the potentially swell future.

You would think that the possibility I was going to get to
shrug off my life as a juvenile delinquent and walk away smiling
and arrest record–free, that I could just hang around and obsess
about Billy Nash pretty much all the time while my so-called
legal problems kind of went poof, like a bunny disappearing into

Mr. Healy's top hat, if I just got with the program, would have been cause for major celebration.

Which could have happened if I had any idea how I was supposed to pull off any of this.

gabs123: r u there nash or is ur computer just on?

pologuy: whatcha doing?

gabs123: filling out forms for my lawyer. huge lawyer.

pologuy: ag only knows famous guys

gabs123: no, literally huge. fattest guy not in the circus.

pologuy: at least he sounds amusing. my guy is frightening. makes people capitulate with dirty looks. u don't do what he says, he looks at u, ur done for

gabs123: well ur guy must b pretty amazing because how come u can drive but I can't?

pologuy: wtf. that sucks

gabs123: so how come?

pologuy: scary lawyer fixed it. changed charge to disturbing peace or some kind of bad mischief with no drinking in it

gabs123: how???????????

pologuy: vaporized from the record? large contribution to the mayor? don't know. u have smashed car and the blood alcohol level of a keg

gabs123: lawyer might be able to keep my blood alcohol level out of it. how would u know my blood alcohol lvl anyway?

pologuy: agnes knows all sees all screws up all

gabs123: consider the possibility that i'm the one who screwed up.

This was so not what I meant to say to him. And I go, *Gabriella, if you don't want him to think you suck, maybe it would be better if you didn't freaking tell him that you suck.*

pologuy: don't say that. hey. miss u gabs

gabs123: me too. castle?

pologuy: can't. agnes is doing her prison warden thing.

gabs123: xx anyway. i just don't know how i'm going to pull this off. how do i even do this so that people buy it?

Which turns out to be so the completely right thing to say.

pologuy: i'm going to walk u through it. u can do this. u have to stay strong

gabs123: as in don't cry and b girlie?

pologuy: as in don't start feeling like u deserve to have something bad happen to u. or something bad will happen to u

gabs123: that is so not what i'm doing. couldn't this just b like the take responsibility thing everyone is so hot and bothered about?

pologuy: no. taking responsibility is like ok i'm sorry and

i'll never do it again. but u can't let yourself get into that
what if i killed a baby i deserve to b locked up frame
of mind

gabs123: what if i did WHAT?

pologuy: point is, u didn't. stay with that. u have to go
hey, i'm the luckiest guy on planet earth. i'm a lucky
duck in a magic pond. don't go spitting in the magic
pond ok?

gabs123: ur scaring me.

pologuy: listen to me g. the universe is tossing u a
free pass. don't u want a free pass? take it. it's not like
someone died

At which point, I completely lose it.

gabs123: shit, i could have crashed into a freaking baby
and i don't even remember it!!!

pologuy: but u didn't. u need to stop thinking about it.
jackman has this technique where u put a rubber band
on ur wrist and every time you think bad thoughts, u
snap it

gabs123: u wore a rubber band on ur wrist? this is hard
to picture.

pologuy: didn't need to—i don't have bad thoughts. i
take what the universe gives me. like i said i'm lucky
and things work out

gabs123: what if i'm not lucky?

pologuy: it's just killer bad thoughts g. u have to stop
it. predators smell fear. they get one whiff of what a
big bad baby-killing girl u think u r, ur screwed

Raising the fascinating question of what I was supposed to do with what a big bad baby-killing girl it felt like I was. How the fact I was a lucky duck in a magic pond with no smashed baby and the universe raining down Get Out of Jail Free cards on my head didn't feel as good as it was supposed to. How I had to go convince the police and the probation office and a platoon of therapists that, even though I didn't remember a single minute of what happened, I was pretty damned sure it was never going to happen again because I was a model girl.

pologuy: wish i could break out of my house and
come get u, do a bonnie and clyde thing, drive down
to rooster shack for deep fry in the hood. get me a
gf fix

Ahhhhhhhhhhhh, GF. GF GF GF GF GF!!!!!!!!!!!!

gabs123: the crips down at rooster shack would
no doubt rush right up to mulholland and break u
out if they just knew how bad u need a chicken and
gf fix.
pologuy: that would be bloods. did u miss the red
bandanas?

gabs123: whatever.

pologuy: just don't mix them up when ur down at the courthouse

gabs123: don't even remind me. i have no idea what to even say at the courthouse. i just have a list of honchos to make appointments with. no idea what to SAY to them.

pologuy: nobody told u what to say?

gabs123: i think i'm just supposed to tell the truth and look sorry.

pologuy: no!!!! ur lawyer was supposed to tell u what to say. what an elephant turd

gabs123: I just have to convince a bunch of people that i'm perfect.

pologuy: that should go well

gabs123: u don't think i'm perfect?

pologuy: ok this is not good. shit. r u home alone?

gabs123: yes. no. i mean, john's here, but he NEVER comes out of the den so it's the same thing. and the door to the laundry room would really work. think about it. you'd come in through the canyon and no one could see.

pologuy: shit, i shouldn't do this. ok. i'll call when i get there and you'll pick up the phone on the first ring but it won't be me ok? i'll be picking up a book from kaplan

gabs123: what do u mean?

pologuy: IT WON'T BE ME. the phone will ring, but it won't be me out there ok?

gabs123: whatever u say.

pologuy: i don't think u get what kind of shit i could be in

gabs123: whatever.

XXX

HE CALLS ME ON HIS CELL FROM THE LANDING JUST outside the laundry room door. There are leaves in his clothes from climbing through the canyon, his hair is flopped down over his forehead in a golden wedge. Black T-shirt and his pupils dilating black as he steps into the dark room and stands between the washing machine and the utility closet and I hold him and he holds me back.

I can feel his skin heating up, his face hot under the stubble, his mouth soft and salty as ever, our breathing matched as ever, synchronized, my head nestled on his shoulder for a minute and then tipped back and kissing him and him kissing my eyelids and my eyebrows and my nose and my cheeks and my lips.

"Okay," he says. "We can't do this now. I have to teach you this stuff fast and cut out."

It's hard to stop. "Billy," I say, catching my breath and trying to sound casual. "The police aren't patrolling my laundry room. I think we're safe."

Billy shakes his head. "I said I was getting Andy's Spanish book. You have no idea how screwed I am. I might have to convince my PO I was trying to leave the bad evil party but I couldn't find my car. I might have to take a freaking acting class to pull this off."

"Okay, I get it. Everyone is screwed. Teach me the stuff."

So Billy sits down on the washer and I sit down on the dryer.

"Okay," he says. "It's not that hard. The way you're going to get out of this is you're going to have a drinking problem and they're going to cure it."

"Oh, please. Do we have to go there? My lawyer won't shut up about my drinking problem. Can't I have some other problem they can cure?"

"Uh, *no*. You're naturally perfect for this because the only way people believe you have a drinking problem is if you deny it. If you wise up and figure out you have a drinking problem too soon, they think you're scamming them. Just remember, you're dealing with fools and deny your head off."

"That shouldn't be too much of a stretch. Except that I got plowed and ran your car into a tree."

"Yeah, there's that. Try it anyway."

"What?"

"You know. Right now. Boo hoo!" he says in a squeaky voice I can only assume is supposed to be me. "How can you say I drink too much? Boo hoo." He pats my leg. "Now you try it."

"Jesus, Billy. You should start an improv troupe. Okay, here goes. Boo hoo! How can you say I drink too much?"

"Boo hoo! I never drink too much!"

"Boo hoo! I never drink at all. The car just happened to crash with my unlucky self in it."

Billy grins, oh my God, *the grin.* "That would be with your unlucky, sober self in it."

"My unlucky, sober self."

"Excellent. Okay, then you keep it up for maybe a month, maybe shorter if they're doing your probation report sooner. You have to stay on top of the timing. Then you fake your big moment of insight."

"Let me guess. Boo hoo. I have a drinking problem."

"You have to get a little enthusiastic about this, Gardiner. You have to sell it. Boo hoo!!!! I have a drinking problem and I'm so upset—how did I miss it?????" He slaps his forehead. "Thank you, wise, helping professionals!!!!!!! A hearty thanks to all you whores for opening my eyes!!!!"

"Boo hoo."

"Then you lean back and let them cure you."

"And people buy this?"

"Babe, you sell it and they buy it. That's what they do for a living."

"Even the lawyer? What am I supposed to say to him?"

"Whatever he wants to hear. Just answer his questions succinctly and look cute."

"Succinctly, Nash?"

"SAT word."

"How cute?"

"So cute he can parade you in front of punk-ass chump cops and probation and they'll be able to tell just by looking at you that it would be a big mistake to try and mess with you."

You can tell that he knows all this from personal experience, which is both reassuring and somewhat less than reassuring.

The reassuring part is: I can more or less do this.

I just can't talk about any of it with anyone else, ever, because the Three B's are a tiny little gossip-riddled world and it could come back to bite me in an anything-you-say-to-friends-or-random-strangers-can-be-used-against-you-in-a-court-of-law kind of way. The whole plan will involve some serious sneakiness, but after seven months of running around Winston School semi-successfully pretending to be hot and, if not popular, not *un*popular, I figure I've developed one or two useful strategic skills I could use in a pinch.

Billy, with his vast bad boy experience, has given me this whole routine, and now it's my turn to dance in well-choreographed circles around the truth.

And then his phone starts to vibrate. "Shit," he says. "Agnes."

"Just turn it off. Tell her you were in a canyon. Sorry, no reception."

He just stares at it. It stops vibrating and then it starts again. I reach for it and he pulls it back out of my reach, not even looking up at me. The phone flashes "Agnes B. Nash."

"You're sure you can do this?" he says, setting the phone on his lap. "You get it, right? You stick to the plan and you don't talk to anyone but me?"

"Completely." I am looking at the stairs that lead to the middle floor where my bedroom is. I am thinking about how close my room is and how John might as well be in Greenland and Vivian isn't going to leave the sale at Neiman Marcus until she's escorted to the door by security because they want to clock out for the night. I am thinking about how I want to feel and who can make me feel those particular feelings.

But Billy is looking at his vibrating phone and then at his Swiss precision underwater watch. He kisses me all along my collarbone, gentle where it is still bruised, holding the vibrating phone against my back. "I want you," he says, as I tilt my head toward the staircase. "You know I do. But I can't do this anymore. I have to bounce."

And he bounces.

Leaving me with the new, improved Billy Nash plan to lie my way out of the whole mess, a hickey that means I am going to have to extend the opaque makeup all the way down the left side of my neck, and no boyfriend.

XXXI

AS SOON AS BILLY LEAVES, VIVIAN, WHO WAS
apparently only at Neiman's in her new role as Highly Organized
Mother, shows up, her shoes clunking around the kitchen floor
overhead and then down the stairs, waving her BlackBerry in a
new, snazzy Prada case.

"You're not doing laundry, are you?" she says.

Unlikely, given that teaching me things like how to work a
washing machine and cook food beyond microwaving California
Pizza Kitchen frozen pizzas is not on the list. If there is ever a
national emergency so severe there's no takeout or housekeepers,
I am going to starve to death in smelly clothes.

"I'm looking for my good jeans," I say, pretending to rub my
neck at the relevant spot.

"No jeans," she says. "We're going to Isabelle Frost. She's the
social worker. I put your clothes on the bed."

"I can dress myself, you know. As God is my witness, I can put a skirt and blouse together."

Vivian does not look convinced. "I was thinking French schoolgirl, not Scarlett O'Hara," she says. Which should at least preclude the matted Amish sweater and the six-inch pleated skirt. Which, for reasons clear only to Vivian and some unscrupulous salesgirl dying to unload the Neiman buyer's more heinous mistakes, involves black linen pants with a waist so high it threatens to meet the underwire of my bra and a tan silk shirt with cuff links.

Think a funny-looking French schoolgirl with no taste.

"I am so not tucking this blouse into these pants. I'll look ridiculous."

Oh yes I am.

I am wearing the outfit with a pair of Vivian's ugly Coach flats, and I am getting into the car with Vivian and John, who has somehow been suckered into wearing a navy blazer with the family crest subtly embroidered on the pocket. We look like a complete joke.

But not as big a joke as Isabelle Frost, social worker to the rich and infamous.

Billy wants me to read my helpful professionals and figure out what they want and give it to them, but it is hard to tell if Isabelle Frost is Botoxed to the point that it limits all forms of facial expression or if she is just trying to look extra stern.

After about five seconds, it's obvious she thinks that I'm some poor depressed alcoholic girl with bad self-esteem craving liquor to drown her alcoholic sorrows.

And she wants me to know that she totally and completely understands poor depressed alcoholic girls such as myself because she had exactly the same Problem when she was addicted to prescription pain pills following an unfortunate series of surgical procedures that you have to assume involved sucking all the fat out of her body and inserting Teflon in places it is embarrassing to look at unless the thought of armor-piercing breasts appeals to you. John would appear to be examining his fingernails, but Vivian is gazing up at her as if she knows the secret of eternal youth.

I still haven't said anything, but after another five minutes, it is also obvious that the only way to get out of this with half a life left is to pretend to *be* some poor depressed girl with bad self-esteem craving liquor to drown her depressed, alcoholic sorrows.

Just like Billy said.

Isabelle Frost has a great many ideas for how I am going to—in a handy two-fer—get my Problem cured and impress the shit out of the Probation Department, with which she is going to personally interface. (*Interface?* Lobby? Bribe? Blackmail? Threaten? Wave a tiny photo of Agnes Nash in the form of a cross? It's difficult to visualize exactly how this is supposed to work.)

"What Mr. Healy wants me to make sure of," Ms. Frost says in between fits of pretending to understand me so so well, her speech slightly slurred because her lips have a limited range of motion and seem to pucker spasmodically all on their own, "is that we have you all set up before the Probation Department even knows your name. They'll see how you've taken responsibility for your Problem and cleaned up your act and you've self-procured treatment and your family is straight out of *Leave It to Beaver* and bingo!"

Bingo?

My mother, by this point, is pacing around Ms. Frost's office picking up and putting down knick-knacks and shredding the tissues. My dad is sitting there stone-still, his eyes half-closed, so you can't tell whether he's super-upset or asleep.

"Absolutely," Vivian keeps repeating. "Of course we can get Gabby treatment! Of course she's not out of control! Of course Gabby can take responsibility for her Problem, can't you, Gabby?"

She is blissfully unaware of what I have to say to fake out everybody, how I have to deny my so-called Problem.

"Sure," I say, really hoping that Billy knows what he's talking about because I am about to launch. Frosty looks up to see where the voice is coming from, given that I haven't said anything, not one single word including hello, for the past forty-five minutes. "Only I'm not sure I have a *Problem.* Are you sure I have a Problem?"

Billy is completely right.

Ms. Frost is so overjoyed that I am sitting there semi-denying the Problem while remaining open to learning all about said Problem, you can almost discern the faint suggestion of a smile at the corners of her Botox-frozen, twitching mouth. Billy is a complete Get Out of Jail Free meister.

Of course I don't appreciate the Problem and that is why all these helpful professionals are going to help me appreciate and come to grips with it! Preferably before the Department of

Probation helps me appreciate and come to grips with it in desert rehab in Arizona.

All I am thinking is: *How do I get out of this and get back to Winston and get back with Billy? Just tell me what to do and I'll do it. Tell me what to say and I'll say it.*

All Vivian is thinking is: *Winston School! Tell me what to do to keep her from getting booted out of Winston School and destroying her chance of attending the sub-regular college of her choice and I'll do it!*

It is hard to tell what my dad is thinking since, even without the Botox, he is almost as poker-faced as Ms. Frost. "Of course we have a stable home life," he's murmuring, his eyes still partly closed. "Of course we know where she is at all times. Of course we don't sanction underage drinking."

Probably he's thinking: *Does this place have a bar?*

Or maybe: *How soon can I get back to Bel Air where we have a bar and several well-stocked mini-fridges?*

The sooner he can get back to a pitcher of margaritas, the sooner he can forget how Winston might hold it against me that I'm a drunken felon car thief, thereby stripping him of any slim claim to status that I had ever offered. Except for my increasingly tenuous connection to Billy Nash.

All I can think about is Billy. How I need to see him and not just to make out to the point of frustration on top of a washing machine and hiding out behind abandoned houses. How I need to see him all the time and I need to make him want me again. How I need to be at Winston even though Ms. Frost says to avoid him and all other cute bad boys—if *I* am at Winston and *he* is at

Winston, what are they going to do, put us in handcuffs if we make eye contact?

Winston School!

For once Vivian and John and I are in perfect agreement.

Only I have to survive the black hole of the legal system first.

XXXII

THE THING ABOUT FALLING INTO THE LEGAL SYSTEM is that even if you aren't ready for it; even if you don't want to deal with it; even if you need to crawl back onto your space-raft bed and float in a gray-green sky; even if you wish you could get your behind-the-eyes documentary going again instead of being stuck with your actual, real life; even if you reach the absolute limits of positive thinking and there's not a single nice thing you can think of to say to yourself that you actually believe, you still can't make it stop.

Vivian and I are parked under a scrubby tree in a parking lot in the Valley. John has bailed, with the completely bogus claim that he has work to do, so it's just me and her waiting in complete silence, which, under the circumstances, probably beats talking.

We are sitting there in the old SUV and not the Mercedes

because Vivian is afraid that the police will hold a Mercedes that big against us if they notice it. Because we are so deep deep in the San Fernando Valley, so far north of Ventura Boulevard and civilization, that we don't even recognize where we are, and she suspects that there's an irrational hatred of rich people—presumably extending to the pseudo-rich—out here.

We are parked by a sheriff's station, waiting for me to go in.

The station is a tan, cinder-block building with windows too high to look out of or see into. All I can think about is how you could go into a building like that and not come out except to ride from one locked room to another on one of those sheriff's buses you stare into on the freeway, wondering what those men scowling sideways at you *did* to be riding in there. And how I could end up in a bus like that with rows of terrifying girls in Day-Glo jumpsuits.

We are not planning to get out of the SUV until Mr. Healy shows up and gets out of his Maybach first, meanwhile avoiding eye contact with any of the tired-looking deputies walking by, or the people going in and out of the station who, from the look of it, have no reason to fear they are going to inspire prejudice by virtue of uppity displays of Westside wealth.

It's the Valley; it is eighty-eight degrees in April; and all I want to do is swim out of there in a conveniently deep river of sweat. Why couldn't I just paddle over to some Westside courthouse where the big question would be what the hell a girl like me was doing in the Valley in the first place, even if it was Songbird Lane in Hidden Hills, which is gated and where all the houses have acres of grassy lawns, black-bottom swimming pools, koi ponds, and a horse?

Leaving aside those pesky questions that are sure to come up in maybe five minutes (if Mr. Healy ever shows) about (1) the drunk driving, (2) the Beemer, and (3) why someone who did what I did should get out of trouble just by having her enormous lawyer bludgeon people.

What I don't want to be doing is the thing I came here to do: get arrested. Or maybe re-arrested, this time adding the element of consciousness.

It turns out that there are quite a few other things I don't want to do, such as getting fingerprinted.

Such as having mug shots taken with numbers on the bottom. Such as surrendering my driver's license—graciously returned to us by the mom of the kid who threw the party on Songbird Lane by FedEx, my wallet still nestled inside my bag and nothing missing—into a big mustard-colored envelope with my number on the front.

Such as getting a date and an actual time on a real day in June to show up in juvenile court.

So I hold my breath and get logged in to the system, with Mr. Healy standing around drumming his fingers as if he's bored and all of this is no big deal. And I say, "I don't remember," in response to every question other than the one about my name and address.

No, I have no firsthand knowledge of where the party was or who threw it or if there even was a party or how I got the liquor or if I drank it of my own free will or if there even was liquor, which I don't remember and therefore I can't admit I drank. Artfully avoiding words like "stole" and "Billy."

The detective looks annoyed as hell but he has the doctor's report about the tree and its effect on my head right in front of him on the table so he can't exactly come out and say *liar, liar, pants on fire* to try to get me to tell him what he wants to know. He keeps cozying up to words that have a great deal of SAT potential such as "stonewall" and "intransigent," but Mr. Healy keeps murmuring "closed head injury," and I just sit there, amazed by the depth and breadth of what I really don't know, and hoping I look dazed and brain-dead enough for them to leave me alone.

What I want to know is why Billy didn't tell me this part of it, the part where you're sitting in a metal chair in a windowless room and it feels like you're an inch away from being sucked up into a whole other life—not in a distant universe, but in a squat, shabby building, with cells and linoleum floors and pissed-off detectives, that you never even knew was there before.

Explain that.

And when I am finally home, alone in my room, all I can think is, *Man, if I did have a drinking problem, this would be the magic moment.*

And then I think: *What the hell?*

And I go into the bar in the living room and get out some vile-tasting twelve-year-old scotch and some ice.

XXXIII

WHAT YOU SHOULD KNOW ABOUT DRINKING A GREAT
deal of scotch on the rocks when you're alone in your bedroom
is that, in addition to making you feel somewhat less preoccupied
with the sorry state of your abysmal, completely wrecked life, it
makes you uncoordinated and a sentimental sap and somewhat
more stupid than usual.

Which might cause you to drink even more scotch on the
rocks in order to take the edge off feeling stupid, et cetera.

So basically I sit on the edge of my bed hugging the ice bucket,
drinking twelve-year-old Glenlivet and feeling like a moron.
Vivian is getting over her traumatic afternoon in the Valley by
getting her nails wrapped in Santa Monica and I, actually *being*
a sentimental sap and also stupid, start rummaging through the
Billy Nash memorabilia in the top drawer of my dresser.

There are movie ticket stubs and shells from the beach outside his parents' place near Point Dume and a ratty wrist corsage that I probably should have pressed instead of shoving it whole into a drawer where the petals are turning into mini-compost.

There are little boxes that used to contain an assortment of Belgian chocolates that Billy bought for me only because he wanted the semi-sweet truffles and if he bought the whole box for me, he didn't have to feel like a goof standing in line at Godiva Chocolatier buying himself romantic candy.

There is the Rule the Pool water polo booster baseball cap that seems like a good thing to be wearing only because by that point in the bottle, I am seriously judgment-impaired.

It seems like a good idea to ponder all the lined up little presents Andie Bennett has mailed me since the accident, and then it seems like an even better idea to kiss the little plastic Flower the Skunk figurine with the pencil sharpener embedded in its belly that she sent last week, only I don't even think about how a person could nick her lip on the metal strip where the shavings get sliced off the pencil.

By the time Anita calls to see if I want her to come over so we can quiz each other on SAT words, I am impaired on several other dimensions too, and she says, "Are you all right? You sound awful."

I say, "I'm fine."

"I don't know," Anita says. "Are you crying? Should I come over?"

"I just cut my lip on a pencil sharpener. Don't come over."

You can hear Anita taking a breath. "Gabby," she says, "if this is wrong, I'll never bring it up again, but are you drunk?"

This seems like the most hilarious thing I've heard all day, which isn't saying much. The only tiny scrap of self-control I have left staunches the impending giggle and leaves me sort of snorting into the phone.

"I'm not drunk," I say, in a vain attempt to sound as if I'm not. "Maybe I went to the dentist so my tongue is numb."

"I thought you were going to see that lawyer."

"Maybe I went to the lawyer and the dentist. Did you think of that? Maybe I went to the dentist and the lawyer and a police station in freaking Reseda. Maybe I should go to sleep."

"Because if you're drinking, if it's more than that one time, you need to talk to someone."

"Anita, all I do is talk to people. And it was just that time and this time. And now I really have to lie down." To demonstrate, I lie down and the Rule the Pool hat falls off onto the pillow.

"Do novocaine and alcohol even go together safely?" Anita says. "I'm going to look this up on the Internet. I'm going to text Sanjiv. Hold on."

But before I have time to hold on, I am asleep.

XXXIV

IF YOU'RE A FAN OF IRONY, MS. FROST'S FIRST project for me, in the quest to look like I am halfway to being rehabilitated before the Department of Probation gets its hooks into me, is going to AA, and Vivian tells me about it when I am still lying on my bed next to the Rule the Pool hat, sauced.

I am pretty sure that Billy would appreciate the irony, but not only has he forgotten to mention AA in the first place, he has been exiled to his uncle's hacienda in Montecito, sharing a room with his nosy little cousin and bereft of electronics, because Agnes had to go to New York on business and doesn't trust Billy at home without heavy-duty adult supervision after it supposedly took him two hours and forty-five minutes to get to Kap's house for the Spanish book, and given that his dad is about as present and as capable of providing supervision as

John, except that his dad is MIA at Murchison Nash Capital rolling in enormous bundles of cash as opposed to passed out in the den.

Fortunately, Billy manages to convince his aunt that he can't stay there for the whole three-day weekend because if he misses any more practice with the water polo team, he'll end up benched and attending a giant state college full of riff-raff, and she has to let him go home.

"Just go," he says, whispering into a prepaid cell phone that he bought at a mini-mart in Oxnard on his way back down the coast while his uncle's driver pumps the gas and cleans the windshield and Billy hides out in the men's room. "Just go this one time and don't say anything. Just sit there. Keep your mouth shut and don't get a sponsor. No sponsor, got that? Gotta go."

What do you even wear to kid AA?

Vivian drives me down the hill and into Brentwood, and she drops me off in front. She seems perfectly happy to consign me to two hours in a room full of alcoholics. But it only takes me thirty seconds in the church hall before I am 100% sure that AA isn't happening for me, even if it is in this very plush church with exceptionally nice-looking refreshments. As much fun and games as it might be to fake out all the sharing caring adults who want to help me solve my so-called problem, it doesn't exactly seem realistic to bank on faking out a whole room full of kids with actual drinking problems.

I mean, it's not as if their bullshit meters are nonfunctional because of an alcohol-induced stupor.

Not to mention, some of them look vaguely familiar and have pretty much the same Marc Jacobs flats and pseudo-military jacket that I have, and might actually turn up unexpectedly in my real life, and then what? My big night of drinking untold amounts might be filed somewhere in the Amnesiac Archives, but other than that, I'm not a drunk, and I'm not about to start lying about it in front of a large, sincere audience.

Not to mention my personal plan, the Gabs and Billy plan, is to suck up to my highly paid professional helpers but trot rapidly in the opposite direction with my lips locked if anybody else wants to Talk About Everything. This is an entire church filled with people who look like they're dying to talk their little hearts out.

What am I supposed to do?

For maybe twenty-nine seconds, I think how probably half the other kids there are in the same stupid situation as me, got caught bombed at a party, downed a bottle of scotch in their bedrooms one time, and *zap*: Go Directly to Twelve Step. Do Not Pass GO. A stop along the way to getting their Get Out of Jail Free cards.

Only then they open their mouths and pretty much no, they're really into it. I feel like a sleazoid Peeping Tom hiding out in the bushes waiting to cop a peek of naked people through his neighbor's bedroom window.

It is actually kind of sad. People who drink before school every day and spend first period sucking on mentholated cough drops to clean up their breath. And who look twelve years old.

And feel like their lives have nothing to offer. And I'm thinking, *No, you're so cute, you could definitely get a boyfriend. You could end up like me, with a totally screwed-up life but, hey, no drinking problem.*

This is probably the only problem I *don't* have.

But no, here are people who can't get out of bed or go to sleep without it. People who are incredibly proud they just spent sixty-eight days without it, even though they constantly want it and think about it all the time and show up at meetings where all they do is talk about it, and have to call up other kids to talk them out of using it.

And I really would have helped them stop it if I had any idea of how to get anyone to do anything. I'm sitting there thinking: *You go, fourteen-year-old drunk boy, get a grip, go another sixty-eight days, call up your fifteen-year-old sponsor* (if kids even get a kid sponsor which, thank you Billy, I don't plan to stick around long enough to find out) *and smoke a lot of cigarettes because if you think this is bad, wait until you grow up and it turns out you're exactly like my dad.*

And then I think, big revelation, giant whoop, silent You Go Girl from the helpful helping professionals who sent me to this godforsaken pastry smorgasbord and confession-fest: *John is the alcoholic. Not me, John. Why isn't he here?*

But it doesn't seem as if it would go over too well to explain that I just drink at parties a couple of times a week, not unlike everybody else at the parties except for the people who just blaze their way into oblivion with weed, and if I belong at this so-called meeting, then we might just as well sink the church into the ground under the sheer weight of the gazillion other kids who all get plowed at the same parties as me and, hello, they aren't alcoholics either.

So maybe there are a couple of other places where I drink, such as at lunch in the Class of 1920 Garden, such as at meals other than breakfast where, give me a break, you really do have to be a drunk to drink anything other than a mimosa, which is at least appropriate with eggs. So send for more chairs. Enough so, say, the entire population of France (where they do drink wine with breakfast; I have personally witnessed this) will have someplace to sit in the Brentwood Unitarian Church.

But I don't say this. Not to people who drink Stoli out of their thermoses in study hall at Paul Revere Middle School. I wish them well. All I want in life is to find some nice way to get out of there without anyone noticing.

Except, of course, that everyone is looking me over, waiting for an opportunity to spring out of their chairs and sidle up to me and make me feel all welcome.

I figure that hanging out in the ladies' room for the next hour and a half would be a bit obvious and somewhat insulting, so I just sit there in my folding chair leaning as far back as possible without tipping over, not making eye contact with anybody, pretending to listen.

Every time another one of them starts talking, I glance up, very fast, and every time they stop, I wonder if this is when they're going to shout out a big Kid AA howdy to all the new people—or for all I know, just me, for all I know, I am the only new person—and force us or just me or whoever to stand up and say something.

I just slink down further in my chair, sliding my eyes over every corner of the room, checking out the emergency exits just in case.

When it is over, I run out of there, not saying hi to anybody, just jumping into Vivian's car and closing my eyes, light-headed and completely clammy.

XXXV

gabs123: i cannot go to AA anymore. get me out of AA. i mean it.

pologuy: shit aa. this is not good

gabs123: kill me now. i'm supposed to go all the time. i mean constantly. daily. i am not going to stand around and talk about myself. did u have to go?

pologuy: long time ago. tiny tot fake aa. i think i got kicked out

gabs123: how does a person get kicked out of tiny tot fake AA?

pologuy: i think i hit someone. doofus buddy geiss. hate that kid

gabs123: buddy geiss!!! wait. isn't this supposed to b alcoholics ANONYMOUS? thus the second a.

pologuy: ok some doofus kid identical to buddy geiss.
not hit. knocked over his chair when he was in it
gabs123: y?
pologuy: who the hell remembers back to tiny tot aa?
maybe he took my donut
gabs123: i don't know if i'm up for knocking over a
doofus to get out of this. what do i do? i'm not a sharing
caring gabfest kind of girl.
pologuy: and that is what we love about u

What we LOVE about you?!?!?!?!

gabs123: ?
pologuy: ok just tell ur social worker u can't do it
gabs123: right. that'll make her happy. frost is the one
who's making me go and she reports to my lawyer.
it's supposed to impress the hell out of probation.
remember probation?
pologuy: think of something else to impress them.
it's not that hard. like i told u before. boo hoo and dig
in ur heels. boo hoo queen frostine I can't go to aa
because . . .
gabs123: because y?
pologuy: it could b anything. b creative. try again. boo
hoo queen frostine i can't go to aa because . . .
gabs123: if anyone sees me there my name will be
mud all over candyland? did u know mudd was some

guy who supposedly helped john wilkes booth shoot abraham lincoln?

pologuy: thnx for the fun fact. will it b on SAT 2's? i'm being forced to memorize all words in english language. and an all purpose essay

gabs123: u wrote an all purpose SAT essay?

Even though it isn't too hard to figure out that life is going on without me in it, the idea that Billy was sitting around writing an all-purpose SAT essay while I was out in the Valley getting mug shots taken is somehow mind-boggling. The idea that he could just sit there and concentrate and write essays about his most emotional moment and his most inspirational hero and his most compelling hope, dream, or extracurricular activity, and soon I am going to have to write about how getting past my Problem made me a Better Person to try to get everyone in some sub-regular college admissions office to love me. The idea that I've wandered into this horrible, alternate world and have to do all this weird stuff to get back, but everybody else is still sitting there in the real world writing their SAT essays and memorizing the Latin roots of SAT words.

pologuy: tutor wrote it. i memorize it and adapt it to 200 stupid prompts. it's inspirational. how i'm on student council and martin luther king and gandhi

gabs123: can u adapt it to getting me out of AA?

pologuy: y not? u need 5 compelling paragraphs. need

reason from literature or ancient history, current events, and deep personal crap that u get to make up. u can make up the whole thing. u can say ghandi was the first indian guy on the atlanta braves, and that's where he met MLK. u can say that you're on council even if ur not. tutor says. what a scam.

gabs123: the deep personal part is i'll die if i have to go again.

pologuy: very compelling. did u make that up?

gabs123: i am not making this up! do something!

pologuy: calm down. tell frosty NO AA. you'd rather have therapy

gabs123: she's already supposedly giving me therapy.

pologuy: ok tell her u need to get super intensive therapy because ur super intensively deranged

gabs123: just kill me now.

pologuy: listen. ur paying the bitch to do what u want and make the court like it. just be smart about it. i can't go to AA because . . .

gabs123: sorry if I'm repeating myself here nash but BECAUSE WHY?

pologuy: ok because being there makes u want to cut yourself. that sounds nice and girlie

gabs123: i want to CUT myself? right, with the plastic knife from the coffee cake on the dessert buffet in the back of the church.

pologuy: makes u want to eat up all the coffee cake,

stick your finger down ur throat, barf, and then cut
yourself
gabs123: ew. like she's going to buy this.
pologuy: u r paying her to buy this. her job is to buy
anything u tell her to buy. trust me on this

So I call her up and cry. And he's right again.

XXXVI

LISA SAYS, "WHERE WERE YOU? I CAME OVER WITH Anita and your mom was very squirrelly about where you were."

"AA." It just slips out.

"Wow," Lisa says.

"Don't worry, I'm not going anymore."

"No," Lisa says. "That's not what I meant. I mean, it could be good for you. You give your worries over to a higher power."

"No offense, Lisa, but I'm not giving anything over to a higher power."

"Well, no offense, but it might be better than giving things over to Billy Nash."

"Did you just say that?"

"Yeah, well, sorry, all I'm saying is that if you're having a problem with drinking, AA wouldn't be the worst place for you to go."

"You can talk when you've been there. I'm going to go to constant psychotherapy instead, are you happy? Could we please talk about something else? Could we talk about you instead? Pretty, pretty please with a rum ball on top?"

"Pretty please with a *keg* on top is more like it," Lisa says.

But as it turns out, she is dying to talk about something else. She is, in fact, dying to talk about Junior Spring Fling, which sounds about as weird and alien to my current life as a potato sack race on Mars but beats hearing one more person weigh in on my so-called drinking problem.

Although it is somewhat odd that now that—instead of festooning the old gym with rolls of crepe paper and watching the Muffins pitch a fit about how much they like pink, silver, and black—I am expanding my range of my fun high school experiences by becoming a lowlife, arrested north of Ventura Boulevard followed by hours in a church full of drunk kids, now Lisa wants to expand her range of fun high school experiences by shopping for a new dress and going to Fling.

You have to wonder what we even have to talk about anymore.

"Huey wants to go," she says. "So I just said I would without thinking and now I'm feeling like maybe this is a mistake."

"Huey wants to go to *Fling*?"

"I know. You wouldn't think he'd want to do anything that conventional. It kind of took me by surprise."

"Are you sure he doesn't just want to use you as cover so he can take pictures that make everybody look like decadent slobs for yearbook?" Huey is a big fan of smoky, black-and-white, decadent slob pictures. Only, nobody can tell he's making fun of them. They think they look gorgeous and artistic.

"Come *on*," Lisa says. She sounds horrified.

"Sorry. I was joking."

"No you weren't."

"Okay, it's not that I don't think Huey would want to take you to a dance. It's just that you'd think he'd be repelled by a rhyming-name dance at Winston."

Lisa sighed. "Well, it's the only dance that's available. Except for his cousin's debutante ball in Paris."

"He invited you to a deb ball in Paris?"

"Like my mother's going to let me go to Paris, France, with Huey? I don't even know if she's going to let me go to Spring Fling."

"You should one hundred percent go. Tell her it's a sock hop, for godsake, with poodle skirts and socks, and all the really old teachers are chaperoning because they like Elvis and all that old stuff. They're going to be dancing the twist. It's going to be completely harmless."

"My mom is pretty sure someone will slip me a rufie."

"She's completely unhinged. It's the Junior Spring Fling, not a frat party."

"I know. I just don't want to stick out in a bad way."

"All you need is a tight sweater." Although not, perhaps, a Little Mermaid sweater. "I'll go shopping with you."

"Thanks. Are you going?"

My first thought is, *of course. Of course I'm going.* Because I've gone to every Winston School social event large and small since September. Because I'm on the committee that has planned and decorated every event large and small since September. Because Billy likes going to parties with a girl who looks damned good and so, of course, I go to parties and I look pretty damned good.

But, of course, I'm not going anymore.

"Doubtful," I say. "I just have to focus on staying out of any form of juvie jail."

"How could you go to jail?"

This makes me remember why I'm not talking about any of this stuff with anyone but Billy and people who are paid to listen and keep quiet about it.

"Not going to happen. Don't worry about it."

"Won't you please, please, please, please let me call my uncle for you? He's a really good lawyer. Listen to me Gabby, don't take this the wrong way, but you really need to have your own lawyer and not Billy's lawyer. My uncle says. You really need to look out for yourself here."

"Lisa, I've *got* my own lawyer. I was just filling out a bunch of forms for him."

"Yeah, but my uncle could really help you. Gabby, this is serious. Don't you want a lawyer who could help *you*? You have to take this seriously."

"Why would you think I'm not taking this seriously? I could go to some kind of jail in Arizona. I could have killed somebody."

"Are you kidding me?" Lisa squeals. An actual squeal, like a piglet having a coronary. "Don't say that!"

It is so clear that I shouldn't say *anything*. Even my best friend can't stand to hear the truth about me. I have to shut it down or I'm going to be too freaked out to get out of bed, eat toast, or implement The Plan. Which is not exactly optional unless I want to embrace a new life as Rehab Wilderness Girl. Billy is so so absolutely and completely right.

You can tell Lisa is getting wound up again, and before she can start, I say, "I'm *not* going to talk about it. Save your breath."

And Lisa says, "I know, I know. And I'm trying to respect that. I am. But this is really hard to watch."

XXXVII

MEANWHILE, MR. HEALY KEEPS CALLING ME ON THE phone. No introduction, he just launches right in.

"Isabelle Frost says you'd be more comfortable with intensive therapy than AA?"

"Yup," I say, "Because—"

But he doesn't even want to hear about it.

I don't know. Maybe all us girls who threaten to gorge ourselves on the entire refreshment table at Brentwood Unitarian AA, stab ourselves with plastic butter knives that aren't even serrated, and thrust our hands and forearms into Brentwood Unitarian's boiling hot forty-eight-cup industrial-size coffeemakers are a lot more comfortable with therapy than AA.

"All righty," he says. "I think I should talk to your mom for a quick sec. I think we need a change of plan here to a heavier-duty therapist, all right?"

"I guess."

"Someone objective-looking with big, bad credentials . . . *hmmmm . . .*"

After this, the frequency of Mr. Healy's phone calls increases exponentially.

He keeps reminding me that I'm not supposed to be driving a car or hanging out with undesirables, by which I assume he means Billy (thank you, Agnes Nash), and to see if anything has *changed*. . . . Pregnant pause.

The only upside to the whole situation is that whenever I need to talk to Billy, apparently it's all right to message him constantly in his new role as legal consultant. He actually seems interested. Even when I don't message him, he keeps chatting me with questions eerily similar to Mr. Healy's.

It is starting to feel as if I exist again, at least a little, in a tiny corner of the outskirts of Billy World. Sort of.

So this is my life:

Lisa is texting me to see if it would be okay to go to Fling in her mother's arguably vintage acrylic cardigan that has sequined sombreros shading little napping men (No, not even close to okay. Tell her that you can't wear racist outerwear to Winston School social events. Tell her *anything*) and me chatting online with Billy to get pointers on how I can stay out of jail.

gabs123: how did u get out of residential? big lawyer says residential is the worst case scenario if therapy doesn't work out. i will DIE in residential.

pologuy: went to this outward bound thing in the rockies summer of 9th after pot in locker room at loyola match. did ropes course. listened to crap about personal responsibility. took other people's ritalin
gabs123: no way.
pologuy: way. no booze no weed. what's boy to do?
gabs123: i will not do a ropes course. just not happening.
pologuy: no worries. u need to knock over lots more trees before ropes course. that's after 4th offense. not now. lawyer's just scaring u so you'll go all o mr. lawyer man, my hero when nothing bad happens to u
gabs123: 4th offense!?!?!?!? u are a very busy boy.
pologuy: what r u wearing right now?
gabs123: i'm going to be wearing a day glo jumpsuit if u don't get me out of this.

And I say to myself, *Gabriella, you have a whole team of highly skilled, high-priced professionals getting you out of this. If you don't stop bugging Billy Nash, he's going to pretend he's offline. You have to stop whining like a big freaking baby and step away from the computer.*

But I don't.

Meanwhile, Vivian keeps slamming in and out of my room without knocking. When she sees that I'm chatting online with Billy, she is somewhat happier.

But Vivian, it turns out, is extremely annoyed about my failure to embrace kiddie Twelve Step.

"Everything was going fine!" she says, tight-lipped. "But could you get with the program? No you could not."

"Mr. Healy says it's fine if I get heavy-duty therapy instead. Billy even said so. What's wrong with that? It's not as if I have a drinking problem."

"Of course you don't!" Vivian snaps. "That's not the point. But I'm not going to stand here and watch you shoot yourself in the foot."

"Yeah, well I'll be sure to take off your ugly Coach clown shoes before I do the deed, so you don't have anything to worry about."

"I am worried. I want this to work out for you, but you have to get with the program. What were you thinking? And now it looks as if you have to go back to that child psychiatrist you don't like, and if that makes you want to cut yourself and tear out your hair and eat it, I just don't want to hear about it."

"What child psychiatrist?"

"That woman at Valley Mercy with the odd hair. The one you said was so annoying."

"Wendy!"

"Not Wendy. Wendy is a playologist. Dr. Berman. With those dowdy Ferragamos."

"Ponytail? Ponytail Doc is a neurologist." But she does have bad shoes. Really expensive bad shoes with bows on them.

"Nuh-uh, she's a child psychiatrist and she went to Harvard, and Mr. Healy has read every word she wrote about you in the chart and it's all good, if you can believe it."

"Why can't you believe it?"

Vivian just glares at me. "That's not what I said. Can't you see that I'm trying to help you? What I said is she's some kind of hotshot who can get you out of this if you'll just cooperate. Can you do that, Gabby? Can you just cooperate?"

As if she somehow doubts that I want to get out of this, short of going to AA all the time. As if she doesn't even know who I am, even though my lying like a rug about my fictional cutting and puking to get out of AA is apparently no secret.

Which is beside the point. The point being that I have to go see Ponytail Doc who is apparently a hotshot shrink in the Valley, which kind of makes you wonder. Like Vivian is going to hop into the car and drive me through the Sepulveda Pass to some strip mall in Tarzana with a Popeyes chicken and a Dunkin' Donuts and a tacky medical building. Fortunately for Vivian, Ponytail, not being completely devoid of taste and discernment, also has an office on the Westside by UCLA, presumably hoping that someone in the B's will notice what a hotshot she is and rescue her from strip mall hell.

XXXVIII

gabs123: whatcha doing?
pologuy: nothing. SAT words. heavily armed warden
with flash cards. what's up?
gabs123: i have to see the therapist later.
pologuy: no worries. jackman is harmless. tries to teach
u deep breathing. very relaxing
gabs123: not ur therapist. big honcho girl therapist.
the one from the hospital. supposedly she likes me,
which is going to make it so so easy to just spill
my guts.
pologuy: as long as u don't plan to spill ur guts
gabs123: i think i have to. nobody came out and said
it but i think if i pass, no residential. if therapy works
out is what the lawyer said. how can u tell if therapy is
working out?

pologuy: didn't ur lawyer tell u what to say on this
one either?

It occurs to me once again that people who write large checks
to the mayor, or whatever it is that Agnes actually does every time
Billy screws up, get a lot more help from their lawyers.

gabs123: i'm screwed right?
pologuy: ur lawyer is lame. he needs to tell u these
things. court ordered therapist tells EVERYBODY what
u say. judge, DA, police. very sneaky. uses everything
against you. DO NOT TRUST THERAPIST!
gabs123: what do i say? i have to pass or i'm going to
rehab jail in the high desert!!!! what do i say???
pologuy: cry a lot
gabs123: a person can't just cry forever. physically
impossible. and she already knows me. i can't just
pretend to b somebody else.
pologuy: stick to the plan ok? complete denial.
followed by maybe u do have the problem. then u
pretend to work on it once a week until your record
gets expunged ok?
gabs123: how do u pretend to work on it? what words
come out of your mouth when u do that?
pologuy: ok like this. oh no dr jackman i have a restless
urge to drink, smoke, and have meaningless sex. yet i
know all this fun stuff my wicked peers are pressuring

225

me to do is self destructive. oh no dr. jackman what should i do? hey i know, what if u put on the cd with the jungle bugs and bird calls and i relax in this nice zero gravity chair?

gabs123: no way.

pologuy: way. and be sure to tell her how much u hate yourself

gabs123: what if she doesn't buy any of this? she's not completely stupid. is there a backup plan?

pologuy: dude u don't need a backup plan. just tell her how u sit in ur bedroom and hate yourself while drinking up ur dad's glenlivet

gabs123: y is everybody making such a big deal about that? it was just that one time.

pologuy: don't tell her that

XXXIX

BACK IN THE HOSPITAL, PONYTAIL WAS JUST AN irritating interruption of *Gabriella Gardiner Presents Scenes from Teen Life in the Three B's*. She was a lot less annoying than when she is sitting in her office in Westwood.

An office in a glass and steel building with a bad metal sculpture in the lobby (convex mother with concave child, only it is hard to tell if the mother is nursing the kid or dropping it).

An office that looks like a set decorator's idea of a professor's lair: the antique desk, the leather chairs, the books and journals strewn across the desk as if Ponytail is so so busy doing important research on the Inner Life of Teens that you ought to be grateful when she looks up for long enough to talk to your seriously annoyed self.

"And so we meet again," she says, settling into her chair.

What, like I was supposed to have kept up with her on Facebook?

"I guess," I say. It is hard to put a finger on why I want to smack her so much except that, oh yeah, I don't want to be here.

She smiles at me and makes the kind of piercing eye contact that feels as if the person can gaze into your mind and see things that you don't know. And I go, *Stop it, Gabriella. She can't see into your mind, for godsake. She doesn't even know you that well.*

But after Billy's helpful pep talk, I am in a complete state of paranoid terror.

Ponytail, meanwhile, is sitting there looking me over, aka staring, as apparently normal social skills are irrelevant in psychiatry. I am sitting there looking her over, too. I am wearing a perky yet conservative teen outfit that looks really expensive and boring but at least I got to pick it out. A denim skirt and a butter-yellow cardigan. She is wearing her standard issue white shirt and a gray pencil skirt and stubby heels with grosgrain bows.

All I can think of to do is fidget. I start buttoning and unbuttoning the top button of the yellow cardigan and pulling on the ends of the sleeves.

"I notice you're wearing long sleeves today," she says.

I am thinking that she is going to turn up her air conditioning when I remember the cutting and the binging on coffee cake and supposedly wanting to plunge my hands into the scalding hot water in Brentwood Unitarian's giant coffeemaker that got me out of AA and into this comfy leather chair in the first place.

Ponytail looks extremely concerned.

I am afraid she is going to make me push up my sleeves and be righteously pissed off when she sees my uncut, unscarred, unscalded, normal weight arms. Not to mention, she has seen me half-naked and half-dead in the hospital and you have to figure she would have noticed that I didn't cut.

"Um, I don't really do any of that stuff," I say. "I just think about it all the time."

"Stuff?" she says, leaning forward. You can tell she knows exactly what I'm talking about.

"I know you know," I say. "Everyone from here to San Diego has read my file by now."

"I know what your file says," she says. "I wrote half your file. But I want to know what *you* say."

I am pretty eager to get to the part where I deny my Problem so she can help me see the Problem so I can go, *Oh yeah, big epiphany, I have a Problem!* and then she can cure me and I can get out of there.

"Okay," I say, in the interest of expediting. "Okay, being at AA and feeling, uh, pressured to talk about myself in front of other people, uh, makes me think about, uh, cutting myself and eating all the refreshments and, you know, the thing with the hot water. But now that I'm not in AA anymore, I'm kind of past it."

Ponytail says she is glad to hear it. Then she goes back to looking me over. "Was there ever a time when you got past thinking about it, and you cut or binged or hurt yourself with boiling water?"

"Ew. No. Of course not."

"And you were at AA because—"

"Oh, all right," I say, in the interest of getting on with it. "If you really want me to say it, I'll say it. I got drunk at a party and crashed my boyfriend's car into a tree. And now I don't remember anything about it. There. Are you happy?"

"Sometimes it's more disconcerting once you get out of the hospital and back to your life. Having your memories gone."

"Not so much. It's pretty obvious what happened. I went to a party. I got drunk. I crashed the car. I grabbed the keys and passed out on the ground. What else is there to know? And it's not like I'm back to my life anyway."

"Do you have any feelings or ideas about why you were drinking that much?"

"Because it was a party . . ." I am trying to come up with the right answers here, but speculating about why you did things you don't remember doing is just not that illuminating.

Ponytail nods as if she were actually listening to me. She is perched on the edge of her seat, deeply fascinated by my every word but so not getting it, patiently waiting for me to enlighten her. "I get that you drink at parties," she says. "Do you often black out?"

"I *never* black out! I hit my head against a tree or an air bag or something. That's not the same as blacking out. If blacking out made me hit the tree, then how did I turn off the car and pull the keys out?"

She just looks at me. More or less as if I'm crazy, which is maybe not that much of a stretch given that I'm sitting in a psychiatrist's office pretending to *be* crazy.

"All right," I say. "All right. I know what you're thinking, but I don't have a drinking problem."

She just sits there.

Really, am I just supposed to repeat this over and over for the entire rest of the session or what? All the time knowing that saying you don't have a drinking problem is supposed to prove you do have a drinking problem, which basically makes no sense, but okay, whatever.

"My dad is the one with the drinking problem," I say. I have to say *some*thing. "You've seen him, right? I swear, the guy basically sits in the house all day and doesn't actually *do* anything and I know I'm not a drunk because I'm nothing like that." She just looks at me. "I'm not."

"So you're not like your dad."

Oh, kill me now. If she's planning to repeat everything I say and sit there looking deeply concerned and fascinated, I might as well just start searching her office for some sharp object I can pretend I'm thinking about stabbing myself with in the faint hope that Mr. Healy will decide that I'm an even crazier model girl than he thought and send me to an even heavier duty therapist who I can stand.

"I really do not want to sit here and talk about my dad. I just want everything to go back to the way it was before."

"And you'd be comfortable with that?"

"I would be totally happy and whistling a merry tune if things could be like before, but my life is completely wrecked."

She nods and looks sympathetic. Really, really sympathetic. Or maybe some shred of Vivian has rubbed off on me through some nasty trick of genetics and I, too, am such a glutton for the smallest scrap of sympathy that a chipmunk would seem sympathetic if it nodded its fuzzy little head at me.

Still, it is hard to believe that Ponytail is going to send me to some residential hellhole in the desert to live in a tent and do ropes courses with gang girls.

"Uh, maybe this isn't what I'm supposed to be talking about," I say. I am thinking that this would be the magic moment for her to teach me to gently close my eyelids, take a deep cleansing breath, and relax, like Billy does with his therapist. Because just sitting in her office staring out the window at the view of Westwood is making me extremely nervous.

Then it occurs to me that I'm doing a pretty damned good job of denying the problem so perhaps this is going well.

"That's the thing, when the courts get involved in treatment," she says. "You're supposed to be talking about whatever *you* want to talk about in this office. This is supposed to be *your* time. But when the courts are going to be involved, it's easy to feel as if, if you say the wrong thing, something terrible is going to happen to you, yes?"

This is the part where I cry for twenty-five minutes straight, which is more or less what Billy said I was supposed to do in the first place, so you have to figure it isn't nearly as bad as it seems.

Which is pretty bad.

The only comforting, affirmative thought I can come up with (*Oh Gabby, aren't you just the most convincing, not-going-to-wilderness-camp patient who ever sat in this big leather chair?* is so not working for me) is that at least it has to seem like I'm being sincere, which, strangely, I am. I mean, who can fake crying for that long?

And it isn't as if I can stop, either.

XL

MY LESS-THAN-FUN SESSION WITH PONYTAIL MUST
have shown all over my tear-rutted, unnaturally beige face because
Vivian, who is sitting in the waiting room in her recently over-
used mauve funeral and teacher conference suit, jumps up and
says she is going to take me for red velvet cupcakes with cream
cheese frosting at Dottie's Sweeties. Which, given all the calories
a trip to Dottie's Sweeties involves stuffing into your mouth, is an
epic offer. Epic and unnerving, given that Vivian never gives me
anything resembling a dessert unless someone has died or there's
an earthquake, not to mention it is hard to visualize her traipsing
around Beverly Hills with a bruised, smeared makeup, red-eyed,
cupcake-chomping kid.

But, of course, it turns out that Vivian thinks she's doing me
a favor when she leaves me in the parking lot and runs in herself,
given that letting me humiliate myself by risking someone seeing

me when I look this wrecked is no doubt right up there in her mind with public flogging.

Sitting alone in the car on the roof of the parking structure, I am completely stumped as to any possible affirmative thing to say to myself.

Losing control and sniveling was so not what I had in mind. If I was going to cry for twenty-five minutes nonstop, I was supposed to be doing it on purpose, not like some out-of-control crybaby who just whimpers on until reaching the point of dehydration.

Not in front of someone I don't even like, in the world's dowdiest expensive shoes, who nevertheless has the potential to make my life worse than it already is.

Not when I've been planning to tell Billy about what happened and how I pulled it off and how everything is just fine and freakishly dandy. I am so not planning to tell him about this, or at least not what this feels like.

pologuy: how was ur day at the therapist?

gabs123: it beats AA. but not by much. and no refreshments.

pologuy: the better to save u from yourself little girl, with ur brand new eating disorder and cutting problem. she bought it right?

I'm afraid that if I lie too much, he won't be able to tell me what to do next, and I'll be doubly screwed. And if I don't lie enough, it will just be too humiliating.

gabs123: i cried copiously. SAT word. vivian got me the flash cards. u said cry—i cried. that's ok, right?

pologuy: what did u say?

gabs123: basically nothing. i cried a lot. very emo.

pologuy: excellent. what do u have to say to her anyway? boo hoo and u don't remember anything right?

gabs123: hence the crying, like you said. no word on when i get to go back to school though.

pologuy: lucky u. stretch it out

Even though Billy might have my best interests at heart, you didn't see him stretching it out in exile at his uncle's hacienda in Montecito despite all the excellent surfing off Rincon Point. And even though my life might currently suck, the only way I have the slightest chance of getting it back is going back to Winston. The only way of getting *him* back.

Which is basically the same thing.

XLI

YOU WOULD FIGURE THAT A HIGHLY TRAINED helping professional like Ponytail would have picked up on the part that I wasn't really at risk for swimming around in the boiling contents of industrial-sized coffeemakers, but apparently she and Mr. Healy had a little chat and now I have to have another deeply meaningful session ASAP so she can clear me to go back to school.

"That's what you want, right?" Mr. Healy says, as if he'd missed the part where I said that was what I wanted every time he made another lame phone call to make sure I hadn't eloped with Billy with me driving.

This seems like a no-brainer until I start thinking about what it will actually be like to slink back into Winston and have everyone looking at me in my current state of being a juvenile delinquent covered with artfully applied beige foundation in a color not approximating human skin all that closely. Gossiping about me as if I were Buddy Geiss coming back to the Three B's from celebrity rehab in Malibu, back from military school rehab in South Carolina, back from holistic-getting-down-with-therapeutic-farm-animals rehab in the Napa Valley.

I, on the other hand, will be back from wrecking Billy's car and messing up my life on Songbird Lane. You have to figure that this could be worse than either my prior state of invisibility or being Buddy Geiss.

This time Vivian takes me to Dottie's for the cupcake beforehand, and when I pull my cupcake out of the little checkered bag, I see that Vivian has paid extra for them to top it with slivers of white chocolate and honey-roasted almonds. In the absence of deaths or earthquakes, it is hard to tell if all the sugary treats are coming my way because she's feeling that sorry for me, or if she thinks it doesn't matter anymore if I turn into a pillar of undulating chocolate-and-honey-roasted-almond-filled fat because any hope of me being anything other than a sub-regular girl is smoldering in Hidden Hills with the last fiery, wrecked bits of Billy's Beemer.

"It's going to be hard on you, going back to school like this," Vivian says when I am halfway through my cupcake and all the way to a sugar rush.

No shit.

Although it isn't clear if "like this" means Billy-less or with a lavender cheekbone and a swollen jawline. Or both.

"It agreed with you to have a boyfriend," she says. "But I

have a lot of faith that you'll be back to being the New You again."

"What?"

And I go, *Gabriella, give it up. She's trying to be extra nice. Don't be a little bitch.*

I say, "I hope you're right," but I just want to scream, *Stop talking about it. Just. Stop.* It's not that I don't totally want what she is saying to be true. I do. But hearing her say it out loud makes it sound lame and not remotely possible. Because I'm pretty sure the New Me crashed and burned on Songbird Lane.

"You will be, Gabby," Vivian says. "You can be anything you want."

Such as the president of the United States, Tinker Bell, and Billy Nash's girlfriend in public?

"Don't look at me like that," she says. "It's hard for a girl to lose her looks, but you'll get back on your game. You'll see. You can get another boyfriend. The swelling will go down and you'll be fine."

Then she hands me a little container of extra white chocolate slivers that I pour directly onto my tongue, partly because it tastes like the god of chocolate made it and partly to keep myself from talking back to her.

Even Ponytail has a plate of what look like homemade cookies on her desk, which she pushes toward me as if she thinks I need some edible comfort too.

This time she's sitting there in a pale-green cashmere sweater, and you want to tell her that even though it might somewhat match her eyes, it is so so not working. I am wearing the highest cut jeans I own to avoid upsetting her with the sight of my thong and an ugly striped shirt with cufflinks that Vivian forced me to wear because apparently she thinks that shapelessness is a good look for the psychologically impaired.

This time, it takes me less than a minute to start crying.

Ponytail hands me a box of tissues, and I notice that this time there is a tiny little leather-covered wastebasket beside the leather chair. The possibility that Ponytail saw this coming, that this is not the result of a slight change in her interior decorating plan, but that she is graciously providing me with someplace to stow my snotty tissues because she knew in advance what was going to happen, completely freaks me out.

After about fifteen minutes of this, she asks me if I can talk about it, and not seeing a downside to telling her the actual truth, I say, "I don't know." Then I realize that this is the perfect opening to tell her how much I hate myself, but then I start crying again.

"I'm wondering if you're feeling reluctant to be frank with me because of your legal situation."

Duh.

I nod my head and try to look as if I want to be there.

"Weeeeeeellllll," Ponytail says, filling my silence, "it's hard for me to imagine anything you could tell me that would harm you in that respect."

For me, on the other hand, it isn't all that hard. To imagine what could happen if I tell her something that makes her hate me, for example. To imagine what could happen if I say the wrong thing and she decides that a few months in the desert serves me right.

Billy's voice telling me not to trust the therapist is playing over and over in my head like a tape loop that won't quit.

"And all this crying tells me that something's hurting," she says.

I just keep sniffling because, basically, I can't stop, and she sits there saying all these inane things about growing and changing and being a re-potted plant turning toward the morning sun and trying to talk to me about how I feel about going back to school after being out for so long, which I can't really tell her because I don't totally know how I feel about it; I just know that I have to do it because not doing it is just going to make my life worse.

"I have to go back to school," I say. "I have to. It's like everybody else's life kept on going but my life stopped and I don't even exist and" (oh yeah, the magic and completely credible and somewhat true moment to throw it in) "I hate myself."

Ponytail's gaze bores through my forehead but is stopped in its tracks by the complete opacity of my completely private mind. She gives me her most sympathetic *mmmmmm.*

"Are you feeling ready?"

No.

I say, "Yes."

So it is finally happening.

XLII

THE NIGHT BEFORE I GO BACK TO WINSTON, PEOPLE are wishing me the kind of bon voyage and good luck you'd expect if you were leaving on a spaceship for a sinister galaxy far far away, not tooling halfway down a swanky hill to finish junior year.

Anita's and Lisa's mothers—who are both very big on being the carpool mom because, as far as I can figure out, it gives them control over the sound system, so Lisa's mom can force us to listen to Jesus radio and Anita's mom can force us to listen to South Asian elevator music—are competing to carpool me, assuring Vivian that it will be much better for me to arrive with my *true* friends.

If I had any other friends, this would be quite the slam, but I don't, so it isn't.

Then Huey's mother calls to offer us a debilitated rescue cat

I could nurse back to health, and when Vivian gleefully assures her that the coyotes in the canyon would eat that cat in one gulp, she offers us an endangered two-foot lizard. This makes Vivian get creative really fast and insist that as much as we'd love to have an endangered two-foot lizard in the process of shedding its mass quantities of scaly skin, our housekeeper has a pathological fear of reptiles.

Then Andie Bennett texts to say that she hopes I have a really nice day, with a smiley face emoticon. I have the feeling my day isn't exactly going to reach the level of smiley facedness, on top of which, all that concern makes me wonder if everybody else somehow knows how spectacularly horrible it is going to be and I am grossly underestimating the depth of the shit I'm in.

And to remind me of the depth and consistency of that shit and how bad an idea everything I thought would be a good idea is, Charlotte Ward actually phones the house.

She does such a good Queen of the Universe impersonation that Vivian doesn't even try to screen her out; she just hands me the phone. And even though Lisa and Anita have spent the past three hours calling to be wildly encouraging, it is pretty clear that some people aren't looking forward to being in the same room with me as much as others.

Council, for reasons clear only in Charlotte's twisted mind, does not seem too eager for me to show up. But given that Billy is on Council, I am not exactly eager to give it up.

The only reason I am even on Charlotte's damned decorating committee is because I heard Mr. Piersol's lecture about leaving your mark on Winston School once too often and I must have been temporarily hypnotized.

And all right, it was unlikely that I was going to leave my mark by leading the charge to adopt a sister school in Botswana. So just after the image of the Slutmuffins tagging the hell out of Winston receded—their mark being giant designer logos and discarded cans of spray paint—I figured that my mark could be the permanent retirement of the vile pink, black, and silver color scheme from all school events involving crepe paper and tinsel.

And after I miraculously got the decorating committee to go along with this, I would change the name of Spring Fling to something reasonable. Something that didn't rhyme or make Billy sneer.

I admit I had visions of walking into this reimagined, nicer dance, resting my head on Billy's shoulder, and swaying to vintage tunes, mostly "My Blue Heaven," while he admired the superior color scheme of the renamed event.

Unfortunately, when I raised the idea of a renamed event, the most popular alternative was Courtney Yamada Phillips's suggestion of Spring Hop, which was kind of the same, only worse. So I went back to shutting up on Council except to support Billy when he talked, which wasn't much. He wasn't even on the decorating committee.

"How are you feeeeling?" Charlotte drawls into the phone, her lips so close to the receiver that her breath rasps and puffs as if she were spitting into my ear.

"I'm getting there," I say.

"Did you get the flowers? The committee sent you peonies. Andie says you like stuff like that, right?"

"They were nice. Thanks. I was kind of out of it."

"I heard. Billy says you don't want to talk about it, so that's cool."

"Cool," I say. Why she would want to talk to me unless she wants me to jump out of bed and run down to Kinko's to pick up giant boxes of dance flyers is a mystery of life.

"So. I'm calling because the committee has to meet and finalize the plans for Fling and I don't want to stress you out or anything . . . so I was wondering how you want to play it."

How I *want* to play it is to show up and explain in detail why her design choices suck and her color scheme sucks and get her voted down and then make fun of her to Billy, which is as close to addressing the extreme folly of him being with a Slutmuffin—his previous companions of choice—as I will ever get.

But abandoning fun fantasies and moving right along, I am more than happy to continue to keep my mouth shut in my role as designated Council slave as long as none of the Muffins tells Billy I suck.

And I say to myself, *Hey, Gabby, look at you! You are right back into high school and your mind is working perfectly. You've got your game on. You can totally play this.* Because: Life with the Slutmuffins really is a lot like a rank game of somewhat challenging, backstabbing Trivial Pursuit.

"What do you mean?" I say, pseudo-sweetly, noticing that it is getting harder to breathe.

"I mean, I know you must have work piling up and SATs are coming up and everything, so I don't want you to feel like the committee is just one more thing you have to do."

"Like an anchor around my neck?"

"Yeah, like that," she says somewhat too eagerly.

Long pause. Long, long pause. I am mostly focused on inhaling and exhaling.

"Nope," I say. "It's fine. Just save me a seat and I'll be there when I get back."

"So, like, when's *that* going to be?"

I know she knows, but I say it anyway, I say, "Tomorrow," just to see if I can hear that little snort noise she makes. And I can. I do.

When I get off the phone with her, it's like I've gone completely numb and breathing doesn't help.

I am so not ready for this.

XLIII

WHICH IS WHEN BILLY JUST COMES OUT AND ASKS
if I'm sure I can do it.

When I'm completely not sure.

And I go, *You know you want this. Just be somewhat cheerful and
get this over with before he figures out that you're pathetic.* Then I simulate normal as fast as I can.

pologuy: earth to g. so can u?

gabs123: can i what, go to school? i've been going to
school since i was 3½.

pologuy: don't get cute g

gabs123: u never complained about how cute I was
before nash.

pologuy: i've been working on this. i can keep the

guys and the andies and the muffins off ur back
guaranteed but u have to stick to the plan with
everybody else

And I go, *Just. Stay. Cheerful.*

gabs123: how hard can it be to say i don't want to
talk about something i don't want to talk about?
what r they going to say? hey gabs i saw u at that
party and man were u drunk? way to drive a car
into a tree?
pologuy: U HAVE TO CUT THEM OFF BEFORE IT GETS
THERE. close them down. all my people know not to
bother u but u have to watch out for the loose cannon
dorks

He sounds seriously seriously worried.

And I'm thinking, *Maybe I should be feeling more seriously worried instead of just numb.*

And then I think, *No, numb is probably a good thing, because if Billy Nash is freaking out, I would be dead on the ground and mainlining Glenlivet if I was actually feeling this.*

And I go, *Okay, Gabriella, take a deep breath and calm the hell down. Keep your eyes on the prize. If you want your life back, you have to go back there and get it. You don't have to feel a damned thing, you just have to go.*

pologuy: r u there?

gabs123: i'm here. i get it. u don't have to worry about me so much. i can handle it. i vant to be alone, dahlink.

pologuy: yeah but nobody really vants to be alone and i can't b with u there. r u going to be ok? can u do this?

gabs123: i get it. ur with me now and I'm fine with it. i can totally do this.

Only what if I can't?

I would so have had a wooden nose all the way out the window and across the street if I were a magic puppet. And I say to myself: *Oh Gabriella, you are such a genius relationship strategist, good breather, and all-round desirable girl, he'll be with you in no time.* At which point the Pinocchio nose extends itself further north, up toward Mulholland Drive.

pologuy: oh and u should check outside ur laundry room

gabs123: ?

pologuy: just do it

I go clomping down the stairs so fast and loud that John yells, "Be careful!" from the den, which has to be an all-time first. I plow through the dark laundry room and just outside the back door, at the edge of the redwood landing, there's a gift bag, the understated ritzy kind with leaves woven into the thick paper of it. Inside the bag, there's a square, gold box that's filled with rows and rows of heart-shaped Belgian chocolates, just the dark mocha ones that I like, and not Billy's usual little box missing the pilfered truffles. This box is entirely full of perfect candies, perfect hearts, completely perfect. And on the gold-striped paper that lines the lid, he's written, "You're the one."

And I think, *Okay, maybe I can do this.*

I'm the one.

XLIV

THINKING THIS IS MAYBE NOT THE BEST TIME TO offend Lisa or Anita by picking one and not the other to carpool with, I say my parents are going to take me to school, even though my parents are not what you'd call thrilled to get out of bed when it's still dark out. Amazingly, John shows up in the kitchen looking like he's dressed for high school circa 1962, in the navy blue blazer and khaki pants, to drive me to Winston.

He keeps saying "Gabs," so at least he has my name right, but I am already so wigged out, the thought of having to live through another bizarro conversation that involves tears running down his face is more than I can take. So I just stare straight ahead of me and clench my teeth when tempted to answer.

He is using his GPS, which gives you some idea of how often he has driven to Winston since seventh grade, when carpool turned out not to be a business op. Navigating the carpool line is completely beyond him, so he pulls into the student parking lot where the clay-waxed German cars get to hang with their own kind. Where I get to watch everybody else get out of their carpools still drinking their coffee and eating their Starbucks pastries.

And I go, *Gabriella, you're the one. You can totally do this.*

But even though Vivian's hairdresser came to the house and re-streaked my hair and I have three-quarters-of-an-inch-thick makeup from my hairline to my collarbone, I still look like a mutant being.

"You're going to do fine," John says, reaching into the backseat to get me my backpack, patting me on the shoulder. Which still hurts. Which makes me wonder, as I climb out of the car and into the open where everyone can see the beige cover-up ooze down my cheeks in the direct sunlight, where they can stare at me as I try to find an unbruised spot where I can put the shoulder strap of the backpack, exactly how horrible this is going to be.

As it turns out, returning to Winston School as a famous screwup is more than slightly horrible in weird ways I never even anticipated. In the first place, there isn't enough oxygen and I keep having to gulp air to the point that reminding myself to breathe is completely irrelevant, and in the second place, walking around makes my legs shiver as if they were cold, only they aren't, and I just want to go sit down somewhere far far away, such as the rings of Saturn.

But I can't sit down because, in the third place, kids I don't know and don't want to know keep coming up to me and expecting me to talk to them between gulping deep breaths.

Not only am I no longer Billy's public girlfriend, which is bad enough, but I'm suddenly approachable.

Back before I was Billy's girlfriend, unwanted attention wasn't exactly my big problem. Now, even though "I don't want to talk about it" is my new mantra, I can't keep people away from me. Kids I barely know the names of have a strange compulsion to share what screwups they are so we can feel bad together between classes.

Like Jenna Marx, who used to be bulimic. What possibly could have made her want to share this with me? By the candy machine in the gym on her way to tennis?

Like Roy Warner, who smokes pot in the chapel before school on a daily basis, who reeks of it, and is still in Winston School only because he is possibly the richest semi-smart person in the history of the world despite the fact that he's stoned maybe 100% of the time and because his dad keeps giving Winston large checks. Extremely large checks. So Roy Warner tells me that he understands completely where I'm at, yeah, hey man, he does, oh yeah, he really does, and I just stand there in a state of stupefaction, going, "Thank you, but I just don't want to talk about it."

The only people who actually seem to want to get away from me as fast as they can without bumping into something and embarrassing themselves are the decorating committee girls, who grimace ever so slightly and go scuttling off in the other direction. The less civic-minded Muffins just kind of look me over and walk away.

I want to tell Billy, just to see him cock his head and raise one eyebrow and be amused by this bizarre turn of events, but it quickly becomes obvious that that isn't going to happen. I might be the one, but not so anybody else would notice.

I keep looking for him, sensing his presence across rooms when he isn't there, glimpsing someone else's shoulder sliding around a corner and thinking it's his shoulder, getting a scent of warm salt and Cuban tobacco and turning, but no one is there.

The first time I actually spot him is when I see the back of his head walking down the hall toward the language lab between classes. When I am sure he has to feel my presence and somehow know that I'm there, and he will have to stop.

But he doesn't.

I feel like the cheesy heroine trying to find her boyfriend in a crowded railroad station in an old-timey World War II movie, only when Cheesy Heroine sees Dashing Boyfriend, he's already on the train and it's rolling away down the track and out of the station and he doesn't even know that she's there. The Cheesy Heroine who racks up offers of monogrammed cloth hankies and faints into the arms of total strangers because she's such a pathetic loser cow whose boyfriend can't even get it together to look out the train window and find her for Pete's sake.

And I say to myself: *Oh Gabby, you are such a spiffy, not-pathetic loser cow, you can totally do this. You can so totally avoid him and not have to deal with this until you stop being such a cringe-worthy whack job. Only perhaps you should stop lurking behind pillars and staring at the back of his head. Like now.*

And it isn't as if I have to skulk around to avoid surprise

encounters with him either. He and the Andies and the Slut-muffins still hang by the fountain in the Class of 1920 Memorial Garden; I don't.

They go to their lockers during the long breaks; I haul so many books around, it feels as if my right shoulder is going to fall off.

In stupid track chemistry, which is the only class we have together, Dr. Berg had already made us stop being lab partners back at the beginning of fall semester because we talked too much. So Billy and Neil Chun are in the back row and I am in front with Lily Branner, who is for some reason so highly moti-vated to get an A in stupid track chemistry, she couldn't have cared less if I'd turned into a werewolf over spring break as long as I could still use my hairy paws to do the experiments right.

All she wants to know is whether I studied for SAT IIs over vacation, and it's embarrassing to admit that Vivian just got me a prep book like a week ago, as if there isn't a lot of point to me prepping for SATs. When I tell Lily I didn't, she kind of mut-ters that it figures, and loses all interest in anything other than whether I'm pouring the right amount of solution into the bea-kers she has all lined up.

And Billy is just busy busy busy with his Bunsen burner, too busy to look over and see me sneaking looks at him. Which is good because that level of being a pathetic stalker cow has to show and I don't want him to notice.

"Aren't you making a lot of new friends?" Huey says at lunch, when Lisa and Anita are nowhere to be found and I'm not about to text them and make them eat with me, and I'm standing in the cafeteria trying to figure out where in God's name I'm going to sit. Huey walks me to an empty picnic table on the deck above the ordinary people's lawn and snaps what turns out to be a photo of Roy Warner looming over me adjusting his crotch while I sit there looking like I just swallowed a live mouse.

Huey says, "Hey, Roy. Did you do the Latin yet?"

Roy mutters something about Virgil and shuffles away.

"Are you all right?" Huey says, just kind of staring at me.

Yes, boys and girls, as if things weren't bad enough, now Jeremy Hewlett III is finding me lunch tables and feeling sorry for me. Ever so briefly, I wonder how I'd look in a Holy Name plaid jumper, and how short they let you wear it.

"My parents are paying hundreds of dollars an hour for professional dimwits to ask me that," I say. "Could we possibly talk about your athlete's foot or something?"

"I don't know," Huey says. "I noticed that suddenly you've become friendly, so I was worried about you."

"What are you talking about?" I say, taking a sip of the cafeteria lemonade, so sweet and cold the first hit gives you sugar shock so bad it makes your head ache. "I was always friendly. I can't help it if everybody wants to turn themselves inside out in front of me all of a sudden."

"Friendly! You've only ever spoken to half a dozen people in the past four and a half years. Now you're gabbing it up with the masses. Gabbing. Gabby. Get it?"

I got it.

"Yeah, well I got mashed on the head. I can't help it." Huey is just staring at me and it is spectacularly weirding me out. "Stop it, Huey. I always talked to anyone who talked to me, such as you."

Only we can't continue the conversation because Jenna Marx and her whole stick-like band of girls who, now that I notice, are pretty much eating only lettuce leaves for lunch, sit down near us and seem to want to stare at me sympathetically in between calculating how many calories there are in a level plastic teaspoon of fat-free cottage cheese. Ashley Haas, who is too skeletal even for extra-small Juicy Couture tube tops, looks deeply into my weirded-out eyes and tells me that they all support me.

Huey doesn't even look up, but you can see his face getting flushed. And then he snaps a picture of five girls with 2% body fat.

XLV

THE PERSON I LEAST WANT TO SEE IN MY NEW ROLE as well-known juvenile delinquent is Miss Cornish. Art is the only class I ever wanted to go to all the time, no matter how I was feeling or what I was going through.

But not today.

It's hard to know how my main art teacher since seventh, who managed to survive my metamorphosis from invisibility to whatever, is going to adjust to my new role as penitent thug.

The problem is, Miss Cornish is personally interested.

Deeply deeply interested.

Deeply and sincerely interested. Not faking it, either. She likes to talk to us artistic young people and it is sort of difficult not to sort of like her. Not to mention I've taken every class she teaches that fits into my schedule, and it turns out she even saw the dorky portfolio my elementary school principal at St. Thomas

Aquinas made for me when I applied to Winston School in the first place since he knew my grades sure as hell weren't going to do the trick.

Just thinking about having to face Miss Cornish in her art room with the kilns and the potter's wheels and the blowtorch and the mallets, where everything smells like warm clay and acid that could expunge anything, makes me stop breathing.

Miss Cornish is always going on and on about how she wants me to nourish my rare gifts and apply for the Interscholastic Art Awards, the Ceramic Federation Honor, the Ovation Fine Arts Scholarship, and the Nobel Peace Prize while I'm at it. But by rare gifts I'm pretty sure she doesn't mean my remarkable ability to play beer pong or turn sports cars into scrap metal. She wants me to infuse my art with my life, but the idea of her finding out anything about the part of my life I am now famous for makes me want to throw up.

It is already hard enough to hold it together, but the minute she spots me slinking through the door to the ceramics studio, she comes scampering up to me and gives me this big, sincere hug in front of everybody in double advanced ceramics and, basically, I want to die.

Miss Cornish drags me into her office, which is this little cluttered storage room off the main art room—unlike Mr. Rosen, who gets a real office with a stained glass window and real furniture upstairs—and she propels me into a metal folding chair.

"I am very proud of you," she says.

I sit there looking moronic and thinking this is probably

not the moment for her to be proud of me. Maybe before I got artificially cute and started hanging out with Billy, it might have helped. Maybe before I got drunk and stole a car and crashed it. Maybe when I was some whole other person who was potentially going to turn out to be someone different from who I am now.

"You don't believe me, do you?" she says.

The thing is, I do believe she thinks I'm just some wonderful young specimen of womanhood. I just think that either she's an idiot to be proud of me or maybe she just doesn't know who I actually am.

I sit there trying not to cry and not to think about how sad this is.

"I'm proud that you came back to school after spring break," she says, gazing into my eyes as if she were kind of daring me to look away. "I'm proud that you're back here taking care of business. I'm proud that you've developed into such a wonderful artist, and no matter what was going on in your life, you never stopped doing the work."

I nod my head but keep my mouth clamped shut. I so don't want to disappoint her, and I'm pretty sure that if she knew me, she wouldn't exactly be so thrilled with me.

"Gabby," she says. "I don't care what happened. You're a wonderful young lady and a wonderful artist. Sometimes at this school it's very easy to lose track of how talented we are and what wonderful people we are. I want you to use this class to express yourself and to use the materials the way you need to use them."

Right, like maybe if I smush enough clay, I'll feel better.

Maybe if I take a nice blue BMW M3 and turn it into a creative, abstract, tree-hugging piece of found art hanging off a eucalyptus tree on Songbird Lane.

Or maybe not.

So I spend the next fifty minutes sitting between Lisa and Sasha Aronson mixing glaze and pretending that everything is all right. Looking down at what I'm doing and not looking up at the windows that overlook the fountain where the Slutmuffins hang out. Not looking up and trying not to see Billy. Trying to see him and trying not to see him. Knowing that it's going to be like this every day and not knowing if it's going to get better or worse.

Seeing him with his arm around Aliza Benitez, seeing his hand slipping just below her waist as they walk toward the lockers. Thinking, *I know this isn't real. You're the one is what's real, I know he isn't actually with her, but how am I going to live through this?*

XLVI

IT IS DEFINITELY TURNING INTO ONE OF THOSE DAYS
that runs on nightmare time, the kind of nightmare where you
start to experience everything in slo-mo, just walking down the
sidewalk takes hours, just lifting one foot is like pulling it up
against the force of a hundred wads of perfectly chewed gum
adhering to the sole of your shoe, and everything is stretched out
and takes forever.

So naturally, before I can make it through the parking lot
and get onto the bus—which would at least let me be by myself
because only kids who live in the hinterlands of Calabasas or
Glendale or Hancock Park take the bus, so the local bus is totally
empty except for the occasional seventh grader whose nanny has
an emergency dentist's appointment—Andie plants herself in
front of me.

All right, you have to give her credit for not totally avoiding me given her aversion to drama and the fact that I didn't return her four hundred phone calls or send thank-you notes for the dozen little presents she's mailed me in the past month. And the truth is, all I want is to be back on the checkered linen blanket on the grass in the Class of 1920 Garden with her and Andy totally into each other and totally uninterested in me and Billy, sitting there drinking Chardonnay from Andie's Dixie cups— *not* standing around feeling awkward and watching her try to talk coherently.

But she looks as if she's going to cry and the Must Help Andie instinct kicks in and I go, "Hey, Andie," given that I don't have any helpful substances to give her if she goes into her catatonic crying state.

"Why didn't you call me back?" she says, looking completely miserable.

"Uh, I didn't know what to say, I guess. Sorry."

Andie blurts, "I feel like it's my fault. I just wanted to tell you that. Billy says you don't want to hang out with us like before," (which, although I instantly understand why he had to say that, is not the funnest topper to what has to be the least fun school day of my life) "and I understand, I really do, but I just wanted to, I don't know, say hi or something."

She stands there gazing at me, looking guilty as all hell, which is a new look for inhabitants of Cute World.

"Are you feeling okay?" she says. "Are you still in pain? Do you need anything for it? Maybe I could help you."

Even the thought of Andie Bennett skipping across campus with an adorably wrapped little bottle of Vicodin does not make this conversation any more bearable. I am in the just-say-something-and-get-this-over-with mode. In the I-don't-want-this-to-be-reality, I-want-to-slip-into-the-alternate-reality-in-which-I-turn-around-and-drive-the-Beemer-back-to-the-party-and-slip-back-inside-and-go-to-the-beach-house-with-Billy-after-he-tells-his-mother-he's-spending-the-night-cramming-for-AP European-with-Andy-and-I-tell-my-parents-basically-nothing-and-everything-stays-exactly-the-same mode.

I am nevertheless not entirely un-curious as to where she is going with this.

"So how is it your fault?"

"Gabby!" she says, widening her eyes, as if of course I know, in a sort of "duh" move. "I was supposed to be the designated driver." She looks down at her hands, which she is kind of wringing in front of herself, as if she could gain comfort from her manicure. "I'm not trying to make an excuse. But Jordie was making those really good margaritas. I mean, who drinks margaritas? But you were drinking them and they looked really good and I guess I kind of started drinking them too."

This is all just so incredibly stupid and lame, and I am already so completely wigged out, I just don't know what to say.

I mean, it's not as if I'm the world's biggest fan of drunk driving, and if you'd ever sat in the backseat while John careened up the hill from Sunset toward Mulholland, straddling the middle line all the way up Roscomare and scraping the bottom of the Benz over the speed bumps, you'd completely believe me.

Because: I don't have a death wish or the delusional belief that cute drunk boys with car keys who say they can handle it can handle it.

And this, boys and girls, is why God invented taxis and Andy Kaplan's pool house.

All right, it's true that occasionally, in a spurt of conscientious zeal, we'd come up with a designated driver, but the only person who ever actually abstained when she was supposed to drive was Andie, which became completely irrelevant when Andy got his Porsche because Andie couldn't turn it on or shift the gears, which put the possibility of Andie driving the Porsche in the basket with ha-ha-forget-it and impossible.

And, anyway, if you've ever wondered why there are no cabs in L.A. late at night, it's because they're all ferrying the rich drunk kids from the Three B's to coed overnights at the houses of whoever's parents are the most clueless or on location in Cambodia. Or occasionally the sharing caring slobbery kind of parents who think it's a testament to their grooviness that their kid and her slightly impaired friends are passed out at home and not in some low-class gutter in the Toy District after a rave.

Andy Kaplan's father is the first kind, which is better; once we ended up in Sasha Aronson's rec room and her father wanted to *rap*, leading Billy to conclude that maybe consuming a truckload of hash in the '60s really could rot your brain. Andy's father, on the other hand, leaves us completely alone out in the pool house, presumably so he and the fifth Mrs. Kaplan can play naked freeze tag all over the hacienda without being interrupted by pesky teens padding down the hall in search of a toilet to throw up in. He is so grateful that we are out cold in the pool house, he sends the housekeeper with trays of brunch-like goodies at noon the next day.

The point of which being that Andie screwing up when she was supposed to be the designated driver of a car that Billy would never let her drive in the first place was kind of irrelevant.

"Right."

I am incredibly tempted to say something really nasty to her.

At that particular moment, it is hard to see a downside to being as nasty as I feel like being, as nasty as I've felt like being all day, and even more so after Billy's hand slipped onto Aliza Benitez's butt and into her pocket while I was innocently staring at the back of his head from behind a pillar.

What was Andie going to do if I just broke down and went for it, drum me out of Cute World?

Get me on the Slutmuffins' blacklist?

"I don't blame you if you're mad at me," she says, scratching her right calf with the toe of her left Chanel ballet slipper, proving the utility of really expensive shoes in times of trouble.

"For godsake, Andie," I say, wanting to be mean but the cute little foot in the cute little shoe is just getting to me and realizing that it isn't *her* cute little butt I want to kick. "It's not like you could have done anything about it. I wasn't exactly looking for a designated driver at the time. It's not like you did anything to me."

Andie says, "It's not?" She bites her lower lip and sniffles. "You are so nice. I never even realized how nice you are. You're like . . ."

(Try to imagine Andie struggling with deep thought.) "Joan of Arc or something. What you're doing is totally amazing."

No, what I'm doing is trying to live through the day so I can come back for more tomorrow. This is probably more stupid than amazing. Or amazingly stupid.

Andie is yammering on and on, goo-goo eyed. She thought she was loyal but I'm the most loyal person *ever*. I'm like a golden retriever, like her golden retriever Duchess who died but she was really a good dog, like a guy in the army who throws himself on a—what do you call it?—hand grenade for you.

This girl is so sweet and so without brains, it's pathetic.

Because, truth be told, I am the hand grenade and *not* the person who throws herself on it. Because if Billy comes near me, his probation will blow up, the shrapnel will rip through his life, and he'll be in Juvie Hell.

I'm not back at Winston School to grow and change like some sort of life-embracing, leafy vegetation turning toward Ponytail's imaginary sun. It's a total fraud.

I'm back because I want everything to stay the same.

My everything being Billy.

Me and Billy.

Because even though I get it, I understand, I'm not brainless, still, my heart does not understand. My body does not understand in the least. Skin, eyelids, fingertips. I want him to play with my hair and the hell with Princeton. Would Romeo give up Juliet for a really good shot at the Ivies? I don't care if Billy blowing in my ear is some form of felony. I want it and it seems to me as if, if I just hang in there and he sees me and my ear is right there in his face, then he'll want it too. He did at the castle, so why not at Winston, every day, just like before?

Because I am the grenade is why.

Because if I get too close to him, I'll mess him up.

I am the grenade and I just have to roll away down the hill and stay away and somehow get by not talking to him or brushing arms with him or holding hands or sitting with him for three more weeks of junior year.

XLVII

BY THE TIME THE BUS DROPS ME OFF ON ESTRADA, I am feeling too much like a person who just crashed a car to drag my backpack home.

It makes you wonder if *maybe* I wasn't emotionally ready to go to Winston, not that I thought anybody ever was, and Ponytail Doc, big surprise, missed the boat on my actual condition. Or maybe, like Billy says, my parents really are paying all these happy helpers to do what I say I want them to do without regard to whether it makes sense, such as sending me back to Winston so I can watch Billy paw my favorite Slutmuffin whenever I look up.

Dragging myself and all the books and the notebooks and the Xeroxed readers I need to make up all the work I missed up the hill to home feels like doing some pointless task on a chain gang in a really boring but disturbing movie just before the jailbreak, dragging giant rocks around for no apparent reason with a sadistic sheriff waving his rifle at me to make me keep trudging uphill. And I'm thinking, *What is the point of this? What am I even doing there?*

And then I get home, into the quiet house, empty except for John, barely there behind the closed door of the den, into my room, and onto the laptop, and *there he is, there is his screen name on my screen,* and *that* is the point.

pologuy: u looked hot today

So what were you doing with your hand in Aliza Benitez's pocket? I so cannot come out and ask him, but what *was* that? All right, it proves to all the world that he isn't still with me, but it's not as if his probation officer is creeping around Winston School with a hidden camera, analyzing the footage to make sure that Billy gets not being with me right.

gabs123: forbidden fruit. want some?
pologuy: duh. only look what happened to adam
gabs123: if adam had ur lawyer, he'd still b running around paradise and eve would still b naked eating apple sauce.
pologuy: ur lawyer is fine. ag says. just don't say anything that anyone could use against u. don't talk to anyone. thought u were going to do ur garbo i vant to be alone don't talk to me thing today but u were miss

popular with the freaks. is this wise miss fruit?
gabs123: strange day. i'm the new patron saint
of freaks.

And what were you doing with your hand in Aliza Benitez's pocket?
I am so waiting for an opening on this one. And so trying to get
myself to back off and not say anything and not care.

pologuy: u r irresistible to one and all

Okay, sort of an opening.

gabs123: tell that to benitez. i totally understand what ur
doing with her and all, but it still somewhat sucks.
pologuy: that must be why they call them slutmuffins.
i miss YOU G

Okay, *totally* worth bringing it up.

gabs123: me too. while u dine with benitez.
pologuy: noticed u dining with baby huey and the stick
girls. u got ur own thing going on
gabs123: give me a break! and andie wants to be my
little pal. pretty weird.
pologuy: she KNOWS she's not supposed to bother u.
brainless twit. i'll take care of it. no worries

Brainless twit? Poor Andie. Drama in Cute World.

gabs123: no biggie.

pologuy: i'll take care of it

gabs123: shit 5:00. gotta go.

pologuy: ?

gabs123: westwood. ponytail. again.

pologuy: have fun. b sure to cross fingers behind back while curling up on couch. wouldn't mind joining u on couch

gabs123: she doesn't have a couch. it's a chair.

pologuy: even better. easier to cross fingers behind chair. just remember not to tell her anything

gabs123: there's nothing to tell.

XLVIII

THIS TIME PONYTAIL IS WEARING A SKY-BLUE pantsuit with a giant white lace ruffle at her neck. I feel kind of sorry for her, watching her wardrobe deteriorate. It's a little hard to take anyone all that seriously in an outfit like that, no matter how expensive the designer buttons are, and you can only hope she isn't planning to wear it when she tells the DA that I'm cured.

She doesn't have any more cookies, either, so I offer to split my Dottie's Sweeties cupcake and she says sure. You have to figure that at least she isn't worried I'm some squirrelly person who might poison her strangely dressed shrink.

"First day back," she says.

"Yup."

"Everything okay in the art room? Hands functional?"

"Yup."

"Any issues with taking in information?"

"Too much information." I shudder a little with the image of Billy with his hand down Aliza's back pocket.

"You're thinking about something specific."

All this cat and mouse is wearing me down. I just want to get my cheese back to the hole in the floorboards and not be harassed by someone who could make me do a ropes course if she felt like it.

The thing is, after you sit in their offices long enough, and you're already totally stressed out, it wears you down. As militant as you are about spending hour after hour explaining you don't have a Problem, it seems as if the time would pass a lot faster if you would just roll over and spill.

I'm sorry, but it does.

Not to mention how hard it is to balance the risk of making her hate me if I tell her any true thing about me versus the risk of making her hate me if I sit there and refuse to tell her anything at all. It's hard to know, if I do tell her anything, if she'll turn around and tell someone else in a chain of revelations that could end up with me in girlie youth jail and Billy in actual prison with under-age gangbangers and a permanent record somewhere else.

"Okay," I say. "Here's the thing. If I tell you about something that someone is doing that might be wrong or like even illegal, do you tell other people about it?" I am staring straight at her. I figure that if she outright lies, I will somehow be able to tell.

"You have some concerns about whether I'll reveal what you tell me and get someone in trouble."

Duh.

So we play this inane game back and forth with her not coming out and answering the question and me not coming out and telling her anything. Because I sure as hell am not planning to tell her how Billy is perhaps still my boyfriend and perhaps not my boyfriend and perhaps sticking his hands down Aliza Benitez's pants (which, when you think about it, is probably the only thing he's doing that could actually benefit him, legally speaking) and get him perhaps sent to out-of-state lockup for violating his probation, where he definitely won't be my boyfriend, until I get a straight answer.

And then finally she says, "Oh dear, I haven't told you if you're safe confiding this thing you're wanting to talk about, have I? Which is so difficult with these juvenile court situations when you're feeling stuck here, isn't it? But let me try. If the illegal thing this person is doing is also illegal for you, for example if he's selling you drugs, then I almost certainly have to mention it. But say he robbed a bank all on his own and then he told you about it, then no. Does that help?"

Talking to your hapless girlfriend online. Robbing a bank. You can't help but notice the difference.

So I tell her, just to have something to say and pass the time.

Then I feel worse.

"Maybe I'm just not trusting enough. I don't know. He *said* I'm the one. He said I look hot, so you've got to think he noticed I'm back. But if he noticed I'm back, what was he doing with his hands all over someone else's butt?"

"You wanted it to be you," she says.

Way to state the obvious. This is so not helping.

"It sounds as if you have to work to interpret what he does and says, but just talking things out with him is off-limits," she says.

As if this were some amazing revelation.

As if there were a universe of teenage girls out there going: *Hey, boyfriend of my dreams, how do you really really REALLY feel about me and are you totally enraptured about being my boyfriend?*

And all these boyfriends going: *Hey, insecure whack job of a girl who I'm about to dump, I'm glad you asked because I long to yap about how I feel about you day and night. Why don't we share our feelings more often, perhaps instead of fooling around, because being interrogated by a clingy cow is more fun than sex on a stick.*

As if.

"You've lost a lot of things very quickly," she says, as if she thinks rubbing it in is going to help.

"You think I've lost him?"

"Well, what you're telling me is that you've lost the ability to be with him openly and the possibility of intimacy."

"You mean sex?" Which is an interesting point coming from someone who looks to be living in some strange, buttoned-up world in which people don't care one way or the other.

Well, it is definitely lost, and I miss it all the time, even more when it looks like Aliza Benitez is getting what I want and I have to sit around and watch her get it.

The point is: I feel like another person when he touches me, and I miss being her.

XLIX

THE SECOND DAY BACK, ANITA AND LISA CORNER me and haul me off to a bench behind the ninth grade lockers where nobody ever hangs out because it's 100% visible from the teachers' office windows and faces the teachers' parking lot, which, compared to the students' parking lot that closely resembles a commercial for European Motor Cars of Beverly Hills, is not a pretty sight.

"Did Billy Nash break up with you?" Lisa says. "We didn't even look for you at lunch yesterday and then it turned out you weren't with him. You were eating with Huey."

"And the stick girls," Anita says. "If you can call what they do eating. And I swear if you say no to this, I'll never mention it again, but you didn't get this thin by purging, did you? Because I can explain the physiology of it to you, and it could kill you."

"So true," Lisa says. "It's better to be fat. Not that you were ever fat."

"No!" I say. "Ew. And I don't see how you call this thin when I've been eating Dottie's cupcakes twice a week."

"Ew to Billy or ew to an eating disorder?" Lisa says.

"Bulimia, thank you. Like I would stick my fingers down my throat. Ew."

Lisa puts her hands on her hips. "Did Billy Nash break up with you or not?" she says. Acknowledging, of course, that the notion I might break up with Billy Nash isn't even worth considering.

"I really do not want to talk about it," I say.

"All right," Anita sighs. "Are you available for lunch?"

"Yeah."

"He broke up with you!" Lisa yells. She looks as if her head is going to explode.

"Okay," I say. "I seriously do not want to talk about this, okay, but sorta yes and sorta no, only you can't say anything to anyone, okay?"

They are just standing there, steaming and speechless.

"Okay," I say. "It's not what it looks like. If he hangs around with me, it violates his probation. So we can't be together or he could get his probation revoked and end up in jail somewhere out of state. He could spend the rest of high school in a prison rehab ward, okay?"

"Billy Nash in rehab," Anita says. "No! What a concept." But at least she remains slightly rational. "That sucks," she says.

"That really sucks, and frankly, I don't see why you're going along with it."

"Hello. Because he could end up in prison."

"I just don't believe this!" Lisa says. "I just don't believe what's happening." She looks like she's about to cry.

"Could we please never talk about this again?" I say. "I just want to live through this, so could you just be like my friends and shut up? I feel bad enough, okay?"

Unfortunately, after this, nothing can prevail on Lisa and Anita to stop glowering at Billy. You would think they were planning to track him down, bare their teeth, and bite him. Which is kind of horrible because it makes Billy think I'm talking to them about him, which I'm *really* not.

> **gabs123:** really, it's nothing. they're just pissed off we aren't the 2nd coming of the andies.
> **pologuy:** we were never the 2nd coming of the andies
> **gabs123:** thanks a lot nash. bite me.
> **pologuy:** that's not how i meant it. and here i thought u were biting into 2½ pounds of belgian chocolate—to think i bought that crap about expressing my undying love with candy! was i supposed to tie it with a bow or something?

His undying *WHAT?*

And I go, *Breathe, Gabriella. It's a joke. LOL. Hahaha. Get a grip.* But he said it. You would think, if he said it, it had to be on his mind, on the tip of his brain, to just slip out like that. And I go, *Gabriella, if you spill, if you give even the slightest hint you're taking this as even slightly meaningful or slightly slightly serious, you are a literal moo cow. An intellectually challenged cow that can't figure out how to chew grass.*

Undying love undying love undying love . . .

And I go, *Gabriella: Get. A. Grip.*

gabs123: r u kidding me? nash it was perfect. not that i would mind if u showed up tied with a bow. or even completely unwrapped.

pologuy: i wish. just b glad i'm up the street. if it wouldn't screw up my transcript for the Big P i'd be in a bunk bed with my cousin henry going to public school in santa barbara right now and i'd never get to c u

gabs123: well that would suck. no me and public school. boo hoo hoo nash.

pologuy: not funny. can't u get those bitches to back off? they're scaring me

gabs123: not bitches. bff's. i just keep telling them i don't want to talk about it. they get it.

pologuy: good. maybe u should put them on hiatus. u don't need to listen to their estrogen crap

I can tell how pissy he's getting, but I totally don't care.

I am the one with the Undying Love candy, and every time his screen name shows up on my screen, which is happening with reassuring regularity, it's like an electronic aphrodisiac demonstrating for all eternity why porn sites gross more than medium-sized countries. And my Billy sightings at school make my heart pound like Cheesy Railroad Girl, and I don't mean in a metaphorical, heart-nailed-by-Cupid's-dinky-arrow kind of way. It is actual weird tachycardia (SAT word) and I feel like some ditz who is going to keel over with a mere glance at Perfect Hot Boy.

It isn't clear if I'm going to live through the rest of chemistry with him in the same room ignoring me. That's how bad it is.

That and the less-than-pleasant daydreams. For example:

Agnes won't let him out of the house after six p.m. so I know he isn't taking Aliza Benitez out for Baby Blues ribs and sweet potato pie on Lincoln Boulevard, listening to Johnny Cash and cuddling up to her, and it's even hard to imagine Aliza as a Johnny Cash–and-ribs kind of a girl. But then it starts bothering me that the place he isn't taking her but would if he could is probably some elegant, expensive place on Melrose or a cute little organic forty-dollar snack at Urth Caffé on Beverly, and not the rib joint where he takes me down in Venice. Even though I somewhat dread going there because did you ever try to look reasonably appealing while gnawing on a slab of ribs with your fingers and chin coated with barbeque sauce?

I am in a complete paranoid snit.

But the fact that he can't leave his house after dark to go out, slumming *or* elegant, doesn't make up for how godawful it is to see him gazing down Aliza's skanky little tank top under her unbuttoned uniform blouse in the Class of 1920 Garden every day, and how totally cat-full-of-cream-and-mice-stew smug she looks.

She is one happy Slutmuffin and I, for all anybody knows, am history.

Within a couple of days, the other Muffins have stopped scurrying off in the other direction whenever I walk by and are actually saying hi to me. This is not a good thing. You can tell that it is only because they feel sorry for me, as opposed to when I was Billy's formerly invisible girlfriend, when they barely even nodded in my direction.

And you have to wonder if being a pathetic delinquent girl with no visible boyfriend is enough to make them start feeling sorry for a person, or if they have actually looked up from their makeup mirrors long enough to see the even more pathetic fact of my life as spectator to Aliza Benitez's bliss.

L

AFTER SPENDING THE REST OF THE WEEK SKULKING around Winston School in my new role as a human magnet for unwanted self-revelations, I get a note from Mr. Piersol at the end of Honors Spanish, and it occurs to me that probably he wants to tell me how he spent *his* teenage years addicted to pornography and smoking crack. Actually, it's kind of amazing to think he would have had enough gumption to drive to a crack house or to do whatever it takes to acquire all the porn you would need to be successfully addicted in the first place, given that he is famous for basically doing nothing but spouting clichés, suspending kids for no apparent reason, and sucking up to parents with checkbooks.

But no, that isn't it. He wants me to resign from Student Council. Not that anybody but the decorating committee will notice I'm gone.

Still, I can't believe it. There I sit in his enormous office in his enormous club chair watching the sun shine through the enormous stained glass window and reflect its colors on the Persian rug. And it sounds as if the tide is coming in inside my ears.

I so didn't see this coming.

The thing is, I am actually sort of good at what I do for Student Council, even though I don't need the Leadership in Party Decoration ribbon for my application to (fog descends, parents moan) Some Random College. Not only that: At the rate I'm going, Student Council is the only place at Winston I'll ever get to sit at the same table as Billy and talk to him, assuming I stop feeling so insane every time I see him and I actually open my mouth and speak coherently, even if it is only about the budget for the homecoming dance and to okay the Junior Spring Fling posters.

At the rate I'm going, if I get kicked off Student Council, our only connection will be at one a.m. on a computer monitor, and he'll forget what my voice even sounds like unless I start raising my hand in chemistry.

"Gabby," Mr. Piersol says, playing what looks to be several rounds of here-is-the-church, here-is-the-steeple with his folded hands, "you have to understand. Eleventh grade rep is a leadership position." Actually, it's about fourteen leadership positions, since Winston has the biggest student council possible with representatives for everything the college counselors could think of so everyone can stick some leadership position on their application to (Hands of God applauding through the clouds) Harvard, but this seems like a bad time to point that out.

"Blah-blah set an example. Blah-blah uphold reputation. Blah-blabitty-blah."

The tide in my ears gets so loud I'm afraid that I'm going to pass out, and it becomes increasingly difficult to make out exactly what he's saying except that it's pretty obvious I'm the bad apple that's going to spoil the bunch, the jailbird that doesn't get the worm, the poor example who is therefore here today and gone from Council tomorrow.

It's just so unfair that *I'm* the one getting beat up with his mindless clichés. Billy is the one whose middle initials are DUI and there is no way Mr. Piersol doesn't know that. I am sitting there thinking how Billy is lucky the Mothers Against Drunk Driving haven't made him their international poster boy, and nobody is asking *him* to resign from Student Anything.

I would never drive drunk.

I would never even let him drive me drunk.

And then I think, *Wait a minute. That can't be right, can it, because I did, didn't I? Somehow I managed to get plowed and wrap a car around a tree.*

But it is still hard to see how any of this makes me unfit to plan how to decorate prom given that I'm the only person on the committee who can see that doing the whole room in iridescent pink and black and silver that looks a lot like tin-foil would be both tacky and disgusting, not to mention I'm completely responsible for the Youth League shelter looking cheery for Christmas.

Which makes this totally unfair.

I look straight at Mr. Piersol, who seems somewhat uncomfortable, his mouth in this tight little straight line, and I just don't want him to be able to do this to me. And I say, "I don't think this is right."

And then I almost do pass out. Because: I don't generally spend my time confronting people. But all I can think is: *Have to stay on Student Council. Billy is on Student Council. Have to see Billy on Student Council.*

"Mr. Piersol," I lie really well after all this endless practice with helpful helping professionals who are supposed to keep me out of jail. "I have a Problem."

He doesn't seem quite as happy to hear this as all the helpful helping drones I am supposed to say it to, but I'm completely shameless.

"I have a Problem and I'm Dealing With It. But the thing is, I'm not the only student here who has a problem, even this particular one. And I think . . ." *Oh God, what do I think? Think think think.* "I think, actually, that this makes me, um, a better leader than I was before when I, uh, wasn't dealing with it."

He is leaning forward in his chair, from the look of it trying to figure out what the hell I'm talking about.

"And frankly, Mr. Piersol," I say very quickly before I pass out or he interrupts me or I completely lose my nerve, "I don't even think I was a true leader before. Like I am now, I mean."

Mr. Piersol just stares at me in absolute silence. It is hard to imagine what cliché he is going to come up with to bash me back into my place as if I were a presumptuous rodent sticking her nose where it doesn't belong in a game of Whack-A-Mole. But then he starts to crack, just a little, and then he's absolutely leering at me like a seriously stoned clown. There it is. The total smile. Mr. Piersol is just sitting there loving every inch of my lying fictional self.

Not that I have turned into a total moron who thinks the man actually likes me, but now he doesn't have to do anything to me—in fact, he doesn't have to do anything at all (an added bonus)—and he can still be Mr. Responsible Headmaster.

I feel like a complete lying genius-child.

Now Mr. Piersol can jump on the bandwagon with my entourage of high-priced rehabilitation experts and embrace my lying fictional self and it won't disrupt his day.

There he sits, embellishing my fictional sad story, and there I am, gazing into my lap and waiting for it to be over. New respect blah-blah . . . thoughtful self-reflection blah-blah . . . newfound maturity blabitty-blah.

Not only am I still on Student Council, but I can see a college recommendation forming before my very eyes, even though you can tell that, deep down, he really hates me and isn't all that happy with himself for getting carried away with the happy idea of just staying inert and not sticking with the original program and tossing me off Council.

It occurs to me that maybe this whole thing really is a Personal Growth Opportunity, just like everyone says, and I have developed the useful new skill of telling people whatever they want to hear, pretending to be whatever they want me to be, while appearing to tell the truth, aka lying, and getting them to do what I want whether they like it or not.

Then it occurs to me that this is what I had been trying to do with Billy pretty much the whole time.

Then I have to go to art, which is fine, because this isn't exactly what I want to be thinking about.

Ever.

LI

BRYNN McELROY IS A SLUTMUFFIN PEON. THAT'S JUST
the way it is, and even her dad calling her "my gorgeous daughter,
Brynn" when he thanks her from onstage at the Golden Globes
can't change it. She's welcome in the Class of 1920 Garden but
not someone whose offer of a lift home confers the possibility of
popularity. But she is on Council with her football-playing boyfriend, Jack Griffith, and she is the lowest status girl working on
the Fling committee. Except for me. So it makes sense that she's
the one who gets stuck calling me to see if they can get me off it
after Charlotte Ward tried and failed.

"Hey," she says.

"Hey."

"So," she says. "Charlotte says you're still on Council, and
you're still on decorating committee, so I wanted to see if you
were still coming to Fling committee."

"Yeah." Three beats of leaving Brynn McElroy hanging there. Three beats of thinking, if I can vanquish Cliché Man, why would I go along with this? And what would be the point of going along with these bitches, anyway? To create happiness in Muffin World? "Why wouldn't I be?"

You can tell, even on a cell phone with the bad reception you get in a canyon, that Brynn didn't anticipate idiot resistance. I feel so pissed off and so like such a righteously indignant moron simultaneously.

"Um, I guess everyone was hoping you were up to it," she says.

And then I say to myself, *Shit, Gabby, even though you are now the reigning queen of assertiveness and will no doubt soon be the elected idol of Winston Women for Equality, you have to stop it. Do. Not. Get. Carried. Away. You do not want to get into a pissing contest with Charlotte Ward and Aliza Benitez.*

Close your mouth and stop screwing with the Fling committee.

"That's really nice," I say, trying to figure out how I'm going to fix this when she knows and I know and whoever forced her to make the phone call knows what's going on and how not nice it is. "I'm doing great. Thanks for the concern."

"Oh. You're welcome," she says. "You know that Charlotte scheduled the meeting for six thirty in the morning, so it wouldn't conflict with the jazz ensemble dance rehearsal, right?"

And also so a person with no legal means of transportation other than legs can't actually get there because last time I looked, there was no six a.m. bus. "So what's happening at six thirty, anyway?"

"No big deal," Brynn says. "Finalizing the decorations and the king and queen."

"You're getting up at five thirty in the morning to set up another election? You just need someone who can count to two hundred. Get Kaplan and sleep in."

"Kaplan? Not likely. No one is up for another election this late in the year. People just nominate themselves and Charlotte picks."

"Are you kidding me?"

"It makes Piersol happy because he doesn't have to force any teachers to monitor the polls and okay the election posters."

"You know what," I say, which seems kind of anticlimactic after vanquishing Piersol and hanging on to Council, but there is only so much unhappiness a person can create in Muffin World and survive. That and I feel so kind of past it. "I'm going to sleep in. Finalize it without me."

"You do know we went back to classic colors, right?"

"Disco balls and tinfoil?"

"I know," she says. "I voted against it. They redid the posters with baby pink."

"They put pink on my posters?"

"Sorry," she says. "They're still good posters. They're at the printers."

"I was supposed to take them to the printer to do the color check."

"Gabby, you weren't here and Nash didn't know if you were ever coming back. We didn't know what else to do."

★　★　★

gabs123: did u tell brynn mcelroy u didn't know if i was coming back to winston? i just had a very weird conversation with her.

pologuy: y would i even talk to brynn freaking mcelroy? don't know what jack is doing with her. other than the obvious thing to do with her. u have to take care of yourself and NOT talk to people like her

gabs123: fling committee screwed up my posters.

pologuy: ok I get this. char wanted to know how long she had to get disco balls or something rammed through committee before u got back and stared her down. this is y u can't talk to people. info gets twisted. everything gets twisted

gabs123: i wish someone had told me this.

pologuy: babe u were in the hospital. ur mom was telling people u were in a coma. didn't think you'd care about party decorations. y do u want to b on that committee anyway? i'm not even on it

gabs123: exactly. i'm not going to their lame meeting. too early anyway.

pologuy: smart move. shit. gotta bounce. AP tutor barking at the gate. FML. miss u

LII

WHEN I AM SITTING IN FRONT OF MY COMPUTER
screen, I can somewhat get myself to feel that pologuy is missing
gabs123. But seeing Real Live Billy grinning his way across the
ordinary people's lawn to get to the Class of 1920 Garden, his
back to me, looking over his shoulder, his eyes skimming the top
of my head, which prickles as if I could feel the very tips of his
fingers along my part, is not getting any easier.

The Aliza and Billy sightings—which he says, in his back-
handed way, mean nothing because I'm the one, that it just makes
the world at large and his mother in particular believe that he's
down with his probation and not with me so maybe someday
she'll loosen her Satanic grip and we can sneak around—are still
miserable. And the Courtney Yamada Phillips and Billy sightings, even though I guess they prove he isn't really with Aliza
Benitez, which is supposed to make me feel fine when he pats

Aliza between the knees for godsake, are not much better.

Courtney, even though she's a sophomore in the *very* firm, *very* young flesh category, is in my Honors Spanish class and I have to watch her heated up and panting about him with Rose Lyons when she comes racing in from the semi-hidden nook behind the teachers' lounge.

"He is so hot," Rose says.

"Awesome," Courtney says.

Awesome. Great. He's publicly nibbling lips that say "awesome" constantly.

And I go, *Suck it up, Gabriella. Wake up and smell the chocolates. You're the one.*

But it is actually a relief to go into painting with Mr. Rosen, who at least doesn't want to have a meaningful dialogue about anything, and whose studio windows face the soccer field so there is no risk of a Billy sighting. Even though I never feel like I'll ever paint anything good enough for Mr. Rosen, at least I'm better than everyone else in there, and he seems to be fine with that.

Mr. Rosen, you have to figure, is just going to keep sitting there in by-permission-only advanced painting, not noticing who I am, having no idea whatsoever about what's going on with me apart from my portfolio.

Not that we're actually *painting* in Mr. Rosen's eleventh grade painting class. Since last semester, we aren't. Just before Christmas break, Mr. Rosen told us that we sucked and we had to start drawing again before we were ready to paint because we had no sense of form. Therefore, we've spent this whole semester drawing a succession of objects Mr. Rosen throws on the little tables in front of us, and there are no paints in sight.

Every couple of weeks, a delegation of earnest artsy girls goes up to Mr. Rosen's office where he sits with his eyes closed listening to music and looking as if he has a headache while they explain in detail how they really really feel about not getting to paint. According to Sasha Aronson, who is head of the petition brigade, no matter how respectful and convincing they are, Mr. Rosen never even opens his eyes.

So naturally, the minute I get back from my vehicular crime spree, Mr. Rosen, who you would think you could rely on not to make a big production about anything short of pure genius, makes a big production out of giving me back the paints. Not the acrylic paints, either.

Oils.

You'd like to think that mixing oil paint on a palette and painting my little heart out would just magically take my mind off things and make everything, if not A-okay, maybe semi-okay. And that I would create gorgeous, angsty art.

But I don't.

I spend a week trying to get the light right on this little table with the remnants of a tea party or something (so not my idea, and the pastry is starting to get moldy and change color) and it just keeps getting grayer and darker until I've completely scrubbed any possibility of life off the canvas. I feel like my paintbrush is going to jump out of my hand, slide down the leg of the easel, and hop out the door in protest.

At least it gives me something to do that doesn't involve scanning the horizon for Billy Nash, both wanting and not wanting to spot him.

Finally, Mr. Rosen comes up behind me and stands there for about five minutes.

"I think you're finished with this," he says. He bundles up the junk on the little table in the tablecloth and takes the paintbrush. Then he scuttles over to his desk and takes out a little framed sketch. Real, and from the Renaissance, a woman sitting in a chair, draped in diaphanous cloth, just done in pencil, perfect.

"Copy this," he says, propping it up.

So great, now that I'm a juvenile delinquent who can't even paint a moldy croissant with rancid butter, Mr. Rosen is preparing me for life as an art forger. Just great. At least it would give me something lucrative to do, something to do other than being at Winston School, where this little sketch is the only real piece of art worth forging.

"Don't think," he says. "Just draw. You'll feel better. You want music?"

He goes back to his desk and sticks a tape into the world's most primitive tape deck. "Young people like this, yes?"

And this is how, for the first time in history, everybody in advanced permission-only painting has to listen to odd German techno all period. And how I find out I'm a really good art forger. Which at least gives me something to do other than visualizing Billy pawing other girls.

LIII

"EXPLAIN THIS TO ME AGAIN," ANITA SAYS, EATING her icy pop at break. "How is it that Courtney Phillips going down on him in the parking lot is supposed to make you feel better?"

"Anita! Just because she's gnawing on his face—"

"Sorry, Lisa." And then to me, even though they can see that I'm tearing up over my icy pop, "Are you completely demented? He's not with other girls to be nice to you and prove he's not with any one of them, he's with other girls because he's an incorrigible player."

"SAT word?"

"Yeah, but that doesn't mean that he isn't one. And it doesn't prove he's not with Aliza, either, it just proves he's a jerk."

All right, so they despise Billy and there isn't much I can do about it.

"Why don't you just tell him how it makes you feel," Lisa says. (Right, that should work.) "Tell him to stop it." (Even better.) "He says he's still your boyfriend so it's not like you don't have a hold on him."

But that's exactly what it's like—like I am powerless and pathetic. Like I'm powerless and pathetic and ridiculously perky and give really good IM. And even repeating *undying love* to myself every time I inhale and every time I exhale can't completely drown out what I'm thinking.

And I say to myself: *Gabby, if you keep this up, you're going to have a whole lot of bad self-esteem to make Ponytail happy. But perhaps you should avoid sharp objects and thinking.*

pologuy: whatcha doing?

gabs123: not a lot. spanish homework.

pologuy: same. do not take AP spanish language. slow death by magical realism. even tutor says so

gabs123: is your tutor living there now?

pologuy: now now. we all have our helpful professionals on the payroll. i'm stuck with him for company. ag is turning me into a hermit. boy needs companionship

gabs123: not a complete hermit. i see u with ur little harem. courtney thinks ur awesome

pologuy: r u saying i'm not awesome? well, i saw u with your scary little witches coven. again

gabs123: that is so not funny again. not witches, bff's. u know this.

pologuy: no seriously. they look like they want to run me down in the parking lot

gabs123: lucky for u they don't have cars.

pologuy: gabs! when did u get so harsh?

gabs123: when did u get ur harem?

pologuy: this is a joke right?

gabs123: duh. i totally understand. i do. u know i do. i'm just getting punchy with all this online cavorting. i miss actual cavorting.

pologuy: me too. miss u Miss G.

gabs123: i've gotta go to sleep. no more irregular verbs. xx

pologuy: u know it

I do know it. But as it turns out, some of the things I know are less true than others.

Because while I am sleeping, drifting through space in solo orbit so far away from actual events on planet Earth that I can't see what everyone is doing well enough to understand anything at all, while I am dozing off thinking that nothing worse could happen, not even noticing when six thirty a.m. comes and goes, I am undone by a rhyming sock hop with poodle skirts.

part three

LIV

IT IS ALL JUST *SO* STUPID BUT I AM COMPLETELY unhinged. It's like having an emotional breakdown over an advertising jingle about aftershave or having your heart ripped out by the Pillsbury Doughboy. And it isn't even the Spring Fling itself, the actual dance, which, when you think about it, has all sorts of genuine dramatic possibilities:

Maybe Huey would grope Lisa, maybe he would play with the buttons of the horrible sombrero sweater that her mom is so attached to, and she would experience extreme moral conflict over slightly spiked punch.

Maybe Anita would break out of her house, show up with her bra straps hanging off her shoulders, and introduce us to the cute French guy from Marseilles who, having renounced his priestly vocation, was holed up at the Bel Air Hotel feeding torn up croissants to the black swans and waiting for her to run away with him.

Maybe I'd lose my mind and go stag and maybe I'd see Billy across the room and maybe we would slow dance to "My Blue Heaven" and we would both remember who I am, swaying to Elvis, and maybe he would want me.

What does not cross the mind of the orbiting space cadet, *my* mind, is that he would nominate himself for King of Fling and not even mention it to me, and Aliza would run for Queen of Fling with not one single other Slutmuffin nominating herself, big conspiracy, so you know that the crowned and anointed couple dancing to "My Blue Heaven" is going to be pologuy, live and in person, with Aliza Benitez and *not* gabs123.

Thank you, Brynn McElroy, for your highly organized and complete Fling committee minutes, distributed to all committee members, present or innocently sleeping through Charlotte Ward's planning extravaganza.

"This sucks," Anita says. "This is a bit much even for him."

We are sitting in the Winston School darkroom, Huey's private domain, where we all go sit in the dark so we can eat inside somewhere other than the cafeteria on rainy days, with the glowing red lights and timer buzzers going off and Huey bouncing around hanging up wet, newborn photos by little clothespin-thingies while Lisa gazes up at him and Anita and I try not to look at each other.

Only it's sunny, and we're hiding out in there because I know if I have to see Billy with *anybody* else, I'm not going to survive the day.

"Wait a minute," Huey says, dipping photographic paper into

a tub of chemicals. "Are you saying you still want this guy to be your boyfriend?"

"Leave her alone," Lisa says. "She's having a hard enough time."

"I'm just saying, I think you'd have a lot easier time if you'd take care of yourself. Like if you'd take care of all the legal things . . ."

"Huey," Lisa says. "She doesn't want to talk about the legal stuff. Leave her alone."

"I am taking care of the legal stuff!" I say. "I'm doing everything my lawyer says I'm supposed to be doing. *Punc*tiliously! I'm staying away from Billy and I'm going to therapy and I'm having a meeting with the Probation Department and I'm pretending to get over my so-called drinking problem and soon I'll have my record expunged, okay?"

"Not okay!" Huey shouts.

Lisa says, "Don't raise your voice, Jeremy."

Huey says, "I'm talking to Gabby."

Lisa and Anita sit planted in their folding chairs.

Huey crosses his arms. "I need to talk to Gabby. Do you *mind*?"

This is a new, improved and updated, Ferocious Huey that I've never seen before. I have the feeling this is the most conflict he and Lisa have ever had in their entire relationship, such as it is—that she refuses to get up out of her chair. So I say it's all right with me and watch Lisa and Anita march out of the darkroom, glaring back at him.

LV

HUEY SAYS, "I THINK YOU NEED TO SEE ANOTHER lawyer."

"I already have a lawyer," I say. "What's your point?"

"I mean a lawyer who isn't related to Billy Nash," he says. "Also, I think you should see a lawyer who isn't brainless."

"I don't see how having Albert Einstein for a lawyer could help," I say. "The facts kind of speak for themselves."

"Well, they don't have much choice, do they?" Huey shouts at me. "Given that *you* don't seem interested in speaking for yourself!"

"What am I supposed to *say*, Huey? Give it a rest. I don't remember anything."

"Right," says Huey, hitting himself on the forehead with an exaggerated, dopey look on his face, his tongue hanging out. "You don't remember anything! How could I forget?"

"Duh. And I don't see how anyone could fix it at this point even if I did remember. I just have to pretend I have a drinking problem and then I have to pretend to get cured and then I have to pretend to grow and change and then my record gets expunged and it all goes away. Even a brain-dead lawyer could figure out this one."

Huey looks amazed. "Is that what your lawyer told you?" he says. "Did someone actually tell you that that's what you're supposed to do? This is almost as mind-blowing as the part where you don't have a drinking problem. Did he tell you that too? What is wrong with you?"

"Stop it, Huey. Just stop it! The lawyer thinks I'm fixing my so-called drinking problem and then he can feel all warm and fuzzy about himself when he gets my record expunged. It's not rocket science."

"Did your lawyer even ask if someone checked the steering wheel for fingerprints? Or did Agnes Nash pay him off before he got to that question?"

"Why would they want to do that? There's no big mystery. It's not like I was wearing gloves."

Something in the darkroom buzzes and Huey starts swooping around sloshing things in big pans of liquid. The only light is this eerie red color and it looks as if he is a red angry burning spirit.

Huey hangs up two sheets of paper with clothespins and he sits down again and he says, "All right. How much do you really remember?"

I say, "Nothing. Nada, niente, zero, zilch, zip, zippity doo dah. This isn't news. Everybody already knows this. Did you miss something when you were locked up in here playing with chemicals?"

"What everybody knows is that you're saving Billy's ass while he's back with Aliza Benitez."

"Are you insane? And he's not really with her. He's the one who's saving *my* ass. In case you didn't figure it out, it turns out that technically I stole his car. Just before I totaled it. For which the Nashes are not pressing charges. Colleges would love that one."

Huey shoves his face so close to my face, my breath could have steamed up his glasses. "Don't you remember anything?"

"No! Don't you get it? *No!* I got hit on the freaking head when I wrecked Billy's Beemer, just after I stole it! Why is this so hard for you to comprehend? I went spinning out drunk in the Valley, all right? There's nothing *to* remember."

Huey shakes his head. Then he takes me by the wrist and he pulls me out of the darkroom. He is such an exceptionally odd person, it's hard to know what he has in mind.

Huey walks me through school and out to the parking lot and into his dopey-looking, ecologically good little car. People are staring at me the whole way. I'm not sure if this is because Huey is dragging me around by the wrist or because I've been crying so much that my eye makeup has run and I look like a raccoon.

A raccoon that's about to cut sixth, seventh, and eighth periods.

LVI

WE DRIVE UP INTO THE HILLS TO HUEY'S HOUSE, which is a giant tan stone château that some captain of industry brought to Bel Air stone by stone from France. It is the size of the Beverly Hills Public Library, and it has matching dogs, three tan mastiffs that come racing and panting up to the car to jump all over Huey and drool on the ecologically good paint.

"This certainly takes my mind off things," I say, trying to open the car door while a large dog pushes on it from the outside.

"Down, Daisy!" Huey says, causing the dog to wag her giant tail and hyperventilate, but not to get off my door. "Yeah," he says, "I live in a parallel universe."

Over by the side of the house, I swear I see a lamb. Two lambs, just walking around eating the grass.

"Is there a shepherd?" I say, only partly a joke, since I figure that if there is a shepherd, he could maybe pull the dog off my side of the car.

"My mother does animal rescue," Huey says. As if this isn't already a well-known fact. Then he climbs out of the car and grabs the dog by the scruff of its neck.

We crunch up the gravel path toward the house with the three dogs and a really pushy lamb. The front door is so tall, it seems as if you would need the eighteen-inch keys from the Pirates of the Caribbean ride at Disneyland to unlock it.

The inside of Huey's castle involves a lot of sweeping, curved staircases and tapestries you could always use to tent normal-sized houses when you spray for bugs and vermin. We climb up a bunch of these staircases while a uniformed lady follows at our heels, offering snack food. Through an open door on the way up, we see Huey's mother in a room with a big table and cages and baskets, feeding what looks to be a tiny ferret with a baby bottle.

She says, "Hi, sweetie," not looking up. You can't tell if she's talking to Huey or the ferret.

Huey says, "Mom? This is Gabby."

This causes Mrs. Hewlett to look up fast.

"Yearbook," Huey says. He doesn't actually say *what* about yearbook, so it's not like he's technically lying.

"Well, keep your door open, Hewbo," she says. *Hew*bo? And then she registers my face and the rivulets of eye makeup and the red eyes, and maybe I remind her of a wounded raccoon or maybe I'm just more pathetically enthralling than the ferret and a box of baby moles put together because she wipes her hands on the sides of her jeans and she hands her little ferret to the accommodating lady with the snack tray.

She is in animal rescue mode for sure and I am the unfortunate mammal.

"Madeleine Hewlett," she says, extending her sticky hand, and all at once she's got me in her grip, pulling me in for a hug. "Hello, dear."

"Gabby Gardiner," I say into her shoulder.

"My cousin Lolo used to visit Gardiner Island!" she says. "Lovely!" As if I were in line to inherit the place, or was in touch with rich and famous Gardiners, or knew them, or could recognize them in a crowd.

"Well then," she says. "Tea!"

You can tell from Huey's whipped demeanor that there's no point in fighting this onslaught of maternal involvement no matter how weirdly crazed he is to haul me upstairs. He kind of leads me back down to his kitchen, which is the size of my house, and sits me down at a grotesquely long rustic table where Louis XVI probably had orange juice with his entire court dressed up as shepherds.

Only probably Marie Antoinette didn't open the backdoor for the pushy lamb to come in and pour it a big bowl of livestock kibble.

The room is filled with black-and-white photos, Mr. and Mrs. Hewlett when they were still young and still hippies, posed in front of what appears to be their house when it was still in Europe, and a bunch of candid photos of someone you have to figure is either the Pope or a highly skilled Pope impersonator.

"I'm going to get your friend some tea," Mrs. Hewlett says, looking at me quizzically, still in rescue mode. This involves silently telegraphing to the other maid that she's supposed to make a cup of tea appear in front of me with a scone and a pot of jam.

"She's upset about her boyfriend," Huey says. It's hard to tell if this is for parental consumption or if he thinks this covers it.

"Oh dear!" Mrs. Hewlett says, in the parental mode of being deeply concerned but even more deeply not getting it. "I was always upset about my boyfriend until I met Jeremy Jr."

Mrs. Hewlett is still pretty without makeup at the age of fifty, wearing jeans and a sweater covered with ferret fur and wet spots you don't even want to think about, a gazillionaire from birth, and married to a fellow gazillionaire who likes the Grateful Dead, writes music for a living, and puts up with a house full of rodents and farm animals because he loves her so much. It's hard to relate to anything about her.

"Remember Buddy Murphy, Huey?" she says. Buddy Murphy is this two-hundred-year-old former studio head who everyone has heard of. "I was crazy about him, and then it turned out he was allergic to dander!"

Mrs. Hewlett smiles with the faraway look of a woman imagining old Buddy Murphy doubled over and sneezing uncontrollably. Then she scoops up a cat and plops it on my lap.

"There," she says. "That always makes me feel better."

There you have it. Billy and Aliza are going to be coronated at Fling and I have a one-eyed cat on me, licking my scone. I can't exactly throw her against the wall. She's a one-eyed cat. So we all sit there at the grotesquely long table watching the cat eat my jam. It so does not make me feel better.

I don't know what's supposed to happen upstairs, and I only like surprises that involve candy, but I hand Mrs. Hewlett back the cat.

"Thank you," I say.

"Yearbook," Huey says.

And I can feel his mother watch me somewhat limp away, trying to figure out if she should report my condition to the Humane Society.

LVII

HUEY'S PHOTOGRAPHY ROOM IS A BIG, SUNNY octagonal place in the top corner of the house with a skylight and a black-and-white tile floor. It is the kind of room you design on purpose, because you want to be able to sit in exactly that space with those windows and that cold, hard floor whenever you feel like it, not a room you just end up with because it's in the cheapest house on a ritzy street and you can just kind of afford it so you buy it and you're stuck with it no matter how dreary it looks.

The room is filled with folding tables and metal shelves and cardboard bankers' boxes labeled by year with the names of events and holidays, like he has records of every Christmas, Easter, and Fourth of July for his whole life. His equipment is strewn over a big, old fluffy couch covered with a faded yellow quilt and sat on by a couple of cats named Pinky and Cocoa Puff. Actually, it's all sort of perfect.

And it's not that I'm jealous thinking of Lisa sitting in this room with Huey doing whatever it is that Lisa and Huey do, which probably entails playing Boggle and Parcheesi and Monopoly and feeding ferrets for all I know. It's just that it's so nice in there.

Huey says, "Wait here."

I walk to the bay window in the corner, which curves in a semicircle and lets you look down to the coast, out to the slate-blue water, and it just strikes me how happy Vivian would be to see me there. I might be a well-dressed slut of a drunken car thief with an unimpressive GPA and no Ivy League prospects whatsoever, but hell, if I didn't mind suffocating Lisa, I could be queen of the castle. So then I stand there thinking about what a bad friend and really bad overall person I am to even be having this particular fantasy, but at least I know I wouldn't actually *do* anything like that.

And then Huey comes back with the album and that particular chapter, the chapter where I knew what I knew and felt what I felt, ends.

LVIII

IT'S ONE OF THOSE CHEAP ALBUMS FROM RITE AID, the little plastic kind with cellophane sleeves that holds the pictures back-to-back. Labeled "April 11, Songbird Lane." Neatly organized. You can tell that Huey is the prince of good organization, and he probably has hundreds of these little albums all lined up in order, and he could just pop open the Cataclysmic Disaster box and there this one would be.

So many of the pictures are shot from behind, you can tell the whole thing involves Huey skulking around and sneaking up on people, blowing his breath down toward his camera so they won't feel him breathing on the backs of their necks. It's creepy, but the pictures are creepier.

First, there is the house. A big, fake Tudor with maybe thirty kids on the front lawn with red plastic cups and bottles. The front door is hanging wide open and you can make out the shapes of more bodies in there, in the white light that seems to have engulfed them and blurred their edges.

"Is it coming back to you at all?" Huey asks.

"This isn't some freaking Alfred Hitchcock movie, Huey! It isn't coming back, all right? *Ever*. Do you want me to look at these or not?"

"You want to look at these," he says.

Huey likes photographs with bodies crammed together in the frame, or maybe that's all the party had to offer. Bodies curved and leaning into one another, arms dangling over rounded shoulders and around necks, hands and wrists and forearms disappearing into the dark folds of each other's clothing. Bodies curved toward each other in doorways, leaning toward one another like arches, shapes with faces melting into darkness.

But you can always pick yourself out. Even years later, photographed from a distance in a group photo at summer camp, you can still tell that that's the left side of your little-kid-self's back in the Camp Tumbleweed T-shirt. Even two months later, you can tell it's your profile, drinking in a corner in a chair and it looks as if you're crying, sobbing actually, at a party you can't remember.

"You need to look at them in order," Huey says.

Why is that? Flipping through them backward and forward, from either direction, they tell the same story.

There I am from behind with Billy and the Andies, weaving our way through the crowd on the front lawn, heading toward the open door.

There we are in the kitchen, going for the bottles arranged

helter-skelter on the counter, the only light reflected off the bottles and my earrings and off Billy's pale hair.

There's Jordie Berger mixing margaritas.

There's Andie dancing for Andy in another corner, a dark expanse of silky skin between the top of her jeans and the bottom of her baby tee.

There are the Slutmuffins, all Louis Vuitton bags and attitude, standing by the pool house, lighting up with boys all around them, their personal fan club. Their heads all bent together, it is hard to tell who's who.

Aliza Benitez on the deck chair with no blouse, breasts and arms and nipples darkened blurs, leaning into someone's shoulder, on top of, under, and entangled with some boy, the boy with light glinting off his pale gold hair.

I appear to be yelling.

I appear to be crying.

I appear to be drinking straight out of a bottle like some bum under a freeway bridge. It is too dark to tell exactly what I'm doing. There I am drinking some more, only the bottle is a different shape. There I am drinking some more.

There I am, being hauled into the Beemer, half-carried, waving my bag in the air. Dropping my bag. Andy has me under the arms and I seem to be made of splayed rubber limbs and a big gash of a sad, drunk mouth.

There I am, getting into the car with Billy and the Andies, with Aliza Benitez kind of sitting on the trunk with her legs hanging over the back. There I am draped over Andy and Billy, who are maneuvering me into the front seat, the passenger seat, no seat belt, all of us looking exceptionally drunk, Billy trying to toss my purse in after me but missing.

There's Billy, walking back around the car, sticking his hands wherever Aliza wants them, sticking his tongue down her throat.

There's Billy opening the driver's side door, holding up the keys, waving good-bye to Huey maybe.

Waving good-bye to me now, to everything I knew and wanted and believed about him and me and everything. Because I knew it was bad all along. I knew it was really bad. I just didn't want to believe it. And I sure as hell didn't know that it could get as bad as this.

And what's worse is the simple fact of what must have happened next. What must have happened after Billy drove the car into the tree. What must have happened just before the sirens started and the police pulled up and I was lying on the ground with the keys in my hand and Billy was gone. Billy and Andie and Andy and Aliza Benitez were gone and I was still there, passed out on the ground.

"Who knows?" I say.

Huey does not look up, flipping forward and backward through the story of my life.

"Pretty much everyone," he says.

"Everyone meaning the computer nerds and the manga club or everyone *us*?"

"Who's us?"

It's true. There is no us. There is my former us. The us in

317

the pictures, the us I poured an entire bottle of vodka down my throat in front of. "Billy and the Andies and the Slutmuffins . . . you know."

"Geez," he says in this sarcastic tone of voice. "I don't know. . . . Do you think they got hit on the head too?" Huey starts pacing around, completely overheated. "Do you think they came down with amnesia too? Do you think so? Because otherwise, yes, *us* knows."

"You knew? Lisa and Anita knew?"

"Everyone knew. I thought you knew. Everyone knows and everyone thinks you know too. Everyone thinks you're doing this on purpose to save Billy's ass."

LIX

WHAT. THE. FUCK.

I am hitting Huey and he's going for my arms and he says that he's sorry and I don't even care.

I am pretty sure I'm pounding the steel pin out of my ulna, pain is snaking through my shoulder, and I pound on him and I wonder, if I keep going, if I demolish the bones in my forearm, if I smash them, if fragments of bone splinter off and slice into my nerves, will I feel better?

Stupid. Stupid. Stupid. Stupid. Stupid.

Huey says, "Don't say that."

I say, "Shut the fuck up."

Then I throw up in the waste basket. Lunch. Breakfast. The lime chunks from an icy pop. Then nothing and nothing and nothing.

And this is the good part. The part where I'm a girl with an excellent grasp on the nature of life, who is not, in fact, a moron dupe. Because: I get what happened. Although it is also the part where the only way to feel better would involve being dead because that would be the only way to stop feeling anything.

To stop feeling this.

To stop feeling.

He *played* me.

He framed me for an actual CRIME.

Beyond cheating, beyond lying, beyond not loving me.

I am so stupid.

I start to slam Huey, but my left arm feels as if the bones already exploded.

I slam him anyway and then there's nothing left, not the old me or the new me or any form of me but stupid stupid nothing me and I can't even throw a fucking pot because I just wrecked my wrist.

Oh Jesus Christ, I really did.

Yeah, I'm the one.

This is the bad part.

LX

HUEY DRIVES ME HOME WHERE I SO DO NOT WANT
to be. There I sit, in front of my house, cradling my arm in
my lap.

Huey says, "I'm sorry. Call me if you want to talk."

Like that's going to happen.

Like I could think or talk or have a conversation.

Billy Nash has taken over my head, his face is sunlit just
behind my eyes, and I am going, *How could you? How COULD
you? HOW COULD YOU?*

And I can't even call him. I can't even ask. Because I already
know. Because listening to him lie some more would only make
it worse. And worse than that, unbearably worse, would be listening to him tell me the truth.

I can't do anything.

My arm hurts and it hurts to cry. It hurts to lie down and it hurts to sit in a chair. My room is hideous and when I see myself in the mirror on the closet door, my makeup looks like primordial ooze, like what would happen if the La Brea Tar Pits were beige instead of black and offering up random eyes and chins and noses instead of prehistoric bird bones.

Vivian spends two days tag-teaming with Juanita, trying to get me to eat food, upping the ante from egg salad sandwiches to delivery pizza to takeout buffalo mozzarella and prosciutto tartine from Le Pain Quotidien.

"You have to eat!" she yells through the door. "You have to tell me what happened to you!"

"I thought you had that all figured out!" I yell back.

"You have to go see Dr. Berman!"

"No," I say, because even if I wanted to go, which I don't, this would involve taking a shower and getting dressed and putting on deodorant and figuring out how to hold my face in an expression that looks like someone who's not posing for Munch's *Scream*. "I don't have to and I'm not going."

I hear her caucusing with John in the hall. She thinks he should get out of the den and do something. He doesn't.

Finally she gives up and goes shopping.

I can't get off the bed.

I am completely and in every way humiliated.

My arm throbs and throbs and throbs and swells around the wrist and all my fingers curl in protest. You can be unnaturally stupid and still know that this can't be good. If I have actually wrecked my wrist, it's going to be like the assisted suicide of the only slim aspect of me that ever had any real reason to get off the bed.

The landline keeps ringing, and John keeps pounding on the door, standing in the doorway, the receiver in his hand. "These are your friends," he says.

I just wait for him to close the door.

"I know," he says. "Sometimes things just creep up on you and then *wham.*"

He is wan and pathetically sober with his eyes blinking too much in a state of utter cluelessness. At least he got the *wham* part right.

What I say is, "Could you drive me to the hospital?"

We tool down to the UCLA ER where I look like such shit that I get prioritized ahead of the crystal meth guy with the stab wound and police escort.

The doctor prods my arm and shuttles me off to x-ray on a gurney.

"So what happened to you?" gurney guy wants to know.

"Car crash and then I fell."

"You *fell?*" the doctor says, when she is signing off on the discharge sheet, when she is giving me prescriptions for three kinds of anti-inflammatory drugs and a sling. When she is telling John exactly how much this is going to hurt and how I can't have any more narcotic pain pills and how I'm not a credible historian. When there is no b.s. about accordion playing, or throwing pots, or my secretarial future, and no stuffed marsupials to blunt the blow. The doctor rolls her eyes, "Well, whatever you did, don't do it again."

And I go, *Listen, Gabriella, if by some miracle Huey was too soft to permanently trash your hand against, things can only look up. Think about it. Really.*

Only then I have to go back to school.

LXI

GETTING OUT OF THE CAR JUST LIKE ALWAYS AND walking across the lawn, climbing the stairs just like always and walking through the domed entryway, all the familiar stateliness of Winston's fake-Gothic architecture and the walk through the familiar buildings does nothing to neutralize the Carnival of Weirdness, tilted floors and fun-house mirrors feel of going to school on Monday.

Knowing what everybody else knew all along and thought that I knew all along makes everything look different, all of the faces more cynical and the buildings as formal and unfriendly as they really are but I'd been pretending they weren't.

I had been back for two weeks, and in two weeks I had been so I-don't-want-to-talk-about-it-blah-blabitty-blah that I'd managed to avoid finding out the *main* thing, the simple fact that would make everything different and worse. I had missed the

Big Kahuna of simple truths. The salient point, as Mr. Monahan would say in history. When you analyze the passage, ladies and gentlemen, be sure to identify that salient point. Underline that salient point. It will be on the test.

I, on the other hand, seemed to have failed that particular test and unwittingly stumbled on the perfect method to evade all those pesky yet salient points. It was a simple three-part plan in which:

1. you run your head into a tree when you're not wearing a seat belt, erasing all relevant memory

2. you share this unfortunate fact with your boyfriend, after which

3. your boyfriend sets you up with the assistance of his helpful posse of adorable Andies, a marauding Slutmuffin, and the entire student body of Winston School.

And Winston School, no-snitch Paradise, was the perfect spot for this simple plan. Everybody knew and everybody believed I would throw myself under the bus for Billy.

Nobody believed I didn't remember, so nobody told me the truth; they all thought I knew the truth already.

No wonder Billy didn't want me to have a meaningful dialogue with anyone.

All of this admiration and bizarre respect I was getting was because of the unfounded Saint Girlfriend aspect of it and, *here comes the salient point*, Billy knew it *all*, knew every bit of it, and now he was spending his time "protecting" me by telling people I didn't want to talk about it while sticking his hands in some other girl's Wonderbra. Not because he loved me and liked me and wanted to protect me, but because he didn't.

Because I was completely expendable as long as it kept him out of trouble.

This is my salient, impossible fact.

LXII

I SIT THERE AT ONE OF THE WHITE METAL TABLES
on the back patio looking out toward the Class of 1920 Garden
and there they are, dripping in salience and conspiratorial friend-
ship. Andie, seeing me, smiles her big smile and gets up and comes
prancing up toward me, waving something orange at me. You
could see Billy trying to keep her there and frowning, turning his
head away.

"Hey, Gabby," she says.

She looks so adorable and harmless and completely evil. And
she is giving me PEZ. Not just a candy, a whole Pebbles Flint-
stone PEZ dispenser. It's like giving me presents is the adorable,
harmless-looking, evil girl's new hobby.

"It's for you," she says. Duh. There is no one else here. "Don't
you like it?"

"Just stop it, Andie," I say. "Go back to your garden."

Andie says, "I don't understand. You were Pebbles for seventh grade Halloween. I thought you'd like it."

"How do you even know that?"

"Yearbook," says Andie, just beaming away. "I love yearbook. Huey takes very good pictures of us, don't you think? I love Halloween. Don't you love dressing up?"

"Andie," I say. "You have to go away."

"Billy keeps reminding me you don't want to talk to me, but I just wanted to give you—"

"*What*, a criminal record? Being cute doesn't give you a free pass, Andrea! You might be cuter than Mrs. God but I *know* what you did and I don't like you."

"What?" I can see the catatonic cry face coming on. Andie scampers off to get Andy, and I watch as Andy gets up and comes toward her with a Dixie cup of *vin du jour* directly from his dad's wine cellar while Billy collects his things and just leaves.

He sees me coming and he leaves basically for the rest of the day.

Because I am following Andie back into the garden with a look on my face that Billy Nash has never seen before. Yes, in pursuit of the salient point, I get up and I walk across the ordinary people's lawn and into the Class of 1920 Garden, which is almost empty because it's so early, and I stand there as Andie slurps down the contents of her Dixie cup.

"Do you want some?" Andy says, offering breakfast wine.

"Haven't you heard? I have a drinking problem."

"Right. Sorry," Andy says. He rolls his head around as if his neck and shoulders were sore. "Sorry about *every*thing."

"Gabby doesn't like me anymore," Andie says, by way of explanation.

Andy looks horrified, maybe because Andie is sniffling and squinting and her face is getting splotchy, and maybe because the idea that a human being is walking the face of the Earth who doesn't adore Andie is too much for him to take.

"What *every*thing would it be that you're sorry about?" I say. "The one where you set me up and then you gave me PEZ?"

I so don't want to be doing this.

I so want to just live through to the end of semester.

"What is she talking about?" Andie says, looking doe-eyed up at Andy as he stands there pouring himself wine out of his thermos.

They look completely baffled, although guilty as hell.

"I'm not saying I expected you to be my actual friends—"

"I am too your actual friend," Andie says. "Tell her."

And Andy runs his fingers through her hair and says, "What's this about? It's cool what you're doing for Billy, but why are you mad at Andie all of a sudden?"

"Were you just going to let this keep on going and never tell me and just hope I never found out?"

"Okay, Gabby," Andy says. "I feel really bad you're the one who got caught, but what is this about?"

So I tell them.

"We thought you knew," they chant over and over, like it is now the lyric of their special song.

Andy, seeing the look on my face, in a vain effort to prevent further drama, says, "Truthfully, at first we thought it was a misunderstanding, and then we thought you knew."

"We thought you were like the coolest person on Earth throwing yourself on a land-mine-thingy to save Billy," Andie says.

"And your sorry little butt," I say.

Andie, dumb as Bambi, says. "What do you mean? *Billy* was driving."

"*We* were in the car," Andy says quietly.

"Do you mean we could get in trouble?" Andie asks, all googly-eyed.

"Let's see," I say. "You dragged me out of the car I wasn't driving and stuck the keys I didn't steal into my unconscious hand and you totally set me up. *May*be you could get in trouble. No wonder you kept your mouths shut."

"What keys?" Andie says, looking up at Andy, who is staring at the ground. "What's she talking about?"

Andy says, "I swear it wasn't like that. We pulled you out of the car because you were passed out and we were afraid it would catch fire. You were passed out before he skidded and you got really banged up. We didn't want the car to blow with you in it, but you started to heave so we put you down. That's all it was."

"Gross," says Andie. Like she never heaved into a cardboard box in the back of the limo on the way back from semiformal.

"Don't forget the part where you ran away and left me there," I say.

"We just went to call Billy's mom on his cell," Andy says. "Because she's a lawyer. And then we heard the sirens and we stayed out of sight. That's all it was. It wasn't personal. And I don't know how the keys got into your hand because I didn't put them there."

He thinks for a minute until his face takes on this amazed and horrified frown, and this time I can tell it's not about whether I like Andie. "That sucks," he says almost to himself, twining his fingers in her curls.

They are so dumb and earnest and into themselves and slimy. Still, it is hard to picture the Andies exchanging looks and prying open my fingers and slipping the keys into the palm of my unconscious hand.

It is hard to see them sitting down over a nice joint and going, "Hey, I know, let's tell Gabby she stole Billy's car. That'll keep her quiet while we go to Dartmouth." (Or in their case, while *he* packs up his lacrosse gear and goes to Dartmouth and she goes to Hanover, New Hampshire College of Fun and Games or wherever girls like that go.)

It is hard to see Andie even understanding the whole complicated plot and it is hard to see Andy making color-coded note cards to explain it to her. How to set up Gabby: Memorize this.

Probably he had figured it out by now, could have figured it out all along if he had given any thought to it. But why would he? He's smart, but why would he even want to know?

I didn't even want to know.

Because as bad as it is to be a drunken teenage felon, it's worse to be a drunken heaving dupe.

Billy's drunken heaving dupe.

LXIII

I GO HOME ON THE BUS, I MARCH INTO MY EMPTY living room, I pour myself a glass of John's Glenlivet, and I drink it straight up. Then I pour myself another one and in a seriously cheesy move, I throw the glass into the fireplace where it breaks into purple splinters, spraying a plume of scotch that smells a lot like a petroleum product across the room. And right on cue, before I can throw up or cry or pass out on the wet chaise, the phone rings.

"So. Kaplan says that you remember part of it," he says instead of hello. "That's good, right?"

And I think of what we're studying in psychology, how when you're shocked beyond what you can take, when your body is flooded with adrenaline, you feel like there's a ten-foot, hulking grizzly bear blocking your path.

That's how I feel.

And you have to wonder if there's some chance that Billy

developed a Problem, such as terminal idiocy, when I wasn't watching. Or if the fumes from the scotch are making me hear voices through my cell phone.

You have to wonder if we're handing off fists full of terminal idiocy like a hot potato, first I had it and now that I am irrevocably smartened and wised-up, he has it instead.

Now he has it and he wants to pass it back to me only my hands are already burned and not exactly open and extended in his direction.

"How come you're phoning me?"

"Gabs, this is important."

"Important to who? Important that you don't admit anything in writing?"

It isn't even a question, that's how obvious it is. I want to strangle him. But still, I want him to be all sweet and sorry, all Imaginary Boyfriend Billy so I can keep on being Delusional Girlfriend Gabby. And even though I can tell this is a sure sign of the proximity of the idiocy potato that I have my fists clenched against taking back, I can also tell that if he gives the slightest hint of wanting to be with me, they will open like pupils dilating in the dark.

"What are you talking about?" he says in his low voice, so quiet you could almost take it for sincere. "I've been messaging you online continuously since you got out of your coma."

There, that sounded almost boyfriend-like, except for the part where you'd expect his lawyer to write a better script for him. That and the pesky, not-true aspect of it.

"I was never in a coma," I say, exerting all possible self-control to make my teeth not chatter, that's how hard I'm shaking.

"Well, that's not what your mother was telling people."

"Jesus, you've got it all figured out. Every angle on this. You're freaking amazing."

"Not, I assume, a compliment?"

"Sorry. No. Not." And then: *How could you? How COULD you? HOW COULD YOU?* Screaming in my head, in my throat, and just behind my mouth. And I know with absolute and complete clarity, if I let it out, that's the end of it, of some powerful, unnamed scary *it*, the end of something, and I have no idea what could possibly replace it, or if my body would just implode, cave in on the vacuum left in there at the former location of my lame, ripped-out heart.

"Listen," he says. "I care what happens to you. I risked my probation to get you out of trouble. I walked you through every step. I snuck out to see you. Don't you see that?"

"Well," it is as if my lack of anger-management skills is eclipsing my lack of discernment-in-boyfriend-selection skills without me having to exert any good judgment whatsoever. "Let me be the first to point out that you wouldn't have had to sneak around to see me because it wouldn't have violated your probation to see me if you hadn't made up your bullshit story about what I did."

"Only, I would have been seeing you when you visited me in *jail*. Don't you get it? Nothing bad was going to happen to you, first offense, cute girl from the B's. And I knew you wouldn't have let anything bad happen to me."

"What are you talking about?"

"If you would have remembered, I knew that you'd take care of it."

And even if you'd been pelted by idiocy potatoes, even if you couldn't think your way out of a bag full of a hundred pounds of moron spuds, you could tell this was probably the truest thing he'd said to me probably ever.

"So you just lied to me and you got everyone else to go along with it? That was the plan?" I say.

"Because you object to lying?"

"Where are you even going with this, Billy? I'm the one who got duped into thinking a lie was the truth. What am I supposed to do with that, anyway?"

There is a long pause and then he says, "You're supposed to keep your mouth shut."

"What, are you threatening me?"

"Jesus, Gabs. I don't know where you got that. All I'm saying is you've got a whole lineup of legal people who think you've been telling them the truth all along. If you change your story now, they're going to think you've been lying to them all along."

"Billy—"

"I mean it, Gabs. No one is going to believe you. They'll think you're just out to get me because I'm back with Benitez."

"Billy—"

"Give it up. Like you didn't notice? Maybe we should talk or something. Castle?"

Because: Knowing me, you'd think I'd go. Because I want to

go. Because I almost go. And I say to myself, *Gabby, do not open your hand and take back that potato. Do not. Just ask yourself what fairy tale this is, and who this guy is, now that he's not the prince.*

Now that I'm not the princess.

Now that we aren't going to live happily ever after until graduation.

And I hang up the phone.

LXIV

THEN I PICK UP THE PHONE AND CANCEL THE ENTIRE week of Ponytail, unlike the last session that I just didn't show up for, because what am I going to say to her? She can leave all the cryptic, where-the-hell-are-you messages she wants. I don't want to talk to Billy and I don't want to talk to her. I want to talk to my real and actual friends.

"Thank God," Lisa says as she plops on my bed. "I thought you were never going to speak to me again. I am *so* sorry. We called your house like fifty thousand times."

At which point, Anita shows up with emergency fudge.

"You talked to Huey," I say.

Lisa says, "We thought you *knew*. I swear to God, we never would have let this happen if—" She kind of peters out, tearing the fudge into little, tiny pieces.

"If what?" I say. "If goddamned *what*? You're supposed to

be my best friends. What, did you think I was *lying* to you?"

Anita says, "We thought you were protecting Billy. You kept saying you didn't want to talk about it. It kind of made sense."

"It would have made more sense if you *believed* me."

But I knew, I absolutely knew, it did make sense.

"Billy thinks I would have done it anyway if I'd remembered. He thinks I would have lied my way right into juvie for him."

"What a self-serving asshole," Anita says.

"Yeah," I say. "But isn't that what you thought I was doing, pretty much?"

That one just sits there.

"It's not that we thought you were *lying* lying," Lisa says finally. "It's more like you never tell us anything. And you were so into Billy."

"As if you ever tell me anything!" I say. As if I were some unnaturally silent sphinx and they're two all-star blabber mouths. "It's not just me. Like, are you doing it with Huey?"

"I'm not even *talking* to Huey," Lisa says.

"How come?"

Lisa starts rolling the torn up fudge into balls. "He was right there," she says. "He could have stopped you anytime for hours. He was taking *close*-ups of you. What kind of friend does that?"

"People who live in glass houses shouldn't throw fudge," Anita says, stacking the fudge balls in a pyramid. "We could have stopped, you know, what happened next."

"We should *crush* Billy Nash," Lisa says.

"It's this stupid school!" Anita says. "We should burn it down

339

for community service." Four and a half years of watching Slut-muffins having a wonderful time, while not being allowed to date or go to kickbacks, dances, or unchaperoned parties, or hang out with evil American boys, has finally gotten to her. "I'd leave tomorrow if I wasn't two days away from a five in AP Bio, which I need for Cal, and it would screw up my plan."

Given that I'm not two days away from AP exams in anything, it's hard to think of why *I'm* not taking off tomorrow. Except that being a disorganized person whose life is unraveling in a festival of messy loose ends, I don't have any plans at all and no place to escape to.

LXV

"LISA SAYS YOU WANT TO LEAVE," HUEY SAYS. HE IS messing with chemicals in the darkroom where I am hiding out avoiding Billy, which is totally unnecessary since Billy is doing such an excellent job of avoiding me. "She says you don't want to do senior year."

It is true that my idea of a bearable future does not involve being a Winston senior, having a big old bittersweet year of pre-nostalgia just before embarking on our big Three B true-life college adventure.

"You still talk to Lisa?" I say because, even now, I'm still the mistress of deflection. "I thought you had The Big Fight."

"You aren't very observant, are you?" Huey says. "It's lucky for you that your artistic interest is still lifes and ceramic bowls and not people."

"I observe people," I protest. "I notice things."

Huey makes a face. "No offense," he says, walking me into the outer photography room full of computers for digital pictures and the yearbook layout, all bright with buzzing light, "but if you noticed things, you'd be leading a completely different life."

Then he snaps a picture of me with my mouth hanging open.

And it hits me: It isn't that I don't notice things. It's that I don't pay enough attention to the things I notice, as if the things I notice aren't actually true or worth noticing. As if Billy was my boyfriend who cared about me. As if the people who actually do care about me don't matter all that much, and the people who don't like me, like me. As if drinking so much I couldn't see or remember or feel anything isn't a problem.

But mostly as if I didn't know I was Billy's pathetic love slave.

As if I didn't know what everybody else had noticed all along and it makes perfect sense to the Andies and the Slutmuffins and even Huey and Lisa and Anita and everybody in the Western world that I'd toss my life out the window just so Billy could be on the water polo team at Princeton.

Because I don't even have a life to toss out the window. I was just Billy's well-trained dog, his tail-wagging bitch.

No wonder Billy went back to Aliza Benitez. At least she's a human being. All right, a disgusting human being, but at least nobody ever accused her of not paying enough attention to all the things she had to know to be able to look out for herself.

Or drinking so much that she careened beyond the point of just being plowed and swerved into the oblivious place of not noticing or seeing or caring or remembering or being the least bit able to take care of herself.

Not like me.

And it occurs to me that maybe I wasn't 100% entirely lying when I copped to the teenage felon drinking problem. It just so wasn't the problem the helpful helping professionals thought it was, so so not about peer pressure or an irresistible compulsion or an impulsive binge. It was pure, cold liquid escape from everything I so noticed but so didn't want to notice. And I just so hadn't paid any attention to it.

"I should have stopped you," Huey says. "Lisa says if I had any balls, I would have stopped you. She thinks I'm like a morals-impaired news photographer watching people in flames jumping out of burning buildings and not trying to catch them because it would mess up his photo op. I should have stopped you. I wish I had."

"So do I," I say. "Duh."

"Are you going to do anything to him?"

It isn't as if I haven't thought about this maybe constantly since hanging up on him, pictured the conversation, pictured myself screaming at him, screaming: *You were supposed to be my boyfriend! You were supposed to care about me just a little!* Pictured slapping his shining face . . . pictured myself crying and him holding me and him apologizing over and over and having make-up sex.

The lameness of my fantasy life is truly horrifying.

And I can't even decide what the most twisted part is, the

part where I can actually picture him being sorry for what he did to me, or the part where I can picture myself believing he's sorry and just ripping off my clothes all glad to have him back.

Even though I know who he is.

Even though I more than notice and I ever so slightly don't even care.

Because: In the sorry, not-going-to-happen fantasy, I whip off my clothes for Billy just like that.

And I know, even with Huey standing there gazing at me expectantly, waiting for me to wise up and do the right thing, I'm not going to do a damned thing about what happened.

Because: Thank you, Billy, for pointing it out, there is no upside to nailing Billy Nash. Beyond pure vengeance, fun as that might be. But so what? After a bunch of drama, he would sink deeper into probation and maybe he'd have to toss his little water polo ball around a swimming pool in the Big Ten and not the Ivy League and so what? It's not like four years at Giant Midwest State U is going to kill him, unless maybe he catches fatal cooties from someone with a dad in middle management.

His mom would have to hide out in a spa with a mudpack on her face for four years, but by the time she got him into law school or biz school or whatever kind of school boys like Billy from the B's are supposed to go to and she undid her seaweed wrap, no one would remember or care what a little teenage shit he'd been. Agnes would hire a consultant in the mid–five figures to rehabilitate his image.

Rock stars and football players get to rape, pillage, and burn and five minutes later the guys are all rehabilitated and fixed and cured and rolling in endorsement contracts. All Billy did was set up a teenage drunk girl from the sketchy branch of her family; he was right back in the Bel Air Country Club for sure.

As for the teenage drunk girl, I'd be more screwed than I already was if I went after him. That's just how things work. I was about to be the Princess of Turning Your Life Around. I was halfway through my plan to make it all go away, the *it* being the stuff I didn't actually do but got arrested for doing, but what the hell? I was skipping down the marathon path to pseudo-rehabilitation.

Why stop now?

The finish line is in sight; what's the point of blowing it?

To the kids who know I didn't do the stuff I'm being rehabilitated for doing, and who think I knew all along: I am the reigning Princess of Not Ratting Out Your Boyfriend. Your really bad boyfriend who is sleeping with Aliza Benitez in your face and Courtney Yamada Phillips behind your back.

This makes me even more heroic to the people who thought that I knew what they knew from the minute Billy did what I said I did.

The so-called grown-ups think I'm a former drunk-driver car-thief who is embracing virtue with the assistance of a pack of brain-dead professional helpers. Everybody else thinks I remember what I don't remember and that I said that I didn't remember in order to protect the Golden Creep Boy.

Billy is the only one who knew what was actually happening

all along, who set it up and sat back and watched it unfold, and he wasn't telling anyone: especially *me*.

No wonder I get along with all the brain-dead helpers so well, I am so totally brain-dead myself. But then, how brilliant do you have to be to make a really good love slave?

As far as I can see, the only way things are going to work out is if I keep my mouth shut. If I open it, if I rat out Billy, if I tell the truth and proclaim my actual innocence, I'm screwed. The brain-dead helpers will think I've been lying to them all along. The kids who thought I was the Joan of Arc of no-rat girlfriends will think I'm finally embracing the truth, only to them, me telling the truth will not be a good thing.

No one wants Billy to go down. That was the point of all this. The only shred of status I still have at Winston School, evidently, comes from the fact that I look like the world's best former girlfriend. And this being the case, there is not a whole lot to gain from making everybody think that I'm Satan the Billy-Slayer.

All I want is to be out of there, to live through pseudo-rehabilitation, and, in the absence of a functional driver's license, walk away. All I want is to be somewhere else doing something else that doesn't have Billy or Winston School in it.

LXVI

"MR. ROSEN," I SAY, BECAUSE HE HAS A LIFE OUTSIDE and beyond Winston and you'd think that he would somewhat get it, so I'm sitting in his office waiting for him to open his eyes. "Excuse me. I need to make a plan."

"What kind of plan?" he says, suddenly scarily attentive. "Is this the college talk? Elspeth, she makes the college talk, not me."

But I don't want to have the college talk with Miss Cornish. I want to have the anti-college talk with Mr. Rosen.

"Is there someplace I could go right now and do art and not be here?"

Which is, I realize, The New Plan.

"Not after graduation?"

"*Right now*, Mr. Rosen."

Mr. Rosen looks straight at me. "Olga Blau is at Santa Monica CC," he says.

Olga Blau is this ancient, genius potter. What was Olga Blau doing teaching at community college? I start to wonder if she's gone totally senile or her hands shake or something.

"Very fine art, Santa Monica College," Mr. Rosen says, staring me down, looking straight through me. Because: Even though Mr. Rosen's portraits bear only the slightest, most abstract resemblance to actual people, you could tell that the man can read faces.

"This would be a *good* decision," he says. And the way he's looking at me puts to rest for all eternity any lingering question as to whether Mr. Rosen's obliviousness extends to some of my less good decisions. "You work with Olga one year, maybe two, you transfer, work with Erik Wertheimer at Northridge maybe?"

Eric Wertheimer is a double-genius ceramics god who gave us a demonstration freshman year.

Except that nobody from Winston ever goes to Cal State Northridge, let alone transfers there from CC. It would be like waving a big white flag that says Defeated By Life. Spit in the Face of Opportunity. Failed to Measure Up. Fuckup of Unspeakable Proportion.

And then I go, *Screw it, Gabs. Just screw it. Don't measure up. So what? You are so good at party limbo, slide under the bar. Then straighten up and walk away.*

And you can kind of see it: me sitting in a room with Olga Blau and a big lump of clay, even if she is bat-shit crazy and I have a scarlet F for failure stamped across my forehead. So what if what I actually want to do makes everyone else wince? Because, you have to figure, things would be looking up if *I* wasn't the one wincing.

"I could maybe do this," I say. Because: You don't need a high school diploma to sign up for SMCC. You don't even need a GED to sign up for SMCC.

"Only Elspeth will be very mad at me," says Mr. Rosen. "Only she does the college talk so I won't tell the artists drop out, go to Europe, learn something, no football, no goldfish, no wasting time!" He is lost in a sad fantasy of U.S. college life.

"Europe?" I say.

"Very fine academies, Europe," he says. "Excellent art academies. The best. But all I'm hearing here is Ivy, Ivy, Ivy."

"Europe!" I say.

"Very late in the year for application, Europe. You want me to make the email?"

Duh?

"Yes, please."

But just when I think I've limboed under the bar and past it, when the song has changed and I think the whole game is over, I turn around and there's a lower bar that even my completely flexible and almost spineless back cannot negotiate.

LXVII

THIS IS HOW IT STARTS TO COME APART: STACKS and stacks of the Winston Wildcat yearbook in its sparkly green, fake leather-covered splendor, on tables along the low stone wall that separates the Class of 1920 Garden from the lawn where the ordinary kids like I am now hang out.

Free dress day. A girl in a slightly orange tank top (homage to her previous, temporarily cute and kicky self) and a pair of ratty jeans sitting with her friends in the ordinary mortal section of the lawn sucking grape icy pops just before, without warning or permission, the naked, unembellished true story of her life appears on the last page before all the blank signature pages.

One full page in black and white, nobody's face blurred out.

Songbird Lane.

Me: drunk and passed out in the passenger seat.

Billy: drunk and driving.

Andie and Andy and Aliza Benitez: drunk and hanging out of the convertible, peeling out toward the crash, toward the amnesiac lie of my dishonest future that was about to end, right here, right now, on the back lawn at Winston School.

The lies I was telling everybody and the lies Billy told me and the lies I was telling myself all burned to ash in the crash I don't remember, in flames I don't remember, but toward which that black-and-white, midnight-blue Beemer is inexorably aimed.

Huey's picture with the date and time printed on the lower right corner in digital indictment.

Who knew the Winston Wildcat was mined? Right now, only Huey and the yearbook advisor, Mr. Bell, who has already had his farewell party and is leaving for graduate school in journalism in the fall, who probably has no idea who Agnes Nash even is. And in about five minutes: everybody and their Uncle Rodney.

Everyone is lined up and getting their names checked off the master list to get their yearbooks, cracking their yearbooks open and pulling out their sharpies and leaning in toward each other and signing each other's books and leafing through looking for pictures of themselves and all their friends.

Until they get past the How We Studied Together, Worked Together, Played Together, Healed the Bay and Cleaned Up the Beach Together sections and make it to the How We Had Secrets and Told Lies Together section at the very end.

"Mother of God!" Lisa says, slamming the yearbook shut as if that would make it go away. "Huey is going to have to go into witness protection."

Huey plops himself down on the grass next to us, looking nervous but extremely proud of himself. Lisa leans over and kisses him on the mouth.

"How could you do this?" I say. Very quietly, since by now three hundred people are turning to stare at me.

"I pasted it in. It wasn't that hard."

"No: *How could you do this?*"

"I did it to bridge the generations," Huey says. "Everybody under eighteen already knew, and now everybody over eighteen knows too." I want to smack him, but Lisa kisses him some more, presumably no longer pissed off over his lack of balls. "Besides, everybody under eighteen already thought you were Saint Girlfriend. You said so yourself. This picture only shows what happened, it doesn't say whether you knew or not."

"Except that now everybody over eighteen is going to believe that I *did* know and I've been letting them think the wrong thing all along," I say, while Lisa and Huey smooch shamelessly and Huey pretends to be the badass king of PDA. "Everybody over eighteen is going to think that I've been *lying* to them all along. I'm screwed. Did you think of that?"

"Mostly I thought of that tool Billy Nash leaving you there by the side of the road."

Oh. My. God.

What's going to happen to Billy now that he can no longer . . . no longer what? Lie to me? Lie to everybody? Set me up? Leave me dead drunk and unconscious, passed out with his car keys neatly tucked into my hand, in the grass by the side of Songbird Lane?

LXVIII

AT LUNCHTIME, VIVIAN SHOWS UP ON CAMPUS, standing outside the door of trig when class lets out. I just follow her out to the car, and there's John riding shotgun with the Wildcat in his lap.

"Where did you get that?"

"Phone tree," Vivian says. "You should have told us. This is not the way we should have found out. You should have told us the truth."

"Why would I even tell you *anything*? All you care about is how good I look and if I have a classy boyfriend and whether I get into some college I'm not getting into!"

"How can you say that to me? Everything I did I did for you, I did it so you would be happy."

"Do I look happy?"

"Don't try to tell me you weren't happy," she says. "You had a very nice boyfriend who happens to be a *Nash* and you felt very good about yourself."

"Uh, Viv?" John says, not merely conscious but coherent. "The point is, he wasn't a very nice boyfriend."

Vivian and John, apparently, do not feel qualified to discuss any of this, and the car is headed not home, where I thought the idea was for me to hole up and hide my head in shame, but is aimed toward Westwood where a highly paid professional is going to help me *process* it all.

"I don't want to freaking process anything," I yell, "I don't even know what that *is*! I just want to go home."

"You don't have a choice!" Vivian yells back. "You have to comply with the reasonable commands of your parent or guardian at all times."

"I do not! I'm not even on probation until the Probation Department finishes the freaking report."

"Well, you will be soon enough!"

Only, John says, "No. I don't think she will be on probation. She didn't *do* anything."

And I go, "Thanks, Dad," which is kind of new and different, and he slightly nods his head and you can tell he likes it.

LXIX

NATURALLY, PONYTAIL HAS THE YEARBOOK TOO. It is lying open on her desk in all its shiny green fake leather-covered glory. And given that there is an extremely fat old black French bulldog snoring in an open crate under her desk and a dog rescue brochure next to the yearbook, it's not too hard to come up with a really good hypothesis about how that yearbook got there.

Apparently Ponytail is so nonplussed by the Winston Wildcat that she isn't playing shrinkish mystery games today.

"Madeleine Hewlett brought this in this morning," she says. "She barged right in and said she knew I couldn't divulge whom I was treating but her son said I was seeing you so I might be interested in looking at the last page. And then she left."

"Right," I say.

Ponytail fidgets with her ponytail.

"The dog," I say. "I'm thinking that she probably said more than one sentence if she gave you the dog."

Ponytail says, "Oh! He's a retired therapy dog." She gives the dog a sideways, hello-doggie kind of sappy look before she pulls herself back together. "The woman is very persuasive. But we did not discuss you."

"Then you're the only person in the B's who didn't. What's his name?"

"Barney."

I get out of my chair and start scratching the dog's warm little head behind his oversized ears, but you can see he's pretty serious about his retirement because he just opens his eyes, gives me a once-over, goes back to snoring, and ignores me.

"I can imagine how shocking this must have been for you," she says.

"My friend showed me the picture last week, but yeah."

"So you'd known for several days before it hit the press, so to speak. . . ."

Then I stop scratching the dog and I just look at her, and it hits me that even with the vast amount of stuff I didn't tell her in the hospital and the even more vast amount of lying I had done in here, starting with why I couldn't go to AA and moving right along, she believes me.

She believed me all along.

The Do Not Trust Therapist tape loop is still going like the annoying, disembodied voice that tells you to please take a ticket when you pull into an automated parking structure, even after you already took a ticket, when you're already driving through the open gate. Billy's voice: Do Not Trust Therapist.

Oh yeah, thanks for that.

The gate is open. I start to talk. Lame as it is, I pretend the empty chair is Billy and I scream at the empty space where he's supposed to be sitting for fifty-five minutes.

LXX

THE ACTUAL BILLY IS GONE.

Nobody sees him after morning break and by that night, his Facebook page is down and his email bounces. He doesn't show at Fling, and Jack Griffith is drafted into being king at the last minute.

Attempts to contact Billy to find out when he's planning to show up are in vain. His cell phone says that the number is not in service, please check the number before redialing. By the end of the week, Andy Kaplan says that Billy is in boarding school in Western Massachusetts and he says he's sorry.

"How?" I say. "I thought he went dark."

"He borrowed some other kid's cell phone."

Andie grabs Andy's arm. "Why didn't he use that other kid's phone to call Gabby himself?"

This is not a rhetorical question.

You can tell that even though Andy knows the answer, he doesn't have the heart to explain it to her. You can tell that the answer makes him sad and uncomfortable, but not sad and uncomfortable enough to hang up when Billy calls him on the other kid's phone.

What was I supposed to say, that it was okay? It wasn't.

That I forgave him? I didn't.

That as good as I was at swearing at empty chairs, the thing I wanted most was to be able to go back to pretending that I was an adorable hot girl and he was my boyfriend who loved me, which made even my therapist look at me as if I were a hopeless case? It wasn't my drinking problem or my closed head injury problem that was interesting to her all of a sudden—it was my Total Evasion of the Truth Problem. How much I wanted things to go back to the way they were even though I knew, I completely knew, that things were never really ever like that.

Andie says, "Well, he should have called Gabby. I'm sorry," she says, looking over at Andy. "I know he was your best friend, but he isn't very nice."

And I think, *How is it that Andrea Bennett gets it but somewhere deep, somewhere that seems impossible to change, I don't?*

LXXI

"IS THIS WHAT HAPPENED?" MR. PIERSOL ASKS, thumping on the Wildcat. "Or is this one of those photoshopped dealies that's someone's idea of a joke?"

Everyone in the picture is there with a full complement of parents, except for, obviously, Billy.

Agnes is there, glaring at everyone, white despite excellent makeup.

"Jim," she says to Mr. Piersol. "I don't see how we can determine what happened, until we have forensic experts. Which I would be happy to provide. Why don't we just collect these Wildcats here and now and hold them in a safe place until we can do that?" You can tell she isn't going to be happy until she has all the Wildcats in a shed with some lighter fluid and a match.

Huey says, "It isn't photoshopped."

"Who authorized you to take that picture?" Agnes snaps.

"Did a faculty member sign off on this? Did you get a release?"

Mr. Piersol more or less cringes. "Well, Gabby," he says, "we seem to have been operating here on some unfounded assumptions. And we know about assumptions—"

"I *really* can't remember," I say very quickly in what turns out to be a very effective attempt to preempt an onslaught of Piersol clichés.

"You can stop saying that now," Vivian sighs. "The cat is out of the bag."

There it is. My own mother still doesn't believe me.

"Well," Mrs. Hewlett says, looking up from the orphan quadruped stowed in her bag. "I have a question, which is, how long have you had this picture, Hewbo?"

Huey looks completely miserable. "When the time stamp says. That's when I took it."

"You're telling me you've had this picture since April and you didn't think to bring it to us or the police because . . ."

At the sound of the word "police" Agnes starts hyperventilating and Mr. Piersol's body seems to gain uncharacteristic muscle tone. This is when Mr. Piersol suspends everybody in the room. He looks very proud of himself.

You can tell that Huey is having to sit on his hands to restrain himself from taking a picture.

Huey's mom, who has abandoned all pretense of paying attention, now has a mole sitting in her lap unraveling her loosely knit angora sweater with its tiny paws.

"I just don't get it," John says, not even slurred, from the back of the room. "If Gabby wasn't suspended when we thought she was driving the car, why is she suspended now that you know it was her boyfriend who was driving?"

Mr. Piersol looks perplexed, possibly because he's never heard a complete, unslurred sentence from my dad before, and possibly because the sentence—the sentence with my dad defending me—makes so much sense.

"What I don't understand, Hewbo," Madeleine Hewlett says, "is how you could have let your friend take the blame when you knew she didn't do it."

At which point Huey and everybody else in the room who is under eighteen recites in unison, "I thought she knew."

I am already on my way out of the room when Mrs. Hewlett says, "I still don't understand. Why on Earth would you think that?"

LXXII

I RUN INTO THE TEACHERS' HANDICAP BATHROOM near the college counselor's office, the only place at Winston School where you can lock the door and actually be alone. I turn on the water and the fan and then I wait to start crying, but I don't. Weeks of crying like a total slob, and now there's nothing left.

I stare at myself in the teachers' handicap bathroom mirror, and I look so strange and so not like myself in all that opaque makeup. Clearly, it's time for something new, but the thing is, I have no idea what new thing that will be.

I put my hands under the cold water and I splash it on my face, not really thinking about it, and the makeup starts to dissolve in sticky clumps. I start to wipe it off, a little at a time, until there are patches of naked skin, mostly beige, some not, some still turning the colors skin turns after it gets pummeled by an imploding car, air bags, and a eucalyptus tree. I look like myself, only slightly bruised. Which is to say: I look like myself.

Someone is banging on the door and I think that unless it's a desperate handicapped person (which, if Winston had one, I would know about it) then it's an extremely rude person who should go away, which I semi-nicely tell them to do.

"But it's Lisa!" she shouts over the fan and the running water.

"Go away!"

"Let me in!" If she doesn't stop, she is going to attract attention and pretty soon there will be a platoon of helpful teachers helping her break down the door, which I crack open, and she squeezes in and turns the lock.

"What happened?" she says. "I was looking for you and I saw you running." You can tell she's looking at my face, at the bruises, trying not to. Trying to lock her eyes into eye-contact-only mode, an eye-lock that won't let them wander along my purple cheekbone and into the hollow of my yellow cheek.

"Well, I might be suspended. Or not. Everybody might be suspended. Or not. They were still duking it out when I left."

"Does that hurt?"

"Yeah. Only when you touch it."

"How did I not know this was going on under your makeup?" she says.

I say, "I don't know," but I kind of do. Then we just stare at me in the mirror some more.

"I was just thinking, Billy did this to me. He got drunk and he stuck me in the car and he didn't put a seat belt on me and he drove me into a tree. I just wanted to look at it. I never think about that part of it but here I am, and I'm such a pathetic loser, I hate him but I still somewhat want him."

There is something about saying it out loud that makes it worse but also better.

Lisa rolls her eyes. "Maybe you're just in love with the idea of him."

"No, I'm pretty sure it's his body."

Then we both start to laugh and Lisa flushes the toilet just to raise the noise level in there to drown us out because we can't stop.

"I am so lame."

"Totally pathetic," she agrees, pulling out her stick concealer because my purse is in my locker. "You want some of this?"

"You know, I'm good," I say.

"You don't even know how good," she says. "That's why I was looking for you. You have someplace to go."

"Even if I'm not suspended, someplace out of Winston, that's for sure."

"Way not to be pathetic. Drop out of school. Perfect."

"As long as dropping out doesn't violate the terms of my impending probation and get me thrown in juvie, I am seriously out of here."

"How can you be on probation for something you didn't do? I thought you said you have a lawyer," Lisa says.

"Ask Agnes Nash. She found him for me."

"Agnes Nash is going to burn in hell," Lisa says, with the

conviction of a truly religious person with a pretty clear idea of how the afterlife works.

I find this extremely comforting, but not comforting enough to unlock the door and go deal with anything.

"We have to go," Lisa says. "People are *waiting* for you. Come on. It's something good. Don't you want to see Mr. Rosen *smiling*? It's kind of frightening. I don't want to give it away, but you really need to get out of here."

LXXIII

THIS IS HOW IT STARTS OVER: AN ARTSY-LOOKING
girl in a ratty smock is lying on her back on an unmade bed in a
room she shares with a Polish watercolor painter named Paulina.
Paulina is the only person whose Italian the girl can understand
because Paulina has a vocabulary of maybe twenty-five Italian
words and she says them all extremely slowly. Through the open
curtains of their room, there are certain undeniable signs: the tile
roof skyline of a Medieval city, the River Arno, and the sound of
people laughing and talking in a language that is slowly becoming
comprehensible.

Paulina, who used to be a gymnast in her former life, has
a suitcase full of skanky little outfits that involve a lot of leo-
tards and cloth that looks like stretchy tinfoil with fringe. Under
the smock, the girl has jeans and a black sweater. The girl and
Paulina look pretty weird together in clubs, where Paulina can

drink entire bottles of anything you put in front of her and still walk a straight line on her hands in skirts so tight they don't succumb to gravity and uncover her upside-down butt.

The girl, having been subjected to the world's weirdest intervention by her three best friends and Andie Bennett—all of whom insisted that anyone who drinks so much that they black out and lose three and a half hours of a highly significant nature has a drinking problem (which she kind of already knew, but she wasn't about to stop drinking because of it)—took a double dare to stay stone-sober for six months. This is somewhat easier to do in Italy than in the Three B's because all you have to do here is point slightly to the left of your belly button and say *"fegato,"* which means liver in Italian, and everyone leaves you alone. Because (*grazie* to her genius art teacher who sent off her slides and attested to her high level art forgery and glazing skills that got her into this amazing art school) the girl turns out to be an art restoration fiend. And it would be kind of horrible to be drunk and debilitated and screw up some ancient priceless artifact. Not that they let her anywhere near ancient priceless artifacts.

Yet.

Anyway, having also accepted blackmail-ish double dares from Ponytail Doc before the woman would sign off on her Get Out of Probation Free card (actually, it wasn't a card, it was a seriously thick legal document), and just to prove that she can totally do it, and because loving Billy Nash was seriously pathetic, the girl has three months, one week, and two days left before she can have Chianti with dinner, streak her increasingly sub-regular hair, or have a boyfriend.

The likeliest candidate for this position is an architecture student named Giovanni who admires her ability to simulate priceless ancient artifact glaze and is almost supernaturally hot for a person who wears turtlenecks and is obsessed with Gothic churches. Although it's hard to say, and probably it would be a good idea to learn enough Italian to be able to have a quasi-intelligent conversation with him and figure out whether he's just another specimen of hot pond scum before removing any significant articles of clothing.

It's not that she's a nun. It's just that she is trying to figure out how to be *me*.

Acknowledgments

Brenda Bowen, because I always wanted an agent who was a goddess, and that would be Brenda. Her intelligence, literary sensibility, tireless attention to text, incisive suggestions for polishing the manuscript ("Incisive" and "polishing" are both understatements), and dead-on savvy made this happen.

Jen Klonsky is the editor everybody prays they'll get—smart, enthusiastic, intuitive, open, completely supportive, and able to see the forest and the trees and the leaves and all the tiny little acorns with perfect clarity. And the whole team at Simon Pulse.

My husband, Rick, Best Husband Ever, who actually read every single version of every single chapter, listened to every draft, and managed to remain kind and constructive and helpful and funny even through the really bad ones.

My kids, Laura and Michael, a writer and a filmmaker, who were raised in the B's but turned out pretty damned great, and whose generosity and talents (and notes) I relied on all the time as I was writing this.

Early readers Suzi Dubin, who gave me hope that I had, in fact, written a novel; Jen Weiss Handler, whose expertise helped me fit seventy-five unruly chapters together; and June Sobel, whose discerning feedback was invaluable.

Electronic communication consultants: Sharla Steiman, Laura and Michael, Sarah Markoff, and Brian and Erik Becker. Thank you!

I am hugely grateful to an emergency room doctor, a pediatrician, a psychiatrist, two lawyers, a Los Angeles County Sheriff's traffic investigator, and two LAPD officers, whom I thank from the bottom of my heart, but who shall remain nameless.

And thanks, Mom, for thinking I was a writer even when I wasn't.

Finally, this is a work of fiction. It is not a roman à clef. My kids are not in it, nor are their friends, or their acquaintances, or my friends or acquaintances, and the most striking thing I have in common with any of the characters (apart from my geography and the tiny fact that I spent a couple of years channeling Gabby Gardiner) is my affinity for Ponytail's Italian shoes. Winston School does not exist, and anyone who has ever set foot at my kid's high school can tell you that that isn't it. I do wish Madeleine Hewlett existed, though, because I like her and I kind of want the one-eyed rescue cat.

Leading me to my dog, Evan, who ate part of one of the drafts, but who sat with me during the entire writing process.